ILLICIT HEIR

MAFIA WARS IRELAND
BOOK THREE

MAGGIE COLE

PULSE PRESS INC

TERMS

Below is a list of some terms used in Ireland and England that ya may or may not be familiar with that ya will find in this series.

A stór - my treasure

Arse - ass, butt, OR a stupid, irritating person

Aye - yes

Bloke is a slang term for a common man

Burd - girl, girlfriend

Garda - police in Dublin

Plonker - idiot, moron

Runners - workout shoes

Da - Dad, father

Mum, mammy - Mom, mother

TERMS

Ya – you

Yea - Yes

PROLOGUE

Devin O'Connor

The ball flies past the goalie, and the pub erupts in ear-shattering noise as everyone jumps into the air.

It's the All-Ireland Senior Football Championship, one of the biggest sporting events of the year, and I've never seen the pub so packed. Normally, the energy would pump up my adrenaline, even though I'm not a huge fan of the sport.

My brothers and I grew up mostly in New York but spent summers and long periods in Belfast. Our father tried to instill the love of what he calls football—and we still want to call soccer—into our heads...and hearts. Yet none of my brothers are overly enthusiastic about the sport.

Boxing's the thing we love more than anything. We've spent countless hours in the ring, so all of us would rather see a boxing match. Or we'd get more excited about American football or even rugby. At least there's more aggression in those competitions, but when we're in Ireland, there's no choice but to embrace what they call football.

Usually, a few pints of Guinness will get me into the sport, and I'll cheer with the other lads, especially for this big of a game. Yet all I keep thinking is one thought: *I'm bored and over Belfast.*

I scan the crowd for the hundredth time, and my frustration only grows. There are at least a dozen women I've conquered in this room. Most of them several times, a few only once. Yet not one of them currently does anything for me.

I'm antsy.

I down my Guinness and glance at my brother, Tynan. He scans the room and then meets my gaze.

One thing is clear. He's just as fed up with Belfast and the current selection of lasses as I am.

One of my longtime friends and fellow clansman, Cathal, steps next to me. His eyes buzz with alcohol and the excitement only victory can bring. He wraps his arm around my shoulder, shouting, "Greatest day of the year, mate!"

I scoff, muttering, "Sure it is."

He pins his eyebrows together and leans closer. "Did ya not see that winning shot?"

"Aye. Course I did."

"Then why aren't ya ordering another round?"

Another clansman, Brogan, steps up to the other side of me and hands me another pint. He grins. "The lasses are going to be wild tonight. I'm calling dibs on..." He glances around and then sets his leer on a brunette he often takes home. He eyes her over and declares, "Her."

Tynan groans. "Mate, you're so fucking predictable."

Brogan's grin widens. "Predictable is good when ya got a lass who can do the things she can with her pretty little mouth."

"Here we go again," I mumble, then down half my pint.

"Which one ya taking home tonight?" Cathal questions me.

I study the pub for another moment, then finish my pint. I set the empty glass on the table and shake my head. "No one."

Brogan smirks, leans closer, and taunts, "Is your cock not working? Got issues ya need to discuss?"

"Fuck off!" I scowl.

Brogan, Cathal, and Tynan all chuckle.

I point at my brother. "What are ya laughing at? There are no birds in here you're interested in leaving with tonight either."

Brogan looks at Cathal and states, "Have our O'Connor boys switched sides?"

Tynan slaps him on the side of the head. "Watch your mouth."

"Ouch!" Brogan grunts.

Cathal asks, "What's wrong with you two? The pub's crawling with lasses ready to spread their pretty legs. It'll never be easier than tonight to get what or who ya want."

I cross my arms, sniff hard, and scan the room once more. Then I announce, "I've reached my limit of boredom. I'm heading to Dublin tonight."

Tynan's eyes light up, and his lips twitch in approval. He declares, "Thank fuck. Let's get on the road."

"Dublin? Have ya gone mad?" Cathal accuses.

"Why would ya go to Dublin when ya can get everything ya need right here?" Brogan questions.

I shake my head. "You two need to expand your horizons."

"My lass over there will expand my horizons just fine tonight," Brogan insists, then winks at her.

Tynan groans and scrubs his face. "She'll be here tomorrow too. And the next day. And then the day after that, dumbass."

"Your point?"

"Exactly what Devin said. Ya need to expand your horizons. It sure as hell isn't going to happen here."

Cathal cautions, "Dublin's asking for trouble."

Adrenaline finally pumps through my veins. I can't stop my grin from growing as I affirm, "Exactly."

His eyes darken, turning to slits. "Brody and Alaina won't give us approval to go to Dublin."

"That's why we aren't telling them," Tynan interjects.

Cathal's head jerks backward.

Brogan blurts out, "Have ya both gone mad?"

My brother and I exchange glances as my adrenaline finally kicks into high gear. I nod at everyone's pints, ordering, "Drink up."

"Ya have to be joking," Brogan mutters.

I grab his pint.

"Hey!" he protests.

I down it, set it next to my empty glass, and order, "Grab a couple eight-packs from Sarah, and let's go."

Cathal whines, "If Brody and Alaina find out—"

"They won't. Now, are ya going to be a pussy, or are ya coming along?"

"He'll be a pussy," Tynan jeers.

"You're asking for it," Cathal warns.

"Ya have two minutes to get your asses in the car," I assert and push through the crowd, ignoring everyone. I get to the front door and step out into the brisk air, taking several deep breaths.

My vehicle isn't far since all my brothers and I have designated parking spots. I reach for the door and pause, almost forgetting I'm not in America.

I spin, and before I can ask anything, the parking lot bouncer, Declan, informs me, "No one's been near it."

I nod, then open the door, slide in, and turn on the engine. After a few seconds of quiet, I relax, even though he gave me the all clear. If guys I trust aren't watching my vehicle, I usually take out my special pen that can detect bombs. Even though we haven't had an incident in a while, you can never be sure in Ireland. The O'Learys will do anything to kill us off, just like we'll do the same to them.

Which is why Brody and Alaina will have a fit if they find out we went to Dublin. Plus, our other brother Aidan's also warned Tynan and me several times to stay in Belfast. So he'll be pissed too.

But a man has to do what a man has to do, and I have to get out of here. Besides, we took a lot of O'Learys out when we hunted down Tommy Ahern. Over the last month, we've claimed some of the territories on the outskirts of Dublin, but my brother and Alaina need to be more aggressive. The window to seize the O'Leary territory could close at any time. So, it's time we start taking over whatever we can, and I don't understand why they're not capitalizing faster on our opportunity.

Tynan opens the passenger door and slides in with an eight-pack. Cathal and Brogan get into the back seat, each holding another box of Guinness.

Brogan mutters, "Can't believe ya made me leave my lass."

I reiterate, "She'll still be here tomorrow, so stop your bitching." I reverse out of the spot and pull onto the road.

"How deep into Dublin are we going?" Cathal questions.

I glance at Tynan's mischief-filled grin. I assume it matches mine. My endorphins ignite, and I answer, "Pick a pub in Coolock."

"Coolock? Have ya lost the plot? We only took over the territory north of there!" Brogan points out.

Tynan turns his head, smirking. "Such a pussy."

I add, "It's prime to take over. The O'Learys have no one there, based on all the intel Alaina received."

"But they haven't ordered the clan to move on it," Brogan argues.

"Pussy," Tynan taunts again.

"Shut up," Brogan scolds.

The pop of a Guinness can fills the car and Cathal mumbles, "I need more alcohol for this."

6

Zings fly down my spine. I veer onto the motorway and head south, finally feeling alive for the first time in months. I demand, "Find a pub, Tynan."

He pulls his phone out of his pocket, and several minutes pass. Then he declares, "Got it."

"Where to, little brother?"

He programs an address into the GPS and states, "The Confessional."

Brogan grumbles, "Reconciliation would be a better decision right now."

I snort, claiming, "Oh, we're going to need reconciliation. But not until after tonight."

Tynan chuckles and opens a can of Guinness.

Cathal points out, "There're going to be O'Leary women in that pub. This really isn't a good idea."

Tynan and I exchange another glance. The heat in my blood grows hotter. I state, "Guess it's time."

"Time for what?" Brogan questions.

My brother and I exchange a knowing glance. It's part of the conversation we've had too many times between us to count.

We need to know why our other two brothers couldn't stay away from their O'Leary women. And as far as I'm concerned, tonight's the perfect night to find out. So I answer, "Time to learn what it's like to be inside an O'Leary lass."

1

Lauren Byrne

"Y ou're being irrational and playing hard to get," Caleb claims, giving me an arrogant look, as if he knows what's best for me.

I glare at him. "No, I'm not. It's over, Caleb. Stop coming in here and expecting it to be any different."

He grunts, takes another shot of whiskey, then slides his hand over my cheek.

My skin crawls. I jerk my head back. "Don't touch me."

He chuckles. "Ya know what happens when women play hard to get with me, don't ya?"

My blood turns cold. The worst thing I ever did was get with Caleb O'Leary. Now he's head of the entire clan, and for some reason, he won't get me out of his mind. It's probably because

I'm the only woman who defied him and turned him down. And his ego is big enough to make him believe he can cheat on me with multiple women and I'll willingly come back.

I assert, "I think it's time ya left."

He shakes his head. "I'll leave when I'm ready. Now go pack your bag. You're coming back with me."

My pulse skyrockets. I firmly state, "No, I'm not."

"Sure, ya are," he insists and strolls to the end of the bar toward his brothers.

My mum comes up behind me. She quietly directs, "Ya need to marry him, Lauren."

Rage fills me. It's a never-ending conversation that I can't seem to win. And while I understand she's from a time when things were done differently, it irritates me more than anything else. So I spin on her, ordering, "Stop saying that. I'm never marrying him. It's over between us."

"He'll protect ya," she claims for the millionth time.

I sarcastically laugh. "From whom? Tommy's dead. No one protected him, and everyone thought he was bulletproof."

Her face turns dark. Tommy was my mum's brother. He was also the underboss of the O'Learys and one of their most powerful men. Everyone thought he was untouchable until the O'Connors hunted him down.

The clan found his headless body burned in a field. His bloody head turned up at the registrar's office, making it clear Aidan O'Connor killed him to marry Tommy's wife, Scarlet.

So I don't know why my mum believes Caleb could protect me or why she even thinks I need it. In all reality, she should be worried about who would protect me from him. The little act he put on when we first started dating didn't last very long until I saw his true colors. He showed me enough of his temper. I want no part of him, and my mum is aware of his wrath.

The pub erupts in angry shouts, tearing me out of my standoff with my mother. I turn, and dread hits me. The score on the TV displays that our football team lost against a team in Belfast, who is also their biggest rival.

I glance at my mum with the hairs on my arms rising. I mutter, "This isn't good."

Her expression mimics my thoughts. Anytime there's a loss, the pub pays the price. The men drink too much and get rowdy, and tonight is no different. I cringe at the thought of how badly we're already in the hole from the destruction our patrons create when they get emotional over anything, whether it be sports, clan losses, or their frequent over-intoxication.

It's another fight I often have with my mum. If people can't control themselves and respect our property, we should ban them. But she lives by a set of clan rules I find ridiculous. The biggest one is that O'Leary members are always welcome, no matter what happens.

My sinking gut doesn't mislead me. Things turn ugly quickly, with fights erupting all over the bar.

"Stop it! Stop it, all of ya!" my mum shouts, but you can barely hear her.

Caleb and his brothers, Dagon and Grady, are in the middle of everything. They're tossing out punches faster than I can keep track. Blood, beer, and whiskey swirl among sweat.

A pint comes flying toward our heads. I grab my mum and pull her behind the bar, ducking but barely missing the glass before it shatters against the register.

My heart slams against my chest cavity, and more pints crash into shards, bursting everywhere.

"Ouch!" Mum cries out as glass falls over her.

I cover her with my body and lock eyes with my cousin Emily, who's closest to my age and barely peeking between her fingers. I look for my other younger cousins, Jessica and Alison, and find them huddled together on the other side of me.

Time stands still as men's grunts, shouts, and other loud noises surround us. Our security finally breaks up the fights, announcing, "Ya can get up now, lasses. It's safe."

"Mum, you okay?" I question, slowly moving off her and holding up her hand. Blood drips down it, and a piece of glass sits wedged between her palm and wrist.

She puts on a brave face. It's not her first injury, but it only irritates me further. She rises and lifts her chin, glaring at Caleb and his brothers. She claims, "I'm fine."

"Ya aren't."

She yanks her hand out of mine and insists, "I've had worse injuries."

"Ya shouldn't have any!"

She grabs a bar towel and pulls the shard out of her hand, wincing. Fresh blood oozes down her arm. She wraps the towel around it and states, "I'm going to tend to this."

"Mum—"

"Time to call it a night, lads," she shouts.

The O'Learys stay quiet.

Mum disappears into the kitchen, shooting daggers at the bloody men with her glare as she passes.

Fresh anger fills me. I'm tired of these animals disrespecting our property and putting my mum and others in danger. I've had enough. I jump up, yelling, "Everyone, get out. Now!" My voice shakes with rage, and I pin my eyes on Caleb.

He smirks through his swollen face, demanding, "Go get your bag."

"Get out," I say through gritted teeth, pointing at the door. I nod to our bouncer, who gives me a look of distress.

It's a bad position to put him in. He's part of the O'Leary clan, but his job is also to protect this pub.

There are few rules that the head of the clan still has to obey, and one of them is listening to security in our pub. It's always been that way, and it's for the good of the clan.

Yet it's no secret that at any time, Caleb could not obey the rules. He's the ruler now. And not a moment goes by that he doesn't let everyone know he has all the power and can change any situation to his advantage. And that means there is nothing I put past him.

Ronin, the head of our security, pats Caleb on the back, stating, "Best if you go now."

He gives him a look of death, and Ronin does his best to stand tall, but he shrinks under Caleb's dark scowl.

Again, I scream, "Get out, all of ya! You're animals!"

My statement only makes the O'Leary clansmen prouder. They don't move, but the other patrons do. One by one, the bar slowly empties until all that's left are O'Leary men.

Caleb steps closer to me, demanding, "I said to get your bag."

I cross my arms. "Last warning and then I'm banning ya from the pub."

He grunts. "Ya can't ban me."

"I can, and I will."

"It's against the rules. Or have ya forgotten the O'Leary ways?" he challenges.

My insides shake so hard I feel queasy. He's right, but I'm not backing down. I do everything in my power not to flinch or back away.

Dagan quietly states, "Let's go. This place is a dump."

"Aye. This place is a mess. Fucking clean it up," Grady adds, picking up a pint that somehow didn't get broken, and downs the rest of it. He slams it on the counter, belches, then saunters out of the pub.

Caleb's gaze follows him, then he pins it back on me.

Tension fills the air with neither of us moving.

Relief fills me when Caleb finally budges, walking toward the exit, but he stops at the door and warns, "The next time I come back for ya, I'm not going to ask nicely. I won't forget this, Lauren."

"Go," I repeat. My insides quiver harder than ever before. They finally leave, and I glance around the pub, grimacing. My gut drops even further.

Glass is everywhere, lying in puddles of bodily fluids and alcohol. Scattered broken chair pieces lie all over the wood floor. Half of a table is missing. I look around and find it smashed against the back wall.

Mum reappears with a broom and dustpan. Stress fills her worn, tired face. She frets, "This is going to cost a fortune."

I angrily shake my head. "You should send the bill to Caleb."

She glares at me. "Ya know that's not an option. And ya shouldn't be defying him the way ya do!"

"You're my mum. Ya should understand why I don't want to marry that thug."

"He'll protect ya," she states again.

I shake my head. "There's no protecting me from anyone except him. He's not a good person."

"He's the head of the clan. You'll have things. Things I never had and could never give ya," she states.

"I don't care about material possessions," I claim and yank the broom from her hand. "And I don't want to be in his world."

"Well, ya are in his world, whether ya like it or not. And ya need to be smart. You're a woman," she asserts.

I scrub my hand over my face in frustration. I'll never win with Mum. She's too engrained in how things have always been. So, I give up arguing and order, "Go home, Mum. We'll clean this place up."

She argues, "I can't leave it like this."

"We've got this, Ruby," Emily declares.

"Yea, take the rest of the night off," Alison chimes in.

"Ditto," Jessica chirps.

Mum hesitates, the weary lines on her face deepening. She pins her gaze on me one last time.

"Go." I nudge her with my elbow, wondering how many hours she's spent over the years dealing with barfights that left everything she owns in pieces.

She finally caves and pulls her bag and coat out of the cabinet. She puts her coat on, and Ronin walks her to her car.

It takes hours to clean the pub. I send Ronin home, and we're about to turn the lights off when there's a knock on the door.

Emily opens it, announcing, "Sorry. We're closed."

A deep voice sends zings down my spine. "But we've traveled so far."

"Far? Where ya from?" Alison questions, stepping next to Emily.

"Cork."

"Well, that is far south. What made ya come this way?" Emily asks and opens the door wider, but I still can't see who she's speaking to.

"We're on a lads' weekend. But we heard about The Confessional, so we had to come pay our respects."

"Well, sorry, we're closed," I interject. I step forward and freeze.

A gorgeous man with a chiseled jaw, dimples, and chestnut hair stares at me. He has a powerful, arrogant expression that is somehow different but also the same as Caleb's. I can't put my finger on why, but I'm sure of it.

He studies me and whines, "Aw, lass, you're going to deny us when we've come this far? Surely ya can let us have one drink?"

My pulse skyrockets as his eyes drift over my body, lingering until he once again pins them back on my face.

He glances behind me, questioning, "Why is the pub empty? I would think you'd be full-on tonight."

"We just cleaned up after a fight," Jessica tells him.

His eyes narrow. "Fight? Ya got some trouble in here we can help ya sort out?" He scans the room.

I stand taller. "No. We have everything under control."

He continues assessing the pub and then nods. "Aye, I see." Then he leans into my ear. His hot breath tickles my neck. He murmurs, "I promise ya, we won't get into any fights. All we want is a pint. Maybe a few shots of whiskey too. What do ya say, lass?"

My butterflies take off. He smells like sin and sex. And it's been way too long since I've had anything exciting happening in that area of my life. I clear my throat and lift my chin. "Ya said you're on a lads' weekend?"

His lips twitch. "Aye. Golfing and hitting the town."

I eye him over, blurting out, "Ya don't look like a golfer."

He puts his palm over his heart, as if I insulted him, and winces. "Am I not fancy enough for the golf course?"

I shake my head, confessing, "No, ya aren't."

He smirks and leans closer again. "So why do I get the feeling that ya prefer me this way?"

Heat travels to my cheeks, and butterflies explode in my stomach.

He adds, "I'm Devin, by the way. What's your name, lass?"

I stay quiet, debating whether I should tell him. His intense gaze never leaves mine.

"I say give him one drink," Jessica calls out.

I spin and glare at her. It's not her place to make the call. I'm in charge when my mum's not here, and she's always inserting her opinion where it doesn't belong.

A man who could pass as Devin's younger brother steps forward, declaring, "Huge tips for all ya lasses. Plus, we'll be buying rounds for ya as well."

Two more lads hang in the background, chuckling.

"Let them in, Lauren," Jessica states again.

"Ya need to learn your place," I reprimand.

She beams and holds her hands in the air, claiming, "They're harmless."

I almost ask her how she knows that because she doesn't. She's naive and stupid. These men could be anyone.

"Aye. We're harmless. We won't be getting into any trouble here. We just want some drinks. Plus, looks like ya can use the money to recoup some of your losses," the one who looks like he could be Devin's brother states.

My gut dives, thinking about the hole we're in that only got deeper tonight.

"See, they're harmless," Jessica claims.

I give her another dirty glare but also cave, knowing I shouldn't turn money away right now. I step back, stating, "Fine. Ya get two rounds. I'm charging ya double. Then you're out of here."

"How many shots of whiskey does that include?" Devin asks, arrogance filling his expression again.

"Ya can buy the bottle and take it with ya on the road," I answer, deciding I should take whatever I can get from his wallet.

He chuckles. "I don't know if there will be anything left. After all, aren't ya drinking it with me?" He gives me another look that sends fire all through my blood. I don't know why I find this man so attractive, but I can't deny it.

I also get the feeling he's dangerous. Yet I'm always around dangerous men. It's what happens when you're Tommy Ahern's niece and part of the O'Leary clan.

And that makes me suddenly remember my caution. I quiz, "Who's your allegiance to?"

He freezes. "My allegiance?"

I cross my arms, the hairs on my neck rising. "Yea, your allegiance. If you're coming into my pub, I need to know who your loyalties are with."

His scrunches his forehead. "Lass, is this a trick question?"

In a firm voice, I answer, "No, it is not."

He glances at the other men, asking, "What am I missing?"

They shrug and look just as confused as Devin.

Emily puts her hand on my arm, stating, "They're just nobodies on a lads' weekend."

Devin's head jerks backward and insult fills his expression. He declares, "Nobodies? I can assure ya we aren't a bunch of nobodies!"

"Then who are ya?" I repeat.

He scratches his head. "I thought I already told ya my name is Devin."

I peer at him closer.

"It's fine," Emily quietly states.

"Is there something we need to know?" Devin's possible brother asks, crossing his arms.

I glance at Emily. She gives me a reassuring smile.

Relief hits me, but something else fills my stomach.

Is he lying?

I glance closer, studying him, and decide he's harmless, even though I feel he'd break someone in two if needed. I declare, "No. Two rounds. Get moving. I don't want to be here all night."

The two other men brush past me. One of them claims, "Well, I'm ready for a Guinness, and I want two shots to start with it." He pulls a bar chair away from the counter.

"Aye, go take the table. We're not sitting at the bar," Devin orders.

I tilt my head, inquiring, "What's wrong with the bar?"

He shrugs. "That table over there fits eight. One, two, three, four, five, six, seven, eight," he states, pointing at everybody in the room. "If we sit at the bar, how will we have a good conversation?"

"Who said we're going to have a conversation?" I retort.

He sniffs hard. "Do you always fight back, lass, when there's no reason to fight?"

"Do you think this is fighting?" I challenge.

His lips twitch again. "No, but something tells me I might want to see ya fight." He gives me another dirty stare that lights up my core.

Jesus, help me.

I turn and walk away, trying to cool the heat rushing to my cheeks. I call out, "Two rounds. Then you're out of here. Don't try to get any more."

He calls back, "Sure, lass. Now don't forget your rounds as well. And come put your pretty self in this chair." He pats the wooden seat next to him and adds, "It would be a shame to let us drink alone."

"Pretty sure ya can handle drinking with your lads without us involved," I say back.

His smile twists. His eyes darken so much I shiver, and he catches it. The intensity of his expression only grows, and his arrogance expands. He challenges, "Are ya scared to have a few drinks?"

My mouth turns dry, and my heart races faster.

"Well?" he questions, arching his eyebrows.

Jessica interjects, "She doesn't drink a lot."

"Shut up," I mutter, glaring at her.

Devin chuckles.

I snap my head back toward him.

"So, you're out? Ya can't handle a few tiny drinks?" he provokes.

I take a deep breath and lift my chin, answering, "Of course I can."

"Great. Round for everyone," he states, pats the chair again, and the feeling I just got myself into something I shouldn't be in erupts within me.

But I don't know how to get out of this situation if I tried.

Nor do I know if I want to stop whatever's about to happen.

Devin locks his challenging stare back on mine, and nothing within me will allow me to do anything but prove to him I can handle whatever it is this night is about to bring.

2

Devin

I introduce the others. "This is my brother Tynan. And these two plonkers are Cathal and Brogan."

They grunt, but I can tell they're pleasantly surprised by all the women's looks.

Niceties are exchanged between everyone. Then I pull the lass aside, the one who can't seem to keep her mouth shut, deciding she's an asset for me to have on my good side.

I ask, "Lass, what are your friends' names?"

I glance over at Lauren, who's obviously in charge. Her allegiance is to the O'Learys, and I know I should hate her, but nothing but adrenaline is bouncing through my veins. She's a looker, and everything about her makes this entire trip worth it. I just have to figure out how to get her alone.

The barmaid gives me an innocent smile. I assume she's only twenty-one, maybe twenty-two. Lauren can't be much older, but her confidence makes me question her age, and she's definitely in charge. For some reason, she's also extra cautious, but I can't say I blame her. The state of the pub is horrible, even though they've cleaned up.

Cracks splinter the mirror behind the bar. There's barely a stack of pint glasses left compared to what I assume used to be there. A bare area gives me the notion that a table's missing, and multiple others need more chairs around them.

It shouldn't surprise me. It makes sense that the O'Learys would destroy the place when the game was lost. We wouldn't stand for it in O'Connor pubs if it would have been our loss, but everything's different with the O'Learys.

And somehow, we lucked out that none of them are here. It makes everything feel like karma, fate, or whatever you want to call it.

Lauren warns, "Jessica, if you don't learn to keep that big mouth of yours shut, I swear to God—"

"Easy there," I interject.

Lauren spins on me.

"I asked her a question. Ya can't ignore your patrons, now can ya?" I slowly lower my eyes over her body once more, unable to stop myself from gawking. Her wavy, beautiful strawberry-blond hair is in a ponytail. She has blue eyes, which I'm a sucker for, and her legs... Jesus, they go for a mile. Her meaty thighs fill out her jeans to perfection. It's everything I like in a lass. All I can imagine is her squeezing her thighs around my head.

She snaps, "Ya want to keep your eyes up here?"

I chuckle and realize she's fierier than I originally anticipated. My cock hardens, and I tease, "Are ya sure you want me to?" I give her another lewd once-over.

Her cheeks burst into flames. She puts her hand on her hip, squints, and accuses, "Ya sure are cocky for a lad who's never been in here before." Mistrust fills her expression.

I stand straighter, declaring, "I'm not a lad, I'm a man. But maybe you've never had the chance to understand the difference." I wiggle my eyebrows.

Her blues widen further. It's not much, but I don't miss it. Then she swallows hard, and all I can think about is putting my hand around her neck and squeezing while I pound into her. My erection strains against my zipper, and I have to hold in my groan.

Fuck, I need to get her into bed.

I glance over her head at an open door. All I can see are a set of stairs leading into darkness. I ask, "What's up there?"

"A flat."

"Whose?"

"Lauren's," Jessica answers, which only infuriates Lauren more.

I put my arm around Jessica, tugging her into me, ordering, "Easy, Lauren. Jessica's just appeasing me when I'm asking questions. No need to get upset with her. She's just doing her job."

Lauren tilts her head. "Her job isn't to open her mouth constantly when she shouldn't, now is it, Jessica?"

She smirks. "No, dear cousin, it's not."

I turn my most charming smile onto Jessica, stating, "Ah, cousins. You're related. So, you're stuck with her regardless, huh?"

Jessica giggles and puts her hand over her mouth, nodding.

"Stuck with me? If that's how you see it, then ya can find another job," Lauren fires at Jessica.

"Easy," I say.

Lauren crosses her arms.

Jessica giggles again, confessing, "She gets like this. She's actually a really cool person most of the time."

Lauren gives her another exasperated look.

I decide that Jessica is my new favorite person, so I pull out a chair and motion for her to sit. Then I do the same for Lauren with the chair across from Jessica but next to me. We sit, and once everyone's at the table, I slide a shot over to Jessica, then hold mine out. "Cheers, lass. It's nice to be greeted with a friendly face when you're from out of town."

Jessica's cheeks flush crimson, and I can tell she's got a little crush starting to form. I note to work that to my advantage.

"Thanks," she shyly peeps and clinks her shot glass to mine.

We down our whiskey, and I refocus on Lauren just in time to see a hint of jealousy flicker over her expression. It only excites me further.

I tug her chair closer to me and put my arm around her.

She yelps, "What are ya doing?"

I hand her a shot. "I saved this one for ya."

"Don't do me any favors," she spouts.

I softly chuckle, clink her glass, then wait to down mine until she tosses hers back. She swallows and winces.

I take mine and ask, "Ya really don't drink a lot, do ya?"

"No. Not that it's your business," she claims.

I chuckle. "I can tell, lass."

"So? Is it bad that I don't drink? That I don't want to be an alcoholic like most people who frequent this pub?"

"No, it's not bad," I answer, unable to stop my grin from forming.

She tilts her head and her eyes shoot me another round of daggers. "Then why do ya have a look on your face that I want to slap off?"

I lean closer. "Are ya always so defensive?"

"I'm not defensive," she claims.

One of the girls giggles. Lauren snaps her head toward her, claiming, "I'm not."

"Ya kind of are," another lass argues.

Lauren groans. "Is everybody in this room against me? Even you, Alison?"

I tug her closer to me. "No, no, no. Ya just need to relax a little bit."

"I am relaxed."

I arch my eyebrows and stare at her until her cheeks turn redder than Jessica's. I move a pint in front of Lauren, then take a mouthful of mine. I nod at it. "Go on."

She takes a sip and cringes, but not as bad as with the whiskey.

"What do ya do for fun, Lauren?"

She singsongs, "Still none of your business."

"She works," a lass with dirty-blonde hair blurts out.

Brogan declares, "Cheers to Lauren's working pastime."

Lauren groans. "Not you too, Emily!"

Laughter erupts. Everybody holds their pints out, and clinks fill the air.

I turn back to Lauren, rubbing my thumb on her shoulder.

She eyes it, then turns her gaze on me. "You're awfully handsy."

"Are ya complaining?"

She stays quiet.

I state, "Surely ya do more than work. Tell me, what are your hobbies?"

She just stares at me.

I insist, "Ya must have something that ya like to do. Surely ya don't just work, work, work, and not have any fun. Not a girl like ya."

Her eyes turn to slits. "A girl like me? What does that mean?"

I assess her again, trying to keep a straight face. "Aye. A girl like ya."

She sighs in frustration. "You're annoying."

"So, I've been told."

As always, I can count on Jessica. She announces, "Lauren loves to ride horses. She used to compete too. She was an equestrian champion in show jumping."

"Are ya going to tell everyone my entire life?" Lauren accuses.

Jessica giggles again and takes another large mouthful of stout.

Emily laughs, nodding toward Jessica. "Ya know how she is. Sorry, cousin, you're in for it all night. Ya know there's no shutting her up."

"No, there isn't," Lauren agrees.

"Why'd ya stop riding?" I inquire.

"Ya mean competing. She competed," Emily corrects.

"Sorry. Why'd ya stop competing in show jumping? That sounds scary," I admit.

Lauren's lips twitch for the first time. "You're scared of horses?"

"I'm not scared of horses," I claim.

"Ya just said show jumping sounds scary."

"Well, getting on a horse and jumping sounds a little intimidating if ya don't know what you're doing," I confirm, even though I don't like confessing any of my fears.

She turns a shocked expression on me. "I didn't think ya'd be such a baby."

"I'm not a baby," I declare.

"Aren't ya? It's just a horse," she chirps, smirking.

I ignore her remark and push, "So ya didn't tell me why ya stopped competing."

Lauren's expression turns into a mix of nostalgia with a possible hint of regret, along with some sadness. She shrugs, finally stating quietly, "It was time."

Jessica rambles, "She was so good. Ya should have seen her. Everybody in town loved to watch her."

"Wow. Sounds like you were amazing at it. I don't understand why ya would let it go," I add, wanting to know why she quit.

"Let's change the subject," Lauren says, looking at me with pleading eyes.

I decide to show her some mercy and let it go for now. Then I slide my hand under the table and onto her thigh.

She freezes but doesn't swipe at it.

That's my girl, warming up to me, I think and down the rest of my pint while slowly caressing the inside of her thigh.

She remains frozen.

I point at the table, ordering the women, "Drink up. We're about to start pint two."

Tynan passes out more shots.

After everyone finishes them and Lauren forces the rest of her first stout down, I question, "Got any cards, lass?"

Her forehead wrinkles. "Why?"

"So we can play a game," I state.

She points out, "You're only here for two rounds. Why would we get started on a game?"

"Are ya scared to play? A horse-jumping world equestrian champion is fearful of some cards?"

"I wasn't a world champion," she states.

I shrug. "Ya are in my book. I don't know any other horse jumpers. And your cousin said ya were a champion. Is that true or not?"

Embarrassment fills her face.

Jessica insists, "No, she was. She really was!"

"Jessica," Lauren groans in annoyance.

I ask again, keeping my gaze on Lauren, "Well, were ya a champion or not?"

She squares her shoulders. "Yea, I was."

"Okay, so a champion horse jumper is scared to play a little bit of cards. Makes zero sense to me."

She lifts her chin in defiance. "Of course I'm not scared to play cards. But I'm not sure how there's enough time for a game when you're only here for two rounds of drinks." She smiles and bats her eyes.

Adrenaline bursts into all my cells. "I'm sure ya can't beat me."

"At what game?"

I shrug. "Any one ya choose."

She scoffs. "That's a dumb bet."

I squeeze her thigh and lean closer. "Then let's place a wager."

Her face hardens. "I don't gamble."

"Why? Ya just said that I made a dumb bet. You don't want to place a wager with me that ya can win?"

She glances around the bar and shakes her head. "I'm not gambling any of my cash. If ya haven't noticed, this place requires an investment to fix it up, and money doesn't grow on trees."

"But if it's a dumb bet, ya have nothing to lose," I point out.

She stays quiet.

Jessica gets up, reaches over the bar, and tosses a deck of cards on the table.

Lauren gives her another dirty look, which I'm becoming a sucker for. All I can think about is how I want to wipe that pissed-off glare off her face while she's coming with my cock inside her.

"Play, Lauren! You're great at cards. Place a bet. Who cares?" Jessica chirps and takes another shot of whiskey.

Lauren accuses, "You're getting drunk."

Jessica shrugs. "So? After the night we've had, we all deserve to get drunk."

"Agreed," Alison says and grabs another shot off the table.

I ask, "How much will it cost to fix this pub? My guess is maybe 5,000 euros?"

Lauren briefly closes her eyes and sighs. She avoids my gaze, but I can see the worry on her face.

Leave it to Jessica to tell me everything I want to know. She blurts out, "Last time, it cost seven. The time before that, six. Oh, then that one time it was eight. The lowest we've ever gotten away with is three."

Oh, how I'm starting to love Jessica.

"Why don't ya just tell everybody all of our business?" Lauren seethes.

I move my hand up her thigh.

She holds her breath and slowly meets my gaze.

"10,000 euros if I lose," I challenge.

Her eyes widen. "I don't have 10,000 euros to gamble away."

"But ya said you could beat me," I taunt.

"No, I didn't."

"Ya did. Ya said it was a stupid bet," I insist.

"Yea, ya did make a stupid comment," she claims.

"So, is it a stupid bet or not a stupid bet?" I ask.

"What does it matter? I'm not betting money I can't afford to lose. Maybe you have tons in the bank, but we don't. This is my mum's pub, and I'm not going to do anything to risk hurting it further," she declares.

"I'm not asking ya to hurt your pub," I claim.

She huffs. "I'm not betting money."

"I don't want your money."

She squints, peering at me closer. She cautiously asks, "If ya don't want cash, what's in it for ya?"

My lips twitch, and my cock aches so much that I take an extra few seconds to answer. I point to the stairwell and announce, "If I win, I get an hour with ya upstairs."

Shock fills her expression. "What?"

"Alone," I add.

She seethes, "I am not a prostitute. I don't know what ya thought coming in here, but none of us"—she points to her cousins—"including myself, are prostitutes."

I hold my hands in the air. "Easy, lass. Did I say any of ya were?"

More anger fills her expression.

I quickly assert, "I didn't say we had to do anything. I just said an hour with ya alone. Now, if there's something that ya want to do with me, we can talk about your deepest desires." I grin at her.

She crosses her arms over her chest, still angry. I sit back in my seat and move my hand from her thigh. I point around. "Ten grand might come in handy. Seems more than a fair exchange. An hour of your time versus ten grand of my money."

"I'm not sleeping with ya," she claims.

Sure, you're not, I say in my mind. But I reply, "Then don't lose."

She scoffs. "It has nothing to do with sleeping with me, my arse. Ya just admitted it."

I put my hands in the air. "It's a joke. Come on. Really, relax a little bit." I push her pint closer.

She stares at it.

"Have a sip. Think about it."

She doesn't.

I pick up the pint and hold it toward her lips. "Take a drink and let go of your anger."

"You're annoying."

"Aye. Now have a yummy mouthful of stout."

She gives me another fiery glare but grabs the pint out of my hand. She takes several sips, then puts it on the table.

I continue, "One hour of your time alone with ya if you lose. But if I lose, I will give ya ten grand. Ya can fix this place and put some extra money in a rainy day fund. From where I'm sitting, it's a win-win. Lasses, what do you think?" I stare at her cousins.

Emily's mouth is practically on the table.

Jessica's eyes beam brighter.

Alison has her hand over her mouth, stifling her giggle.

I goad, "Lasses, help me out here."

"Ya should do it," Jessica encourages.

"Of course you'd say that," Lauren mutters.

"I'm with Jessica. I think it's a great idea. Ya always win at cards anyway," Alison states.

"I'm not sleeping with him," Lauren declares again adamantly.

"All ya have to do is win, and we get ten grand. He confirmed you don't have to sleep with him," Alison argues.

"Exactly. I just said an hour of your time," I reiterate, even though as soon as I get her alone, I'm putting the moves on her so swiftly she won't know what hit her. And she won't be able to resist.

Lauren turns toward Emily.

Her face falls. She admits, "Ya know that we don't have a lot of options right now. Just do it. Win the money. You'll be fine and then we can fix the pub without the extra stress. Think of how much it'll help your mum."

I taunt, "Am I that bad that ya don't want to spend an hour of your time with me if ya lose?"

Lauren tilts her head and studies me with distrust in her eyes.

I add, "It's just an hour. All we have to do is sit up there and talk. That's it."

She cautiously asks, "Talk only?"

I nod. "Aye. Talk. Or whatever ya want to do. But if ya just want to talk, we'll just talk."

Her mistrust never leaves her face.

I pick up the cards and shuffle them. "Are ya really that scared you'll lose?"

"I'm not scared," she insists.

I grin at her. "Great. Then what game are we playing, and are you dealing or am I?"

3

Lauren

*D*evin keeps his arrogant, yet challenging, expression pinned on me, but I keep debating.

Ten thousand euros would solve our problems.

But I'm not a prostitute.

He said we can talk for the hour if I lose.

"Play Irish Switch! Ya always win that!" Jessica blurts out.

"Irish Switch? Never heard of it," Devin states.

My pulse rises. If he's never played it, that gives me an advantage.

It's still a risk.

He declares, "Let's not take all night. It's decision time. Do we have a bet or not?"

My jitters increase. I don't answer him.

"If I walk out that door, you're going to kick yourself for not attempting to earn 10,000 euros," he warns.

He's right.

I can do this!

I take a deep breath and lift my chin, holding my hand out for the cards and asserting, "I'm dealing."

His lips twitch. "Ya don't trust me?"

I scoff, admitting, "Nope!"

"But I said I don't even know how to play."

"Doesn't matter."

He chuckles and places the deck into my palm. He leans closer and asks, "How do I know ya aren't a cheater?"

"She's not!" Jessica insists.

For the first time all night, I'm not annoyed with her. I keep my eyes on Devin and state, "See. Even your buddy Jessica can vouch for my honest playing skills."

His eyes dart to my lips, and he states, "Well, if my buddy Jessica says it, then it must be true." He once again pins his gaze full of mischief on mine.

Zings fly to my core. I reprimand myself for reacting to his sexy, dirty expression and squeeze my thighs tighter. I sit back in my chair and shuffle the cards.

He asks, "What are the rules?"

"Don't worry. It's easy and doesn't require a ton of brainpower, so ya should be good," I tease.

"Are ya saying ya don't think I'm smart?"

I tilt my head, smile, and bat my eyes, declaring, "I never spoke those words."

"Hmmm," Devin replies with a deep, grumbling sound.

It intensifies all the sensations inside me that I wish would go away. I ignore the heat creeping up my neck and smirk. "What does hmm mean?"

He points to the cards. "Are ya going to let me cut the deck at least?"

I slap it on the table.

He puts his palm over the top card and fans the deck. Then he slowly drags his finger over them, stopping three-quarters of the way. He divides it into two piles and puts the bottom on the top.

I arch my eyebrows. "Was that a magic trick?"

He grazes his knuckles over the side of my thigh, answering, "Nah. I keep those for private times."

Tingles explode under his touch, racing to places inconvenient when he's a stranger I need to only be thinking about beating.

Tense silence builds between us, and more arrogance grows in his expression.

Why do I think his cockiness is so hot?

It's not.

Yes, it is.

Concentrate!

He taps his fingers on the table. "How do we play? Let's get this going so I get my hour of alone time."

Butterflies overpower all my logic.

Maybe I should lose on purpose.

What?

No! No! No!

I bet he's an animal between the sheets.

Stop it!

Ten grand. Get the ten grand.

I order, "Ya better put your money on the table where I can see it. Don't want ya losing and running out of here."

"Ya think I'd not make good on my bet?"

I admit, "I don't put anything past ya."

He leans into my ear, teasing my lobe with his hot breath, declaring, "There's a lot of things ya shouldn't put past me, lass. Paying my debts isn't one of them."

I turn to face him, demanding, "Still want ya to put it on the table where I can see it. Ten grand's a lot of cash. How do I even know ya have it?"

He studies me, and my heart thumps so loud in my chest that I think he must hear it.

Tynan calls out, "Well, get on with it. When your game ends, Emily and I are making a wager."

Surprise fills Emily's voice when she squeaks, "We are?"

"Aye. Unless ya don't want to take your chances of winning some cash. I'll double my brother's bet." He slams down a wad of euros, and my cousins and I stare at the money with our mouths hanging open.

These guys are seriously crazy for making these types of wagers.

Tynan wiggles his eyebrows and adds, "But I get *two* hours of your time. I like to take my time..." He eyes her over, then adds, "Talking."

Emily bites her lip, her blues sparkle brighter, and her cheeks burst into flames.

My instincts kick back in. I inquire, "What did ya say ya all do for a living?"

Devin answers, "Technology."

I turn my gaze back on him. "Technology?"

He nods. "Aye. Boring stuff."

"What kind of boring stuff?" I push.

He shrugs. "Software. Like I said, boring stuff."

I assess him further.

He crosses his arms over his chest. "Sorry. Do I not look posh enough for technology either?"

I wince since my previous golfer's comment must have struck a nerve with him. Still, I'm not going to apologize. These men are strangers and in my pub. It's my duty to be skeptical and question them on who they are, especially when there's so much chaos in my family. So, I respond, "Can't say I'm an expert on techies. Not sure I've ever met one, but maybe a pair of sexy specs would be appropriate."

He chuckles. "Sexy specs?"

"Yea. Don't all tech nerds wear glasses?"

"Who said I'm a nerd?"

I shrug.

"But ya think glasses are sexy?"

"Depends on the pair and who's wearing them."

"Why are ya all talking about glasses when none of us wear them? Let's get on with it," Tynan blurts out.

"Agreed." Devin gives me another cocky look, then removes a wad of cash from his pocket. He sets it next to Tynan's. It's half the size, and I once again gape.

He demands, "Let's get on with this, lass. How do we play?"

Jessica interjects, which is good because my mind turns mushy again. She announces, "It's easy. The first to run out of cards wins. You can match numbers or suits. So, if ya get a six of spades, ya can put down a six or a spade. If ya don't have one, ya have to draw another card."

"It's like Uno?"

"Yea," I confirm.

He leans back in his chair, cracks his neck, then his knuckles, and rolls his shoulders. He commands, "Deal it up, lass."

Jesus, help me.

Why did that turn me on?

Focus!

I obey, then put the remaining cards on the table and flip the first one over, which is the queen of hearts. I state, "Ya can go first."

He purses his lips, shaking his head. "Nope. Lasses first."

"But I dealt."

"And I'm a gentleman." Mischief flies into his expression.

I tilt my head. "Sure, ya are."

"Well, it depends on the situation," he confesses and points to my hand. "You're up."

My butterflies reappear, and I refocus on my hand, adding a queen to the pile.

For several rounds, we put cards down until we each have three left.

Jessica states, "I don't think you shuffled very well."

I toss her some daggers with my glare. Her inability to keep her opinion to herself annoys me more than normal this evening.

"Crap," Devin mutters and picks up a card.

My adrenaline spikes. Then I assess my hand, and my gut drops. I double-check, but I don't have an eight or diamond. I groan and pick up a ten of clubs.

Devin adds a two of diamonds.

My stomach dives further, and my insides turn to a soft quiver.

Everything is fine.

The game's not over. This is part of the sweetness of victory.

Three to five. Not good.

I've been down to one and ended up winning before. I can do this!

I pick up a two of spades and lift my chin, giving Devin my most intimidating look.

"You're making me all hot and bothered with your glare," he teases.

"Funny." I smirk.

He glances at his hand and reaches for a card from the pile.

Relief hits me. I add my two.

He groans and adds another card to his hand.

We go back and forth for two hours, ignoring the grumbles from the others to get on with it so they can play.

After each round, our intense stares relock, challenging the other. And with every minute passing, every feature he possesses becomes more alluring.

Several times, I reprimand myself. Throughout our game, his suggestive comments get more daring.

I find myself having a harder time focusing and not wondering if I could get an hour alone with him even when I win.

We get down to one card each. He glances at his hand, then grabs the wad of cash. He drops it on top of the pickup pile. He leans closer and suggests, "Want to change the terms?"

Rage flares inside me. Of course he's going to try and not pay me what he's about to lose. I blurt out, "Don't try to get out of our deal!"

"Ya don't want to do best out of three, double or nothing?"

I firmly state, "No. I do not. Now, take the money off the cards and make your move."

His lips twitch. "Are ya sure that's what ya want, lass?"

I point to the deck, ordering, "Play it."

He drags his eyes over my body, resting on my chest, then lips, and finally back on my gaze. With no emotion in his expression, which somehow makes him appear cockier, he tosses his card onto the discard pile. "Don't say I didn't give ya another fighting chance, lass. Time to go upstairs and give me my hour."

My gut sinks. Blood drains from my face as I stare at the card and the ten grand I desperately need for the pub.

"Ya lost," Jessica blurts out in disbelief.

I snap my head toward her. "No shit."

"But ya never lose."

My insides quiver. I scoot my chair back, blinking hard. I move toward the back entrance.

Devin calls out, "Are ya backing out of our deal?"

I freeze, squeezing my eyes shut.

Tense silence fills the pub. My pulse pounds between my ears.

He adds, "I didn't take ya for a lass who doesn't keep her word."

My pride conflicts with wanting to run. I hate that I lost, but I also am a woman of my word. I know better than to gamble. My da lost everything we had to his addiction. The only reason my mum got to keep the pub was that her father still owned it at the time, so my da couldn't gamble that too.

Regardless of my error, I agreed to this, so now I have to pay the price.

I shouldn't have drunk.

The alcohol had nothing to do with me wagering my time with this stranger.

I didn't need those extra shots while we were playing.

Dammit!

I say nothing, forcing myself to climb the stairs, cursing myself every step over how stupid I was to engage in his bet. Catcalls from his lads ring through the air, making me wince. I arrive at the top, reach into my pocket for the key, and unlock my flat.

The sound of the *woots* from the others gets muffled and his heavy footsteps get more prominent.

I close my eyes, trying to regulate my heartbeat.

I'm just talking.

He's going to try something.

Take control of this situation.

I glance around my one-room flat and more panic hits me. My tiny place consists of a small kitchenette against the wall, a bathroom, one sofa with enough room for two people, and my unmade bed.

"Nice place," he states, and sets down the fifth of whiskey, which is three quarters gone, on my side table.

I spin, pull my phone out of my pocket, and set the alarm. "Your hour starts now." I quickly go to the bed and pull the covers up.

"No need to make it when we're just going to mess it up again," Devin taunts, shutting the door and locking it.

Anxiety erupts in my chest as tingles race down my spine. The mixed signals in my body only make the situation worse. I freeze, gripping my duvet and staring at him.

He takes two steps closer and reaches for my hand.

A wave of sensations I don't want to have right now rushes between my thighs. My lips tremble, matching my hand.

He closes his long fingers around mine and suggests, "Take a breather, Lauren. Let's have a seat on the sofa and talk."

"Talk?" I question, tilting my head and squinting at him.

He softly chuckles. "Didn't ya say ya wanted to talk for our hour?"

"That's not what ya wanted when you bet me an hour of my time. I think you've made that clear," I blurt out.

And now I've become Jessica.

I turn my head away from him and take a deep breath.

He tugs me into him, wrapping his arm around my waist and sliding his hand through my hair. He gently yanks on it so I can't escape him.

I gasp, shaking harder, wishing I could control anything in my body that seems to have gone rogue on me.

His gaze intensifies, flaring with fire like nothing I've ever witnessed. He turns it on my lips.

My mouth waters, and I swallow hard, taking shallow breaths, feeling his heart pounding against my palm.

He demands, "Tell me ya want to talk, and we'll talk. I don't force lasses to do things they don't want to do."

I stay quiet, willing myself to say it but unable to get the words out.

He moves his chiseled features closer to my face, and I think he's going to kiss me. I hold my inhale, but he brushes his lips against my ear, stating, "Want to know what I think about ya?" His hand drops to my ass, gripping my cheek.

A tiny whimper flies out of me. I reprimand myself again, but I can't seem to speak.

He roughly chuckles, pressing his cheek against mine, and I close my eyes. He murmurs, "I think you're my type, and I'm yours."

I force myself to open my eyes and snap back into reality. I turn toward him, asking, "Now, why is that?"

Assurance is all over his expression, as if there's no way he could possibly be wrong. He unbuttons my jeans then slides his hand behind me. He bypasses my ass, gripping the back of my thigh.

I inhale sharply.

"That right there."

"What?" I barely get out.

"Ya can't help but respond to me. Ya did it all night."

"I... Why do ya think that?" I ask, trying to deny it.

"I'm a man. I know. And these thighs of yours are driving me crazy, angel."

"Angel?" I question, my voice growing stronger. And what's he talking about regarding my thighs? They're a tad juicy, so I've never considered them my best asset.

He kisses my neck, trailing his lips to my ear. Then he pushes his palm against my leg, moving me closer so his erection digs into my stomach, and states, "Vixen might be more appropriate." He positions his face in front of mine and adds, "You're a mix of naughty and nice, aren't ya, lass?"

My butterflies flutter so hard that I feel dizzy. Or it could be from the scent of his woodsy Meghann cologne mixing with whiskey and Guinness. I respond, "Ya seem to think ya know me well."

He confidently replies, "No. I don't know ya. I only know what I've wanted to do to ya since I stepped through that door and how I think you'll respond."

How I'll respond.

Jesus.

My heart races faster.

His fingers climb up my throat. They curve around it, pressing tighter and surprising me. I've never been into neck play.

When Caleb tried, I hated it and told him to never do it again. He didn't listen, of course, and the last time he did it, I went into a full-blown panic attack. Yet it didn't faze him. He loved watching me panic to the point I thought my heart and lungs would explode.

So, to my shock, something about this stranger gripping me with dominance turns me on. I can't comprehend it, but there's no denying how my pussy's throbbing with need.

Devin adds, "Aye, my little angel-vixen. I want to know what sounds come out of this pretty mouth of yours right before ya beg me for everything you've never felt before."

His arrogant statement should turn me off, but it doesn't.

He lowers his voice, continuing, "Imagine your body shuddering against mine, helpless to what I release upon ya."

"You're awfully sure of yourself," I mumble, which is the wrong thing to say.

Devin's lips curl. His fingers slide between my thighs and into my pussy.

I gasp.

He thrusts slowly, squeezing my throat tighter, brushing his lips against mine, challenging, "Tell me to stop."

A moment passes. He inches closer and glides his tongue into my mouth, urgently flicking it against mine, the sweet remnants of whiskey bursting on my taste buds.

My good sense flies out the window and can't resist him any longer. I return his kiss, grinding my body onto his hand.

He removes it, circles it around my body, and unfastens my jeans. He mutters against my lips, "I haven't heard ya protest, angel."

There's a split second where I tell myself to stop this, but the fire in his eyes and his body against mine make it impossible to listen. I stick my tongue back into his mouth, lacing my fingers into his hair, barely getting air into my lungs.

He shoves my pants to the floor, along with my thong. He releases me, tearing my pub shirt over my head and unfastening my bra. His large palm presses my shoulder. I fall to my ass on the mattress, and he pushes me onto my back.

He kneels on the ground, lifts my thighs over his shoulders, and thrusts two fingers inside me.

"Oh!" I moan, gripping the edge of the mattress.

"What do ya taste like, my little vixen?" he taunts, then kisses the inside of my thighs.

Delicious sensations hit me so hard that I squeeze my insides against his fingers.

"Fucking good lass," he praises, then tornadoes my clit with his tongue.

"Oh Jesus!" I cry out.

He chuckles but doesn't remove his mouth from my body; instead, he reaches up and once again circles his fingers around my throat, adding more pressure than before, and lifts my head off the bed. His lips curl around my clit, and he pins his steely gaze on mine. He demands, "Watch me eat you, my angel."

I couldn't disobey him if I wanted. He has me in a tight hold, but I wouldn't look away if I had the chance. The way he's manipulating every sensitive part I have, dominating me while studying my every reaction, turns me on even more.

Heat explodes in my body to the point sweat bursts out on my skin. I tighten my hold on the mattress, using it as leverage to grind my hips against him.

"Ya want it? Ya gotta earn it," he mumbles and slows everything down, moving his mouth back to my thighs.

A whine slips out of my mouth. Desperate. Incoherent. Needy for everything he's just done to me to resume.

Satisfaction flashes in his eyes, and he moves to my other thigh.

More of my whimpers fill the air, and I shudder.

He licks all around his fingers, then toward my clit, but he stops before he gets to it.

I reach for his head and try to hold him there, grinding harder. But he's too strong. He only stays where I want him when it's his plan.

He creates a pattern, sucking and licking me to the point I'm going to fly over the edge but always stopping me before I do. Then he moves back to my thighs or teases the rest of my pussy.

No one's ever spent so much time focusing on my pleasure yet not allowed me to have it. Any man I've ever been with was only worried about theirs. And even though adrenaline fills my cells, I haven't hit the crest. My body quivers harder and harder with sneak peeks of what's to come until he releases his grip on my throat slightly, and I beg him, crying out his name.

Then it happens. He tightens his grip on my throat to the point I can't breathe, sucks my clit hard, and a surge of endorphins consumes me.

My body convulses so violently I see stars. A gush of fluid bursts from me, pushing me higher.

My alarm blares into the air, alerting us that the hour is up. I blink hard, returning to reality.

Devin's gaze comes back into view. He softens his grip on my throat. His expression flares with more heat. He grits his teeth and demands, "Tell me to keep going, angel."

My orgasm withers. I keep shaking but want nothing more than to get back the sensations he's given me. So, I swallow hard against his fingers, giving him a pleading look.

"Tap into your vixen side and tell me." He sucks again on my pussy.

Another round of adrenaline rushes through me, and he tightens his grip once more. I arch my back and cry out.

The alarm grows louder.

He lets go of my throat. He reaches for the phone, turns off the alarm, then, in a quick move, flips me onto my stomach. He spreads my thighs, slides his arm under my waist, and thrusts into me with one push.

"Jesus Christ!" I yell in a shaky voice, loving how his body fills mine.

He thrusts a few times, and everything is different but just as tempting as his mouth.

New quivers erupt within me. My walls try to grip his erection, spasming with every inch he moves.

He grabs my hand and laces his fingers through mine, then stretches my arm above my head. He murmurs in my ear, "Tell me to stay, my little vixen."

There's only one answer. My voice cracks as I desperately answer, "Stay."

4

Devin

*L*auren's wet body throbs against mine, driving me to the near point of insanity.

Everything about this girl's taboo. She's way too young for me. What is she? Twenty-three tops? Her blood is linked to the O'Leary's, which makes her my enemy. If she knew who I was, she'd hate me.

Yet here I am, quenching my thirst to understand why my two older brothers couldn't walk away from their O'Leary brides.

And I'm no longer confused. If their experience is half as good as mine is right now, I can't blame them.

Except I won't make their mistake.

I'm leaving this town tomorrow morning with my itch scratched. There won't be any O'Leary woman in my life long-term except my sisters-in-law, who have taken an oath to no longer have any loyalty to their bloodline. But my brothers can deal with the headaches that come with that mess.

"Devin," Lauren moans, making it harder for me to keep my current pace without ending our little rendezvous too soon.

I slow down my thrusts, bite her collarbone, and wrap my hand around the back of her neck.

"Jesus," she whimpers, her cheeks flushed, skin coated with sweat.

I mutter, "Take it like a good little vixen."

She closes her eyes, ordering, "Faster."

"Shh. I'm in charge. Your pussy's going to take me all night now that you told me to stay," I inform her, slowing it down even more.

She pins her heated gaze on mine. Her voice cracks as she pleads, "Please. Too...too slow."

I kiss her lips and pull away when her tongue flicks out of her mouth and into mine. I move to her ear and taunt, "Ya want it faster, angel?"

"Mmm..." she whines.

I glance around her small space, wishing I had the luxuries of my bedroom suite. There's not much to restrain her with, not even a headboard. But if I'm going to last longer, I need some relief.

I pull out of her and jump off the mattress.

"What—" she starts.

I tug her onto her feet and move her to the kitchenette.

"Why—" she tries again.

I spin her against the fridge.

"Devin!"

I press against her, ordering, "Hands on the top."

She turns, scrunching her flushed face. "What?"

"Is it your role to ask questions, angel?"

She takes a deep breath, but the defiant expression she's had all night reappears.

I answer for her. "No. It's not. So put your hands on top of the fridge and don't take them off. If ya do, there will be consequences."

She huffs. "What would those be?"

I reach for her wrists and position them over her head and on the appliance. I press her palms flat and threaten, "I only give warnings once. This is the time to be an angel and obey. If your vixen shows up and ya try to disobey, I won't ever make ya come again. I'll leave ya dripping wet with no way to quench your needs. Understand?"

She smirks, batting her eyes, claiming, "I can always take care of myself. Or did ya forget?"

I softly chuckle, keep her arms pinned with one hand, and grip her chin with my other. I move an inch from her lips and ask, "Is that what ya prefer? A night with ya satisfying yourself or one with me doing the work?"

She stays quiet, but her answer is all over her expression.

Still, I'm not letting this slide. "This isn't the moment to let your pride rule ya, my little vixen. I need an answer, or I'll assume you want me to end things now."

She still doesn't answer.

I slide my thumb over her jaw and add, "Let me assure ya, if I walk out that door, I'm not coming back. So what's it going to be? Me or ya on your own?"

She closes her eyes.

"Oh, how stubborn my little vixen is," I murmur in her ear, grazing my mouth against her neck.

She shudders.

"Three. Two—"

"Ya," she confesses in a barely audible tone.

My grin can't be stopped. I demand, "Louder. I couldn't hear ya."

She glares at me.

I slide my hand down her arm, over the curve of her torso, and in front of her body. I cup her pussy and press my thumb over her clit. In my most authoritative voice, I assert, "Tell me. Do ya want me or yourself on your own?"

She swallows hard, then clearly admits, "Ya."

I give her a chaste kiss on the lips. "That's a good angel. Now, don't move unless I permit ya."

She scoffs. "Permit me?"

I warn, "Your defiance is only going to bring ya consequences. Decide right now if ya want rewards or punishments."

She gives me an insubordinate expression.

My cock throbs against her back, and I chuckle. "Two choices. Keep your hands on top at all times..." I take my ankle and move her legs farther apart, then continue, "Or all this stops." I fist her hair and tug so she's facing the ceiling.

She inhales sharply.

"Don't move," I reiterate, placing her hair over one shoulder so it's out of the way. I step back and stare at her, taking in her long torso, round ass, and those juicy thighs that exceeded all my expectations once her jeans were off. I mutter, "Jesus, you're perfect."

"Why am I like this?" she asks.

So I don't come in you within two minutes like a little pussy.

"Shh. No more questions," I declare, then press my lips to her shoulder, make my way across them, then down her spine while dragging my fingers over my kisses. I get to the top of her ass, and she's quivering. The scent of her arousal swirls around us. My erection continues to ache, but I push it out of my mind, focusing on every inch of her backside.

I nibble on her ass, and she moans. I kiss her to her ankles, caressing her legs and licking the drops of her juices running down them.

"You're being a good angel," I praise, glancing up, impressed with how she keeps her position without restraints.

Her chest rises and falls in short bursts. The sound of her ragged breath echoes in the air.

I rotate between licking and kissing her legs while sliding my palms over her body after my mouth's left it. Her whimpers get louder, and her tremors turn more intense. When I reach her spine, I flick my tongue against it, gripping her hips, until my mouth hits her neck. I murmur, "Ya react well to me, my little angel."

She keeps breathing hard, staring at the ceiling.

I close any gap between us and move so her head's resting on my shoulder. I press my cock against her and ask, "Do ya still not appreciate slow?"

She says nothing.

"Do ya still want it fast?" I taunt, palming her ass cheeks and positioning my cock against her spine.

"I...I don't know," she whispers.

I kiss her cheek. "But ya want my cock in ya?"

She pins her blue eyes on me over her shoulder. They're as needy as before and drive me just as crazy. She mumbles, "Yea."

I lift her off the ground by her ass cheeks, pinning her between the fridge and my body, securing her with my forearm. Then I thrust deep inside her.

"Holy fuck!" she cries out.

"There's nothing holy about me, angel. And now's the time for ya to be a vixen and work your sweet little pussy on me as hard as ya want," I declare.

She reaches across the top of the fridge and grips the back of it so tight her knuckles turn white.

I thrust several times before she begins working her hips faster.

This time, I let her control the speed, matching the pace she sets. It only takes a few thrusts before her walls fight to grip me. I bite her shoulder, and she cries out. I growl, "Is this what ya want? Fast and hard?"

"Yea! Jesus, yea!" she whimpers.

I pound into her harder.

She cries out, "Like that! Don't stop!"

"Ya want to come, my little vixen?" I say through gritted teeth.

Her voice cracks as she breathes out, "Please!"

I squeeze her ass cheeks and kiss her neck. I murmur in her ear, "Squeeze your fucking pussy on me, then. Come hard on me like a good little vixen."

As soon as the words are out of my mouth, her body violently convulses, and she spasms so hard on me that I barely keep it together.

"Fuuuuck," I mutter.

"Oh...oh..." A bead of sweat rolls down her red cheek. Her hand shakes as it lifts and slaps against the fridge door.

It's the best goddamn thing I've ever seen.

I tease in her ear, "Ya want me to stop?"

"Don't ya dare!" she cries out.

"Then ya better keep working my cock," I threaten.

She doesn't disappoint me, continuing to keep our pace, working me like we've been together for years and are perfectly in sync.

Fire races through my veins. Another round of spasms hits her, and she squeezes my shaft so hard it overpowers me. Adrenaline floods my body.

"Fuuuuuck! Ya, naughty little vixen," I grit out, burying my face into her hair. I convulse harder than I have in the past, and my orgasm seems to last double what it normally does.

When it finally subsides, she's still shaking, slightly spasming against my depleted erection and gripping the top of the fridge.

Her tiny whimpers turn quieter but don't disappear.

I don't move except for kissing her cheek and murmuring, "Such a good angel."

She inhales a ragged breath and pins her gaze on me over her shoulder. Her lips tremble, and I press mine against them, slowly exploring her mouth.

When her body relaxes more, I carefully step back to ensure she has her footing. I reach for her hands, remove them from the appliance, and spin her into me. Her flushed, exhausted expression only riles me further. "Ya were exceptional. Now ya get rewarded."

Confusion fills her expression. She barely manages to get out, "Wh-what do ya mean?"

My lips twitch. I give her a chaste kiss, then circle my arm around her waist, guiding her to the couch. "Sit down."

She obeys and gazes up at me with the same perplexed expression.

Everything about her looking at me like that riles me up again. She's beyond beautiful, and she has an innocence about her, even though she's a spitfire.

I kneel in front of her and slide my palms over her thighs. She shudders, and I chuckle.

She stutters, "Wh-what are ya d-doing?" She bites her lip, tilting her head.

"It's time to give ya your reward."

"I-I still don't understand."

"Just relax, angel," I croon, then glide my hands over her inner thighs. I extend my thumbs and pull open her pussy lips.

She gasps. "Devin—"

"Relax," I reiterate, then lick the bottom of her pussy to her clit.

"Good God," she mumbles.

I eat her out, suddenly feeling famished, needing to hear and feel her coming against my mouth. And while I took my time before, there are no lazy licks now. It's a full onslaught of anything I can do to get her there quickly.

She's already sensitive from all we've done, so it doesn't take long. When her moans and cries get louder and her quivers become more intense, I squeeze her throat, glancing up at her.

Her blues widen. Her body convulses into a battleground of tremors, and she doesn't take in any air.

I suck her until her eyes roll and a faint choking sound fills the air.

I wait another moment, then soften my grip on her but don't remove my hand. I lower my mouth and glide my tongue inside her pussy, reaching as far into her as possible.

A new sound I haven't heard flies out of her mouth. It makes me think of a mix of pleasure and relief, which drives me to explore her insides slowly.

"Oh God. Jesus, you're good," she says, so quietly I question if she actually said it. She laces her hand over the side of my head, gently caressing it as if she's finally relaxed.

It makes me wonder what it would be like to have a lazy Sunday with her, with nothing to do but manipulate her body.

I stay inside her for a while, loving how she smells, how she tastes with me mixed in her juices, and the soft moans that never seem to stop.

It's a perfect recipe, and my cock grows hard again. I flick faster until she's gripping my hair and circling her hips again, then I retreat, wiping my forearm across my mouth.

She looks at me in question.

I rise and swoop her into my arms.

She shrieks.

I take her to the bed and place her on her back, caging my body over hers.

"Devin—"

I quiet her with my mouth, kissing her with everything I have.

She responds, holding me tight and sliding her hand through my hair. She parts her legs and lifts her hips.

I thrust into her, loving her long moan that fills the air.

In three thrusts, we're back in sync, fucking each other as if the only reason we're on Earth is to be together in this capacity.

I kiss her, murmuring between her lips, "You're fucking gorgeous, angel."

She kisses me harder and clasps her arms around me tighter. Her spasms intensify, and she mumbles, "I'm...I'm going to come again, Devin!"

"That's good, angel."

Hesitation crosses her expression.

I freeze, searching her eyes. "What's wrong?"

She opens her mouth and then shuts it.

Panic hits me. I tuck a lock of her hair behind her ear. "What is it?"

She scrunches her forehead, glancing away.

"Tell me," I demand.

She pins an embarrassed and slightly confused expression on me, answering, "Choke me when I come. Please."

I arch my eyebrows, surprised she's asking me but figuring she doesn't understand why she enjoys it. No one's done it to her before, is my guess.

"Forget I said it," she blurts out.

I slide my palm over her neck. "Don't take statements back when they're things ya like and want." I press my mouth to hers and resume thrusting.

She falls in line on thrust two, and her spasms quickly resume.

I increase the pressure on her neck, staring at her, ordering, "Blink once to keep it like this. Blink three times if ya want more."

She blinks three times, and I almost erupt within her. I barely stop myself and tighten my hold. She can still breathe but barely.

I kiss her for a bit, enjoying every sensation consuming my body, then pull back when I'm sure she's about to go over the edge. I demand, "One or three, vixen."

She blinks three times, and I cut off her air supply, pounding into her at full speed.

We come at the same time. Endorphins dump into my system, sending me into a new high.

I fight through my haze to closely watch her, ensuring I don't go past a point I shouldn't. When she gasps, I wait another moment, then force myself to reduce my grip so she can get air.

She takes several short breaths.

I give her a moment, then ask, "Ya good?"

She nods.

I kiss her, slowly lift my body, and roll onto my back. I stare at the ceiling, trying to regulate my own breaths. When I'm almost normal, I turn my head toward her.

She's twisting her fingers and biting her lip, glancing away from me.

She's too fucking adorable.

I slide my arm under her body and tug her into me.

She yelps.

I chuckle, then drag my knuckles over her cheek, teasing, "Why do ya look nervous all of a sudden?"

"I'm not," she claims.

"No?" I arch my eyebrows.

Her confident expression returns. She adamantly states, "No."

I study her for a moment.

"Why are ya looking at me like that?" she questions.

"Ya appeared a bit confused."

"When?"

"Before ya asked me to choke ya."

Her cheeks return to crimson.

"Ya don't have to be embarrassed about it," I assure her.

"No?"

"No."

Silence fills the air.

I add, "Ya don't understand why ya like it, do ya?"

She slowly licks her lips, then shakes her head.

I tug her closer to me and kiss her forehead. "Ya don't have to understand it. Just don't let any bloke do it to ya. If they don't know what they're doing, they'll kill ya. I would hate to see a pretty lass like yourself end up in a grave."

"I already learned that lesson," she blurts out.

I freeze, then tilt her chin so she can't ignore me. I question, "Another bloke has choked ya before?"

Disgust fills her expression. She doesn't answer.

Anger fills me. "Aye. I see. I take it that it was a bad experience?"

Her silence tells me everything.

I swallow my rage, wanting to kill the bloke, but remind myself that come tomorrow, I'm out of here. Her life will be her life, and mine will be mine. So instead of pushing to find out who this amateur is, hunting him down, and paying him a visit to teach him a lesson, I tell myself it's better to let it go. I tug her closer and kiss her head, reiterating, "Be careful going forward. Don't ever let that bloke touch ya again."

She curls into my chest and mumbles, "I have no intention of doing anything of the sort."

5

Lauren
The Next Morning

"Y a sleep like a rock," a deep voice states.

The morning light breaks through the darkness, and I slowly blink a few times, forcing myself to wake up fully.

The voice chuckles.

I look over, surprised to still see Devin here. I don't know why I should be. Where would he have gone in the middle of the night?

I can't believe I slept with a total stranger.

Cockiness is all over his expression. He reaches over and curls his fingers around my neck, which is tender from the night before.

I inhale sharply, still not understanding why I liked it so much or how I had the audacity to ask him to choke me while we were having sex.

Before I can think too much, he leans closer. His lips brush against mine as he orders, "Stop thinking bad about what you want, my little angel."

Angel? Vixen? I'm unsure which one I like better when he calls me those names, but he seems to know which one to call me at the right time.

I don't say anything. We stare at each other intensely until his lips overpower mine and he slides his tongue back into my mouth.

I don't hesitate, kissing him back. Something about Devin makes me feel like I've known him forever. Our bodies curve into each other just like the previous night, and I don't understand how it's even possible.

He's still a stranger. I know nothing about him, and now that it's morning, he's going to leave. He doesn't live anywhere near here. This isn't his life. I'm fully aware of it, yet something about him makes me want more than I know he can give me.

So I kiss him back with everything I have, and he pulls me on top of him. I sink over his cock.

He palms my ass, controlling every motion I make. Neither of us speaks. Unlike the night before, where everything was frantic, this morning it's slower...lazy in a way.

It's another example of how confusing he is to me.

How can having intense sex with him, like when he put me against the fridge, feel just as good as this slower experience?

It doesn't take long for me to get lost in him. He grips my throat, squeezing to the point I get dizzy, and we're soon coming together, just as good as the previous times.

He curls his arm tighter around me, keeping me close to him as our bodies shudder against each other and our incoherent cries fill the air, muffled by our kisses. When the aftermath hits, I lie on top of him, breathing just as hard as him.

He releases his hand from my throat and asks, "What do ya have going on today?"

I rattle my brain, trying to think of something coherent to say, but I'm still fuzzy from the rush of endorphins that took over my body.

He waits for me to speak.

It's Monday, so I'll be starting my week. I answer, "Just working at the pub later on."

"Ya work every day?" he asks.

I shrug. "Sometimes. It just depends. My mum needs to retire, but she won't, so I try to take whatever I can off her plate."

"You're a good daughter."

No. A good daughter would've won that money, I guiltily think, cursing myself again, that I could have had our problems fixed last night if only I had won.

"What's wrong?" Devin asks, but my pride returns. The last thing I want to do is remind him I'm upset about losing. So I shake my head and roll off of him. "Nothing. I'm going to go take a shower."

"I should join ya."

It's tempting, but I suddenly have the urge for a few minutes by myself to get a grip on this situation. So I point at him, ordering, "No, you stay here. My shower isn't that big."

"Trying to wash me off ya?" he teases.

I tilt my head. "Well, I'm not going to stay smelling like ya all day if that's what you're implying I should do."

"That's a shame, lass. Once I'm off of ya, you'll wish ya hadn't stepped foot in your shower," he arrogantly declares.

I roll my eyes, but a laugh comes out of me. "You're so full of yourself."

"I didn't hear ya complain last night, or this morning for that matter."

My cheeks turn to fire. I groan. "You're impossible." I escape into the bathroom, shutting and locking the door. I put my hands on the countertop and look in the mirror.

My heart races faster.

What the heck have I done?

I don't even know this guy.

Why am I feeling guilty?

I'm not a one-night-stand type of girl.

Maybe I should be since it was so good.

Stop it.

Why am I judging myself over what we did? It's not the Dark Ages.

Is it really a bad thing?

I sigh, turn on the shower, wait for the water to heat up, and get in. I quickly wash and condition my hair, pour soap on my loofah, then drag it all over my body.

I rinse, turn the water off, and step out of the shower. I dry off, wrap a towel around my head, and secure one around my body.

I open the door, and Devin's sitting on the bed with his back to me and his phone to his ear. He says, "We leave in thirty. Get moving." He hangs up.

My heart sinks. I knew this was coming. It was one night and never meant to be more. So why am I feeling so disappointed? It's not like we were going to live happily ever after.

Still, I can't help the sinking feeling in my gut. Maybe it's because he's so nonchalant about leaving.

I'm sure he has one-night stands all the time.

This is nothing new for him.

I'm not anything special. I'm just another lass he'll leave behind.

Jesus, why did I agree to let him touch me?

The thought of being a notch on his belt doesn't make me feel good about myself. As much as I hate to admit it, I want to be something special to him, but this is my reality.

So I lift my chin, grab some clothes from my dresser drawer, then return to the bathroom.

He calls out, "What are ya doing, lass?"

"Changing," I answer, shutting the door.

He shouts, "I've seen ya naked—a lot. In fact, that's all I've seen of ya for the last eight hours. Ya can get dressed out here."

I ignore him and put my clothes on. I take the towel off my head, comb my hair, then hang my towels up. I open the cabinet, pull out a fresh towel, and set it on the sink. I open the door and jump.

Devin's standing in front of it, his palms on the doorframe.

I blurt out, "Whoa, trying to scare me?"

Amusement fills his expression. "Now, why would I want to do that?"

"Standing in front of the doorway is a little freaky, don't ya think?"

"Is it?" he asks, with an expression like he's genuinely confused.

"Yea," I say, then nudge past him. "Towel's on the counter for ya. Use whatever's in my shower that ya want."

"Who said I'm showering?" he questions.

I spin and arch my eyebrow. "Ya don't shower? Are ya a dirty bloke?"

His lips twitch. "I think ya know the answer to that."

More heat permeates my face. I put my hand over it and groan. "You're impossible." Yet I can't help but smile. Something about him is charming, even though he's annoying and so damn arrogant. I'm sure if I added up the cockiness of all the men in my entire village, it wouldn't equal the amount in him.

"Ya love it," he claims.

I ignore his statement and ask, "Ya really don't want to shower?"

He shrugs. "I'd rather smell ya on me all day, but I guess I'll shower. Got a long ride ahead of us."

I freeze, and the hairs on my arms prick to life. I question, "Long ride? I thought ya were on a blokes' weekend."

His expression changes, and I'm unsure what to make of it.

Is it surprise?

Did he just get caught with his hand in the cookie jar? What is it about that look of his?

He recovers quickly, not giving me much time to decipher his expression, and says, "Aye, we are, but we're still an hour out from where we're going."

"An hour's a long drive?" I ask, still not buying his lame excuse.

He nods.

"So where exactly are ya going?"

"North."

"That doesn't answer my question."

He shrugs. "I don't know the town. My brother's picking a place."

"Why do I not believe ya?"

He shakes his head. "Not sure, but that's your issue. Like I said, we're on a blokes' weekend. That means we get in the car and decide where to go. And it's Tynan's call. All he said was that he wants to go farther north and will let us know today where he decides to go."

I squint at him.

"What's that look for?" he questions.

"That sounds like the dumbest thing I've ever heard," I admit.

"Well, my brother's not the smartest tool in the shed, now is he?" Devin claims, his lips twitching.

I put my hand on my hip. "He doesn't seem too stupid to me."

He steps forward, puts his palms over my cheeks, and tilts my head toward him. That expression I can't decipher fills his face again, and he claims, "Lauren, you're overthinking things. I'm on a blokes' weekend. Sometimes it's nice not to have any plans. Have ya ever done that? Not had any plans?"

I contemplate his question, but I can't think of one time in my life I've gone somewhere with no plan.

"Ah, I see," he states.

My defenses perk up. "What does that mean?"

"You're very scheduled, aren't ya, Lauren? Ya haven't lived life to the fullest yet in your youth?"

Somehow I feel like his question's a derogatory remark.

I huff. "Of course I've lived life."

He chuckles. "How can ya? You're what? Twenty-three?"

I stiffen my shoulders. "No, I'm twenty-eight."

Surprise fills his expression. His eyes widen. "You are?"

He really thought I was twenty-three?

He glances down my body and back up to my face until my blood's pumping hot, just like it's been since I laid eyes on him last night.

I confirm, "Yea. I'm twenty-eight."

"I thought ya were twenty-three."

"And how old are ya?"

"Just turned forty."

Shock hits me. I knew he was older, but I assumed he was in his mid-thirties, tops.

"Why are ya looking shocked now?" he asks.

"Isn't it pretty sick that you're okay being with a twenty-three-year-old?" I point out.

He grunts. "No."

"You'd be robbing the cradle a little bit, don't ya think? I mean, ya are, even with me being twenty-eight."

"Is that so?"

"Yea. Do ya always fuck younger women? Is there something wrong with women your own age?"

His eyes turn to slits. "Do ya always fuck older men? Is there something wrong with men your own age?"

I open my mouth, but he snaps his fingers.

"Aye! Don't answer that. Of course there is something wrong with them. They're boys, not men." He lowers his voice and leans closer. "Am I the first real man you've ever had, Lauren?"

"No," I state.

"Ya sure?"

I stay quiet.

"Ah, I am."

"No, you're not. I've been with lots of older men."

"Lots?" he teases.

I nudge him with my elbow. "Stop. Don't put me into a box and turn me into one of your loose women just because we did what we did last night."

He holds his hands out. "Easy. I'm not putting ya in any box. I never said that. I don't think just because ya have sex that makes ya a loose woman."

"Ya don't?" I ask, not believing him.

"Nah."

"Then what would make a woman loose?"

"If you've fucked every bloke that walked in here, I might call ya loose. Just because ya have some casual sex from time to time, I don't think that makes ya loose."

I ponder his statement, wondering if I should trust it.

"Lauren, chill out. Everything's good." He kisses me, but it's quick and leaves me wanting more. The desperate feeling I had when I first woke up and realized he was leaving reappears. I hate it. I'm not a needy person. I definitely don't need a man, and I don't even know why I like him. He's so arrogant.

He takes his fingers and curls them around my neck but doesn't squeeze. Tingles race down my spine. He stares at his hand for a moment and states, "Ya really are a beautiful lass." He gives me another chaste kiss, then releases me and steps back. He declares, "I'm going to take a shower, although I know I'm going to regret washing your smell off me."

I don't say anything and watch him go into the bathroom. He doesn't shut the door and turns on the water. He glances over his shoulder and smirks. "Ya can watch me if ya want."

"You're annoying," I say and shut the door, but I instantly regret it. It would've been nice to watch him shower. His body's like that of a God. I don't think I've ever been with a man as muscular as Devin. He's not over-the-top with the steroid look some guys in our town possess.

No, Devin's body is flawless.

I glance down at mine, and all my insecurities flood me. "Goddammit, stop it," I curse myself. I walk away from the door and pick my clothes from last night off the floor. I toss them in the laundry basket. Then I grab Devin's shirt and pants and toss them on the bed.

His wallet drops to the floor, fanning open. I reach for it and am about to shut it, but the words on his license make me freeze.

My heart pounds harder. I stare at it.

No, no, no.

This can't be true.

No, no, no, no, no, no.

I keep staring at the license, panicking.

It reads *Devin O'Connor.*

It has to be a coincidence.

As the shock wears off, I slowly put two and two together.

Devin.

Tynan.

Oh my God. How did none of us know? How did we not think?

I fret further, pacing the room and holding his wallet.

Devin O'Connor, the head of the O'Connor clan.

Well, not the head. His brother Brody and his other brother Aidan are higher up, but he and Tynan are still super powerful.

How did this happen?

I keep pacing, but no answers come. The longer I pace, the angrier I get. I don't even hear the shower turn off or the door open.

"What are ya doing with my wallet?" Devin questions.

My insides quiver. I spin on him. My voice shakes with emotion that I'm trying to hold in but can't. I accuse, "You're Devin O'Connor."

A quick flash of panic hits him, but then his arrogant expression lights up his face. I suddenly hate it. I want to punch him and erase everything that we did.

He stands taller, answering, "I am. And you're Lauren Byrne, niece of that bastard Tommy Ahern."

My gut somersaults. I drop his wallet, unable to hold it any longer, and grip the side of the sofa, choking out, "Ya knew who I was this entire time?

"Aye. Of course I did. It's my job to know who everyone is," he confesses.

I open my mouth, but no words come out. I put my other hand over my stomach, feeling like I'm going to throw up.

How could I have been so dumb?

He stares at me, his face neutral, as if waiting for me to say something.

When I finally find my words, I can only whisper, "How could ya?"

He drags his gaze over my body like he's done dozens of times since walking into my pub.

"Ya may be an Ahern and loyal to the O'Learys, but we still had a fun night, didn't we?"

I lose it, shouting, "What the fuck are ya talking about? How could ya have done this? What is wrong with ya?"

His smile turns sinister. "Nothing's wrong with me, lass. I saw what I wanted, and I took it. But don't forget ya were a willing participant."

I toss my hands in the air and scream, "I didn't know who ya were!"

He grunts. "So what? Ya still had the best night of your life. Leave it at that." He goes over to the bed and puts on his pants and shirt.

I stare at him the whole time, still unable to move.

He spins and steps toward me.

I back up until I'm against the wall.

He crouches down, picks up his wallet, and shoves it in his pants. He reaches for my face.

I move my head. "Don't touch me."

He taunts, "Aw. Is that any way to say goodbye to me after we had such a lovely night?"

Tears rush down my cheeks. I wish they didn't, but I can't help it. I seethe, "How dare ya? Get out of here."

"I think ya owe me a kiss before I go."

I shove him, and he stumbles backward, surprised by the power of my push. I yell, "Get out of here, and don't ya dare ever come back, or ya will get killed!"

He scoffs. "Killed? Who's going to kill me? Are ya going to kill me, Lauren?"

"I'm warning ya," I threaten, but I know my threats are nothing for a man like him.

He steps closer and puts both hands on my face, pinning me between his body and the wall.

I can barely breathe, hating myself further how I'm not one hundred percent disgusted by him even though I know the truth about the blood that runs through him.

He stares at me for a second, then at my lips. He gives me a chaste kiss. "I will miss ya. I would've liked to have some more fun with ya."

"You're disgusting," I manage to get out, choking on my words.

His sinister smile reappears. "Ya didn't say I was disgusting last night or this morning."

"Get out," I say again.

He gives me another kiss, then releases me. He reaches into his pocket and tosses a wad of cash on the bed, declaring, "Have a nice life, Lauren Byrne." He opens the door to my flat.

I stare at the money, grab it, and follow him down the steps. I call out, "Ya forgot your money."

"Take it. Ya need it."

"I'm not your fucking prostitute!" I scream.

He gets to the bottom of the steps and turns. "Ya don't listen, Lauren. How many times have I said I know you're not a prostitute?"

I toss the wad of cash at him.

He lets it fall to the floor, and it disperses everywhere.

I snarl, "Pick up your money and go." I spin, run up the stairs, then shut and lock the door to my flat. I slide down to the floor and hug my knees.

I cry for too long with guilt, shame, and the most remorse I've ever had flooding my body.

6

Devin

*T*he door slams, and I stare at the top of the staircase with my gut sinking. This isn't how I wanted things to end.

I reprimand myself for not taking my clothes into the bathroom.

How could I have left my wallet out?

Why did she even look at my wallet?

Nosy bird.

I continue staring at the door and almost go back upstairs but stop, forcing myself not to.

It's over.

It was always supposed to be like this anyway.

Well, I didn't want her to know who I was. I wanted to leave things on a good note. Maybe even pop back in one of these days just because she is so fucking good in bed.

Jesus, she's good in bed.

Well, I've ruined that option now.

I finally step back and stare at all the cash on the floor. My phone buzzes in my pocket. I pull it out and answer my brother, "What?"

"We're pulling in right now. I know you said a half hour, but we're ready to go."

"Where did ya stay last night?" I question, glancing at the cracks in the mirror behind the bar.

Tynan answers, "We stayed with the women. Who else would we have stayed with?"

I'd usually give him an *atta boy*, but now isn't the time. We've got to get out of town. My arrogant courage from last night has been replaced with common sense. I don't put it past Lauren to call the O'Learys, which wouldn't be a good thing. We don't have any backup, and the last thing we need is a showdown between them and the four of us.

I glance at the cash, then walk past it and unlock the pub door. I yank it open, then freeze. I glance behind me.

There's no movement from the staircase. I stare for over a minute.

What am I doing?

This isn't the time to linger.

I step outside, slamming the pub door, and slide into the passenger side of the car.

Tynan asks, "Ya get what ya wanted?"

I grunt. "Of course I got it. Dumbass."

Cathal reaches from the back seat and pats my shoulder, announcing, "Have to admit, your plan to get out of town and get some new blood in us wasn't a bad one. That lass knew how to come on my cock like a freight train."

I don't look at him. I lean the seat back and close my eyes, stating, "Aye, ya pussy. Ya should listen to me more often."

He whines, "Come on! Do ya have to put the seat back? Ya know there's no room back here."

"Deal with it, I'm tired," I claim, keeping my seat right where it's at. Then I glance at my brother, declaring, "Ya might want to drive faster."

He arches his eyebrows. "Why?"

I nonchalantly confess, "Lauren might have seen my driver's license."

His eyes widen. "What do ya mean she *might* have?"

Annoyance fills me. "I was showering. I came out of the bathroom, and she was looking at my license."

He groans. "Jesus. What the fuck were ya thinking leaving your wallet in the other room?"

"Shut your mouth and drive," I snarl. I close my eyes again and pretend to sleep for most of the journey. And I curse myself for washing the scent of her off of me. Even though I know I won't see her again and there's no hope for a future between us, everything about that girl turned me on. Keeping a part of her would have been nice, even if, eventually, it would be gone.

I should have grabbed her fucking panties.

I curse myself for wanting any memento. Now that the sun's up, I need to move on with my life.

A long time passes before I finally open my eyes. I stare out the window, ignoring all the banter in the car. I scold myself for having to experience what my older brothers have. Now that I've had Lauren, I only want more. No matter how much I tell myself to forget her, she's consuming all my thoughts. And that look of hatred she gave me is haunting me.

Fuck.

I'm not a man who allows guilt to eat at me, but it sure is right now, and I'm doing a poor job of stopping it.

I finally understand why my brothers couldn't let their O'Leary women go.

Yet I'm not them. I won't be stupid like they were and take that headache on. Besides, there's no way in hell that Lauren would ever come near me again.

So all these thoughts are pointless. She is who she is, and I am who I am. Yet the facts don't stop my brain from running a mile a minute.

I got it out of my system. I fucked an O'Leary, and now I can move on with my life.

I'm full of shit. I could keep her as mine and make her forgive me. I should turn her against the O'Learys like my brothers did with their wives.

No, I'm just having a momentary lapse of judgment, wanting what I know I can't have.

I could get her back.

What am I saying?

My debate and scolding goes on and on until we arrive in Belfast. I order my brother to drop me off at my flat. I step inside and walk to the window, cross my arms, and stare out into the city.

Belfast just isn't New York.

I miss everything about my city, including its busyness, the rude people, and the frantic energy. Belfast is a nice city, but something about New York fills me with life. It's missing here in Ireland.

It only takes a few minutes of missing home to realize something that doesn't help my current predicament.

Last night was the first time I felt like myself in a long time.

It's because of Lauren.

I grumble out loud, "Goddammit. Stop being a fucking pussy and thinking about her."

I go change my clothes and leave my flat. I walk for several miles and finally end up at the pub, feeling just as angsty as when I left my flat.

I need to find another bird to shag so I can get her out of my system.

I go inside the pub, even though it's barely noon. There are only a few people scattered about at this time of the day. I grab a barstool and sit on it.

The barmaid, Chloe, looks up. She chirps, "Devin, are ya hungry?"

My stomach growls, and I realize I'm famished. "Aye."

She bats her eyes, leaning across the counter, stating, "We've got some bangers and mash on special today. It's fresh. Want me to fix ya a plate?"

"Aye," I agree, nodding and motioning to the levers. "I'll take a pint too."

She pours Guinness into a glass and sets it in front of me, offering, "On the house." Her cheeks flush, but I ignore the little advance and nicety. Since our rendezvous about six months ago, she's been dying for a repeat. But I'm not interested.

She's not Lauren.

Jesus, I need to let it go.

I mumble, "Thanks," and concentrate on the TV screen, barely tasting the Guinness as it hits my tongue.

"Can I get ya anything else?" she questions.

I glance at her and sternly say, "No."

Disappointment fills her expression. All it does is reiterate how much I don't want to sleep with her.

She's too eager. I wouldn't even have to ask. I'd just have to cock my head and point at the stairs, the back room, or tell her to lock the pub and kick everyone out. I know she'd do it. Most of the women who frequent this pub would do it.

And maybe that's part of why I can't get Lauren out of my mind. It's just too damn easy in Belfast. In New York, I had to work harder for women. When I first arrived here, I embraced these women, but now, it's too easy.

Last night, I had to work to get into Lauren's bed. There was a challenge to it. She made me work all my angles.

Something tells me that even if there was a chance for us, she'd always have some sort of defiance for me. She would always make it interesting in some way.

I scold myself again.

I have to stop thinking about this bird.

She's just another lass with a pussy between her thighs, and there's plenty of those in the sea.

I drink some more Guinness, and Chloe shoves a plate of steaming food in front of me. She gives me another coy smile and practically sings, "Bangers and mash at your service."

"Thanks," I mutter and focus on my food, eating faster than I should and downing the rest of the pint.

I don't have to ask for another. Chloe sets it in front of me, then inquires, "Where did ya go last night? Ya left pretty early and in a hurry."

"None of your business," I reply, harsher than I mean for it to come out, but I don't apologize, even when hurt lights up her expression.

Tense silence fills the air, and she lifts her chin and replies, "Oh. Sorry. I didn't mean to pry."

I lock eyes with her, become a bigger dick, and state, "Then ya shouldn't have asked."

Her cheeks heat from embarrassment. She adds an additional "Sorry," and then scurries off.

Happy I got her out of my way, I finish the food and the rest of the pint. Then I look around the pub. There are only a few blokes in it, and the two drunk women who are always here. They're way too old for me, and I find nothing attractive about them, even though plenty of blokes do. Yet I wouldn't touch them with a ten-foot pole if they were the last women on Earth.

I quickly divert my gaze from everyone, not wanting anyone to approach or talk to me, and stare at the wooden counter. All I can see is Lauren. Her thighs, round ass, and those blue eyes.

And remember how she held on to me. I can almost feel her shuddering, making me feel like I was hers.

Jesus Christ. What the fuck is wrong with me?

I reprimand myself again for the trip down memory lane. Then I get up, toss cash on the bar, and leave the pub. I walk around Belfast for hours, wondering again how I'll ever get used to this place or if I'll ever stop missing New York. And I wish that my dad or Brody would send me back.

But I know it won't happen. Dad insists that the four of us stay in Belfast and keep Ireland moving in the right direction. And with the headway we've been making, I can't say I blame him.

Things are stable in New York, but not here. Although, they've gotten a lot more so since we killed Tommy and started taking over more of the O'Leary territory.

"Fucking O'Learys. They're such a pain in my ass," I grumble.

As much as I wanted to quench my thirst for having an O'Leary, now that I've had Lauren, I realize how bad of an idea it was to dip my wick where I shouldn't have.

And I can't stop asking myself questions that will never have answers, like why did she have to have a defiant little attitude I adore? Or why couldn't she have sucked in bed? Or why couldn't we have had no chemistry? That would have made all this easier.

Now I'm just thinking about her like a stupid schoolboy in love, puppy dog eyes and all.

"Goddammit!" I bark and kick a can down the road.

It scares a homeless man trying to stay warm against a building. He cowers, putting his hands over his head to protect himself.

I reach into my pocket, pull out all my remaining cash, and toss it at him. "Sorry, mate. I'm just having a bad day."

He peeks through his fingers but doesn't move.

I walk past him and continue roaming the streets until the sun sets and the darkness of night fills the sky.

I return to my flat, and when I step inside, my phone vibrates. I pull it out of my pocket and stare at an unknown number.

> Unknown Number: Why would ya do that to me? What was the purpose?

I freeze. My pulse skyrockets.

It can't be her.

Who else would it be?

It has to be her.

How did she get my number?

I rack my brain, then scrub my face in frustration. *Jesus, I'm a moron.*

I did give her my number. I drank too much whiskey, and in the middle of our card game, I let my arrogance determine my moves. I programmed my number into her phone to prove a point to her. I barely remember what I was trying to reassure her about, but it had something to do with being a stand-up guy and not just a crazy stranger.

Guess I proved her correct on her assumptions about me.

Goddammit, why did I do that?

> Unknown Number: You're going to ghost me now? I know you're reading this. Ya fucking coward.

I program her number into my phone. I write Lauren the Enemy to remind myself who she is and not to confuse the situation.

> Me: I'm not a fucking coward. I'm not an O'Leary.

> Lauren the Enemy: Ya are a coward. You're manipulative. Ya did it on purpose. Ya came into my pub, knowing who I was, with all intentions of hurting me. What was the point? Why did you single me out?

Guilt once again gnaws at me, and I wish it didn't. I stand in front of the window, staring into the darkness of the early evening sky, loathing my actions. The thought of how I hurt her doesn't bring me any pleasure the way I assumed it would.

> Lauren the Enemy: Yea. That's what I thought. Ya are a coward.

I don't reply. What would I say? I wanted to know what it was like to fuck an O'Leary? *Actually, that's exactly what I should say.*

Be a complete dick, and she can move on easier.

> Me: As ya know, my brothers are with O'Leary women, except they're not O'Learys anymore. They came over to our side because your blood is disgusting and they realized that.

> Lauren the Enemy: So ya wanted to convert me?

Me: No. I didn't sleep with ya to convert ya, lass. I just wanted to know what it was like to be inside an O'Leary, and now I do. So thanks for the night. I enjoyed it. I know you did too. Why don't ya focus on that instead of whatever you're trying to get from this situation?

Lauren the Enemy: You're such an asshole.

Me: Aye. And ya knew it before ya slept with me. But I can assure ya, this situation isn't going to change. I am who I am, and ya are who ya are, so I'll thank ya again for a fun night.

Lauren the Enemy: Give me your address so I can send ya this money ya left.

Me: The money is yours.

Lauren the Enemy: I told ya, I'm not a prostitute.

I shake my head. What is with this woman thinking that me giving her the money for the pub makes her a prostitute?

Me: For the last time, it's not a payment for sex. Fix your pub. Give your mum a break. Give yourself a break. It's my parting gift. Now, I think it's best if we stop texting.

Lauren the Enemy: Good call. I'll block ya.

My gut sinks and panic hits me. I don't want her to block me. What if I want to reach out?

"What the fuck am I talking about?" I mutter and then bang my head slightly against the glass window, stating, "Jesus, I have to get a grip."

> **Me:** Ya do what ya want to do, angel, or maybe I should call ya my vixen right now?

> **Lauren the Enemy:** I'm not yours. Don't ya ever call me yours again.

It's another knife to my chest, but it's reality.

> **Me:** Don't say things ya don't want to be true.

> **Lauren the Enemy:** Stay away from me, Devin. If I ever see ya again, I will have the O'Learys kill ya.

> **Me:** Don't make threats ya can't keep, my vixen.

I wait for another message, but it never arrives. All night, I stare at the phone, thinking about things to text back, but I don't. I restrain myself even though I want to send a message just to know if she blocked me.

Several times, I almost delete her number, but something won't let me. I hate the hold she seems to have over me, even though I tell myself she doesn't. Yet I know that deep down, she does, because I should block her number and then delete it.

My pussy self can't.

A million different things go through my mind to message her. All night, every second that goes by that she doesn't send me another message only irritates me further. I become so antsy I have to go back outside. I wander the streets all throughout the night until the sun comes up.

Even then, I'm still answer-less. I don't know what I'm searching for or what I expect to happen. I slept with my enemy. I did it knowingly and willingly, and she found out. There's nothing left for us, yet I can't shake the fact that I feel like there is, and I hate myself for that feeling. I should have never laid eyes on her or made that bet. Sleeping with her was my mistake and one I'm now paying for because all I can think about is how I'm never going to have her again.

I didn't anticipate any of this, and none of it is sitting right with me. Yet I'm clueless about how to change any of it or reverse what I've done.

Now, I just have to live with my mistake and move on. Somehow, some way, I will forget Lauren Byrne.

If it were only that easy to pretend I never dipped my wick into the forbidden zone.

7

Lauren

I hide in my room most of the day, not wanting to face the girls. I texted Emily earlier that I wasn't feeling well and to take care of the pub before Mum arrives later tonight, but I can't wait anymore. I have to get to work.

I stare at the text messages Devin and I exchanged one last time. Then I toss my phone on the bed and groan. I'm still in shock, but I'm also angry.

How could I have been so stupid?

I put on my pub T-shirt, slide on my jeans, and toss my pajamas in the dirty laundry. I leave my flat and go down the staircase.

The loud chaos of the pub grows with every step I take. Normally, I'm excited to go to work. But all I feel right now is dread.

When I get behind the bar, Emily appears. "Ya feeling better?"

"Yea, I'm fine," I reply and grab a towel. I wipe the counter even though it's dry.

She stares at me, lowers her voice, and asks, "Are ya okay? Did he do something ya didn't want him to do last night?"

I freeze. My insides churn faster, and my heart pounds.

Emily puts her hand on my forearm. "Lauren, what happened?"

I meet her eye and force out in my most convincing tone, "Nothing. I'm fine. He didn't do anything I didn't want him to do."

She leans closer. "So ya had sex with him, then?" She arches her eyebrow.

I glance around us to make sure no one's listening, then admit, "Yea. Tell me ya didn't have sex with anyone last night."

Her face flushes. "We all did."

My insides quiver harder. How could I have let my cousins get into a mess like this? I freak out a bit more, then state, "I need to talk to all of ya. Get the others." I go into the kitchen.

Within a few minutes, Emily, Alison, and Jessica step inside.

I nod to the chef, ordering, "Go take a smoke break."

He doesn't argue and leaves.

When it's just the four of us, I declare, "We're never letting strangers in this pub again. Do ya understand me?"

Surprise fills their expressions.

"I mean it. Don't ever open the door and allow anyone we don't know inside once we're closed."

Alison asks, "What happened?"

I answer, "We shouldn't have done that last night. Do any of ya have the phone numbers of the other guys?"

They all slowly shake their heads. Jessica admits, "No. Didn't see the point in exchanging them."

"Good. Do not ever talk to them again."

"Why?" she questions.

I rub my hands over my face in frustration. Leave it to Jessica to drill down my orders. I'm sure this is just the beginning of her curiosity. I bark out, "Because I said so. They're not who ya think they are."

"Then who are they?" she inquires.

I glance around again and swallow hard. My stomach roils. I admit, "They're O'Connors and not just any O'Connors. They're part of the family that heads up the clan."

My cousins' eyes widen, and the shock I felt appears on their expressions.

Mum barges through the door, interrupting us. She questions, "What are all of ya doing in here?"

Emily jumps in, saying, "We're just having a quick conversation."

"About what?" Mum pushes.

"Tonight."

"What about tonight?"

I step into the conversation, lying, "I'm telling the girls what sections I want them in and that I don't want any funny business tonight. No one's to linger with customers. We need to make as much money as possible."

"Speaking of money..." Mum pulls a wad of cash out of her pocket, demanding, "Where did this come from?" Disapproval and curiosity fill her expression.

Guilt overtakes me.

Her tone turns sharper. "Well? Where did this come from? It wasn't in the register when I left last night."

Emily replies, "It was left in an envelope at the back door."

More confusion fills Mum's face, like she doesn't know if she should believe us.

Jessica suggests, "Maybe someone felt guilty for destroying the place."

I have to hand it to my cousins. They always have my back. Thank God. If Mum knew what happened last night, she'd never forgive me.

Still, she stares us all down, making me want to squirm under her glare.

"It's true," I declare.

She squints, keeping her gaze on me the longest.

I add, "We should be happy. We don't have the stress of how to fix this place now after what those thugs did."

Mum waits a minute, then glances at the money and states, "It must be Caleb. He must have done it to make amends with us."

"It's not from him!" I snap.

She tilts her head, asserting, "No one else has this kind of money. If it's not Caleb, who would it be?"

My pulse continues to skyrocket. I hate lying to my mum or anyone else, for that matter. But there's no way she can ever find out the truth.

Alison interjects, "Caleb would've taken credit if it was him."

"That's true," I declare.

"Then who left it?" Mum repeats.

Silence and tension grow, filling the air between us.

She pushes harder, "Lauren, if it wasn't Caleb, who was it?"

I toss my hands in the air, trying to look convincing. "Your guess is as good as mine."

She adds, "I don't know anyone else who has this kind of money around these parts. Do you?"

I shrug. "I don't know, Mum, but the envelope was left outside the door. That's all we know."

"It has to be Caleb," she insists.

Anger fills me. Even though I'm not proud of where the money came from, I'm not going to allow Caleb to have credit for it. I point out, "He would use it to hold over our heads. So it can't be him, but somebody in town must have money and wanted to help."

Jessica interjects again, "Lauren's right. Caleb would definitely make sure everybody in town knew it was him. But it doesn't matter, does it? Whoever left it didn't want anyone to know it was them, so maybe we should just be grateful that we have the funds."

"I agree," Emily says.

Alison adds, "Ditto. Why are we making a big deal about this when we should be concentrating on the fact our problem's solved? It would've taken us months to be able to save enough. Now we can get everything to fix the pub and put it back to normal."

"And we need new rules in here," I declare, crossing my arms, determined that I will not allow these thugs to continue acting this way in Mum's pub.

She frets, "We don't make the rules. Don't create problems for us."

"That's ridiculous. This is your pub. They keep destroying it. We got lucky this time with whoever left this money, but we can't keep fixing and replacing things. We have to set new rules," I insist.

She briefly closes her eyes and shakes her head. She lowers her defeated voice, asserting, "It doesn't work like that, Lauren, and ya know it."

I hate it whenever I hear that tone from her, and now is no exception. She's worked her entire life in the pub and shouldn't have to deal with any of this.

She adds, "That's why ya need to marry Caleb. You'll have way more choices than I ever had."

"I'm not marrying him, and stop saying that!" I blurt out.

Emily steps near me and puts her arm around my waist. "Yea, ya need to stop saying that, Auntie. Caleb is not the man for Lauren. He's not a good person. Ya know this."

"He will protect her," she insists.

"No, he won't. He'll hurt me," I state.

She shakes her head in disapproval again.

Jessica claps and chirps, "We need to get back out there. We have customers. But ya have money now." She points to the wad of cash. "We can fix everything, so let's be happy."

Jessica is definitely winning me over today.

Mum stays quiet and stares at the money.

The guilt flares inside me. If Mum ever finds out where this money came from, she'll think I'm a prostitute.

I might as well be a prostitute. I slept with him, and he gave me ten grand.

An ill feeling expands all around me. Guilt, shame, and horror at who Devin is and that he knew who I was resurfaces.

He set me up.

I still don't understand why.

Because he could.

The more I think about how he used me, the sicker I feel. I swallow down bile.

"Ya look like you're getting sick!" Mum exclaims and puts her hand on my forehead.

I move my head away. "What are ya talking about? I'm fine."

She continues pinning her gaze on me. "Your face just turned green."

"No, it didn't," I insist.

"It did, didn't it, ladies?"

My cousins stay quiet.

It makes Mum's suspicion reappear. She asks, "What happened here last night after I left?"

"Nothing happened," I lie, feeling more guilt for continuing to keep up this charade.

She continues to study us, declaring, "Something had to have happened. All of ya are being too quiet."

Jessica blurts out, "We're not being quiet. We're just listening to ya. Don't ya always tell us that we have to listen to ya more?" Jessica says.

Alison steps next to her. She points out. "Yea, ya talked to us about this the other day. Actually, every day ya tell us that we need to listen better. Now we're listening and you're upset with us, claiming that we did something last night, but we didn't. We cleaned up, closed up, and then went home."

"What time did you get home?" Mum inquires.

"Couple hours after. What's the big deal? Why are ya accusing us of lying?" Emily asks.

Mum doesn't look convinced. She finally puts her finger in the air, motioning to all of us. "If I find out that you're lying to me and that something happened here last night—"

"Nothing happened," I blurt out.

Tension resumes.

Mum continues, "If something happened here last night, and it has to do with this money, you're all in trouble for lying to me. Do ya understand?"

My stomach dives. Jessica once again interjects to my approval. She claims, "Nothing happened, Auntie. We aren't lying. You're overreacting."

"Am I?" Mum questions.

"Yea, ya are. You're fantasizing," I state.

Mum scoffs. "I don't fantasize about anything. I'm a reality person. Ya know that, and something's going on here. I can feel it."

I huff. "Well, you're wrong."

She lowers her voice, insisting, "Ya girls are hiding something from me. I always know when ya are, and I always find out."

I groan. "Mum, we're not hiding anything from ya. Okay? Now, can I get to work? There's a whole bar full of patrons out there, and even though we have this money, we still need to make as much as possible. Ladies, stick to the plan for tonight."

My cousins nod as if we had this big discussion about what they're supposed to do for the evening. I brush past Mum, return to the pub, and grab an apron. I tie it around my waist and get busy serving our customers.

Hours pass. The entire time, I can't get Devin off my mind. Every time the door opens, I expect to see him and other O'Connors pushing through.

I don't know why I think that or what I expect them to do if they did. Yet I hate not knowing where he's at right now.

Lads' weekend, my ass.

How could I have been so dumb to believe that lie?

And golfing. Ugh!

He's definitely not a golfer.

"Guinness." Fred, one of our long-time patrons, an American who moved over here when he was in his twenties, shakes his pint so the edge hits the counter.

I grab the glass from his hand, seething, "Do not disrespect our property."

"I didn't disrespect your property," he declares.

"Didn't ya? Hitting the glass against the counter is disrespecting our property."

He grunts. "Stop being so uptight."

I finally have had enough. Maybe it's because of Devin and my guilt that I fell for his lies. Perhaps I'm just tired of Caleb destroying things in his path and thinking it's okay, just like all these other people who come here almost every day and want to enjoy the place but have no issues being destructive and disrespectful.

Screw this.

I jump up on the bar and yell, "Everybody shut up and put your attention over here!"

Some people stop talking. Others continue their conversations.

I scream louder, "I said, shut up!"

"Lauren, what are ya doing?" Mum questions in horror.

I barely glance at her. "What should have been done before." I turn back to the pub, repeating, "Shut up!"

The pub finally turns quiet, and everyone watches me.

I announce, "There's going to be new rules around here. If ya can't obey them, you're not welcome here."

"Rules? You're not one to make rules," a man calls out, and others praise him for his comment.

I don't see who said it, but it's gruff and arrogant. It's everything I hate about our clan members.

I insist, "I can and I will. If ya want to enjoy this place, so be it. Enjoy it. But the minute ya destroy it, you're done. You're banned, and it will be a permanent ban."

"Lauren," Mum quietly says, but I ignore her.

I point around the room at the broken mirror, the missing chairs, and the space where extra tables should be. I state, "I don't know what your impression is, but we aren't rich. We cannot afford thugs to come in here and destroy our property. So make sure you tell everybody in town. The next time you're a part of any fight within this pub and anything gets destroyed, you will be banned. You will never be allowed back in here."

"Ya can't enforce that," another bloke calls out.

I turn toward where the sound came from, unsure who said it. I square my shoulders and lift my chin, standing taller. "Test me on it."

Groans fill the air.

I glance at Ronin, asserting, "These are the new rules. You will enforce them. Do ya understand?"

I'm once again putting him in a bad situation. The rules of the clan are the rules of the clan, and everyone knows Caleb is the only one who can change the rules. But this has to stop.

In my most determined voice, I question again, "Do ya understand, or do I need to replace ya as well?"

He finally comes to his senses and shakes his head. "No, ya don't need to replace me. I understand."

"And what are the rules? Why don't ya tell me and the rest of the pub so we're all clear?"

"Lauren!" Mum tugs on my leg, but there's no stopping me. I'm over people doing whatever they want and thinking they can get away with it.

Ronin repeats, "If anyone gets in a fight or destroys property, they're banned."

"For how long?"

His face hardens.

I wait for him to answer.

He finally says, "For life."

Outbursts fill the air.

I shout, "That's right," looking around the room again at the shocked faces. I add, "If ya don't like it, then don't come in. This pub will be a place ya respect, or it won't be yours to utilize."

"You're being harsh, Lauren," Paddy, a clansman calls out.

I snarl, "Deal with it. This pub serves a lot of purposes. Ya have parties here for birthdays, baptisms, and wedding receptions. Over the holidays, ya come here with your families and children. You're here several times a week, if not daily. So I'm warning ya, if you want those privileges to continue, you will obey our new rules, or ya will never step foot in this pub again. I promise ya that."

"Caleb won't stand for this," Paddy declares.

The pub fills with agreement.

My stomach flips. I insist, "If Caleb has an issue, he can take it up with me." I jump off the bar and go into the kitchen, then through the back door. I step into the alley, needing to breathe fresh oxygen.

The crisp nighttime air hits me as soon as I step outside, cooling the heat in my cheeks. It does nothing for the anger or the worry that fill me.

There's going to be some backlash for what I just did. Caleb won't like it. I have a battle in front of me.

My mum comes tearing out the back door, fretting, "Lauren, what did ya just do?"

I spin on her. "I did what ya should have done years ago. We are not going to stand for this anymore."

"Ya can't—"

"I can and I will! I've had enough, Mum. We will not live like this. We will not be taken advantage of, and we will not have our things destroyed and disrespected. These are the new rules."

"It's not your place—"

"Bullshit! And I'm tired of it. I know you are too. Now, I don't know who left that money, but thank God they did. However, this is the last time we will replace our things due to these imbeciles. There has to be consequences. If they disobey our rules, they don't deserve to be here."

Mum shakes her head. "But Caleb is the only one who can make rules."

"Screw Caleb!"

"Shh! Ya can't say that," she says, looking around as if other people are in the alley with us.

"I can and I will," I state through gritted teeth, brushing past her to return inside.

I work the rest of the evening, ignoring the unhappy comments and whines of men who should know how to act in public. A few attempt to argue with me, but I stand firm. They can either learn to live with the rules I've set or they don't need to be here.

Somehow, I will enforce it.

Even if Caleb isn't on board with what I'm insisting is the path forward.

8

Devin

I've almost nodded off when my phone rings. I glance at the screen and groan, answering, "What do ya want?"

Brody's voice is harsh when he orders, "My place, now." He hangs up without another word.

"Shit," I grumble.

I lie in bed for another minute. Then I force myself out, toss on my clothes, and go to his house with my gut diving.

He must know.

Of course he knows. He always finds out.

Still, how did they find out?

Maybe it's something else, I tell myself, but it's wishful thinking.

The minute I step inside, I lock eyes with Tynan, and he gives me a knowing look. Cathal and Brogan are next to him, and it's clear we've been caught.

Brody and Alaina step into his office.

She puts her hand on her pregnant stomach and snaps, "Want to tell us what ya were doing at The Confessional?"

"How did ya know?" Tynan asks, which is a stupid question. Alaina never tells us her secrets. She has her thumb on everyone's moves, and no one understands how she does it. I suspect even Brody can't figure out how she does what she does.

Alaina answers, "We know everything, and ya shouldn't ever underestimate us. I thought all of ya were smarter than that."

I don't respond and cross my arms, sniffing hard. I'm tired of living my life according to Alaina's rules.

Brody barks, "What were ya thinking? I want answers now. Ya had no right to be in a pub in O'Leary territory."

"Territory we should have taken by now," I mutter.

Brody slams his hand on the desk. "Goddammit! That's not your decision to make."

I meet his scowl. "It's prime for the taking, and ya know it."

He repeats, "Not your decision! Now, what were ya doing there?"

"It seems like ya know everything. So why are ya asking me?"

Alaina seethes, "Did any of ya sleep with any O'Leary women?"

The room turns silent.

She steps in front of Cathal. "Well? Did ya?"

My heart races faster. From the corner of my eye, I catch the guilt in his expression.

Fucking pussy.

He's never been able to go neutral.

She erupts, "Ya stupid assholes! How could ya sleep with them?"

"Sorry. Were they wearing chastity belts we weren't aware of?" I ask.

Alaina steps in front of me. She jabs me in the chest. "This isn't a joke, Devin. Ya put all of us at risk, and ya had no right to do anything with an O'Leary woman!"

I tilt my head. "For someone who made a pledge to the O'Connors, claiming to be done with the O'Learys, you sure do seem to still have a lot of loyalty toward them."

Alaina's eyes darken.

Brody steps next to her. "Ya better watch your tone and remember who you're talking to."

I groan inside. I hate how both Alaina and Brody rule our family. I would've liked it better if he did it alone. Alaina's way more ruthless than he is, in my book, not that I'd ever tell her that. My brother just looks like a pussy in my eyes. I wouldn't let any woman rule next to me.

But I have to give her credit. Alaina's a badass. We're way better off as a clan with her than without her.

Alaina seethes, "You know damn well O'Leary women don't have choices."

"Says who?" I ask, arching my eyebrows, and then I glance at Cathal, Brogan, and Tynan, questioning, "Did we not give them choices the other night before they spread their legs?"

Alaina reaches back and slaps my cheek so hard my face turns toward the window.

A sting flares across it. I clench my jaw, put my hand over my cheek, and slowly meet her eye.

Fire ignites in her expression. Her green eyes glow like a wild animal ready to kill its prey. She lowers her voice, but it's shaking. "The women in the O'Leary clan do not have choices. It's not right for ya to do what ya did and take advantage of them."

I maintain my ground. "I didn't take advantage of anyone. Nobody did anything to anyone that they didn't want to do. So can we make that clear? Unlike the men in your clan, we don't force women to do things."

"It's not my clan anymore," Alaina reiterates.

"Isn't it? Ya seem a little bit loyal to them for a bunch of barmaids," I repeat, in an effort to upset her further.

"Barmaids?" The color drains in Alaina's face.

"Don't tell me ya have extra respect for barmaids," I mutter.

Brody warns, "Don't ya keep talking to my wife that way. Show some respect."

My face hardens and I clench my fist at the side of my body. This is exactly why I don't need any O'Leary women in my life. They're just a pain in the ass.

Alaina puts her hand on her belly again and says, "Tell me ya didn't sleep with Lauren."

The hairs on my neck rise. "Why?"

Alaina shakes her head in anger at me. She wags her finger near my face and snarls, "Of course it would be you! Ya idiot. Caleb will kill ya!"

I grunt. "I'm not afraid of Caleb."

"Ya slept with his girlfriend!"

My chest tightens. "Girlfriend? What are ya talking about?"

She glares harder at me.

Brody declares, "There are consequences to your actions. Ya all knew ya weren't allowed to go anywhere below our territory line. Ya went without our permission, knowing it was wrong. So now you'll have to serve your punishment."

Tynan groans. "More bodies to cut up?"

A twisted look fills my brother's face. Brody's lips twitch, and he shakes his head. "No, we've got something way better for ya."

My chest tightens, and my stomach drops. I don't know what would be worse than being on body disposal duty.

Alaina grabs her phone, types something on it, and my phone buzzes. She orders, "Go ahead. View where you're spending the next day or so."

I pull my phone out of my pocket, and my gut sinks further. The address of the sewage tunnels flashes up at me. We use them to distribute our firearms to other parts of the city, but guys low on the totem pole run it. It's the most disgusting job and one I never wanted to get.

I stare back at Alaina, wanting to tell her off but knowing I've officially pissed her off big-time. This is way worse than body disposal duty.

Tynan asks, "What is it?"

I keep my stare on Alaina, not wanting to look intimidated or to let her know she's affecting me. In a nonchalant voice, I relay, "We're on firearm duty in the tunnels."

"The sewage tunnels!" Cathal blurts out.

Alaina's head snaps toward him. "Do ya have something to say about your punishment?"

He shuts his mouth and stares at her forehead.

"Aye. I thought so."

Brody warns, "All of ya better stay in O'Connor territory from now on. If I catch any of ya disobeying us again, you'll wish you could live in the sewer after ya see what I do next to punish ya."

We don't say anything. The four of us leave and get in my car.

"I told ya we shouldn't have done that," Cathal says.

I bark, "Shut the fuck up. Stop being such a pussy."

"Pussy? Excuse me for not wanting to work in the sewer. Have ya ever been in there? It's disgusting," he whines.

"No. Why would I go in there?" I ask.

"Exactly. Ya have no idea what we're about to have to do. I had to once, and it's revolting. We'll smell sewage for weeks, unable to get rid of it no matter how much we shower," he claims.

"Stop being a fucking baby," Tynan orders, then pulls his hoodie over his head and puts the seat back.

"Ow, do ya have to do that?" Brogan barks.

"Shut up! All of ya. I need some sleep," Tynan declares.

"Aye. Shut up," I order and turn on the engine.

The rest of the way to the sewer, everyone stays quiet. All I can think about is Caleb putting his dirty hands on Lauren.

Girlfriend.

How can she even allow him to touch her?

When we get to the entrance point, our men are there. The man in charge, Jackie, looks us over with his eyes widening. He questions, "What are y'all doing here? Something wrong?"

Shake my head. "No. Alaina's on the warpath. We've been summoned to take over for tonight."

"What the fuck did ya lot do?" he asks.

"None of your business," I reply.

"Sorry," he mutters. Then he opens the door to tunnels. The stench creeps into the city air, and I hold down my bile. He motions to the ladder and then disappears down it.

"Fuck's sake," I mutter. I put a handkerchief over my face and follow him into the dark hole. When I reach the bottom, I use the flashlight on my phone and glance around the space, but I can't see very far. Sewage swirls around us, and even though the water's low, it's still knee-deep.

Brogan has a coughing fit.

"It'll take a few minutes to get used to it," Jackie declares.

Tynan belts out, "Get used to it? How the fuck do ya ever get used to this?"

"Ya just do."

"Doubt that."

"Jesus Christ, I can't stay down here," Brogan says and tries to climb back up.

"Ya will stay down there, or you'll receive the next consequence," Alaina's voice fills the air.

He freezes on the ladder, pushing his mouth into his arm, gagging into his sleeve.

"Jesus, is she everywhere?" Tynan mutters.

"I can hear ya," Alaina threatens.

"I told ya going to Dublin was a bad idea," Cathal complains again.

"Said like a fucking saint. I didn't see ya complaining when ya were sitting in front of that lass ya banged," I point out.

"No bird's worth this," he states, pulling his scarf tighter, his face turning even greener.

Jackie whistles. "Ya'll went to Dublin? That's some balls!"

"Don't get any ideas," Alaina booms.

He holds his hands in the air, stating, "I'm not."

I glance around but don't see where the speakers or cameras are, then give up and ask, "Jackie, how far is it?"

"A few kilometers."

"You've got to be kidding me."

Jackie shakes his head. "Nope. Ya got at least two and a half kilometers."

Alaina's voice comes back over the speaker. "Jackie, take the night off and thank your four fellow assholes for the big bonus that you're getting."

Confusion fills his face. "Bonus?"

"Yep. Their wages for today are going to ya. Go enjoy the night with your family."

Shock fills Jackie's face. The bonus is probably more than he makes in a month. He freezes.

I motion to the exit. "Get going." He nods and scurries off, closing the tunnel door, and the air grows thicker.

Cathal mumbles, "I can't believe ya got us into this."

"Stop your fucking complaining," I order. I move the flashlight around and find the containers that need to be moved. They're full of ammo, guns, and bombs.

"We better get going," Tynan says, grabbing one of the cases and putting it on a cart.

We spend hours moving all of the illegal items. When we finish, it's early into the next evening.

I climb the ladder and step back in the crisp air, which barely relieves me. The stench seems to have seeped into my pores.

As soon as I get to my flat, I scrub my body half a dozen times with soap, but it barely touches the stench. I finally give up and crawl into bed, exhausted but unable to turn off my mind.

All I can think about is Lauren and Caleb. How could she be with him? Is he the one who choked her? Then my cock aches, reminiscing about how she came on it while I cut off her air supply.

"Fuck, I got to get this lass out of my head," I scold myself.

I try to sleep, but I can't. So I get out of bed and hit the floor, doing rounds of push-ups. Yet I can't shake the thoughts of Caleb putting his hands on her neck, kissing those plump lips, or taking her in all the ways I did.

Does she like it as much as she liked what I did to her?

No, she couldn't.

What if she does?

It doesn't matter.

What if she's into Caleb?

Who cares?

Get a grip, I order myself, but I can't shake it.

I roll over and start doing sit-ups until my torso can't take anymore. It doesn't help either. Then I stand and do jumping jacks until I'm covered in sweat.

I take another shower, wishing I could smell Lauren on me instead of the rotten sewage stench that seems to be clinging to me.

The more I think about Caleb, the more intense the sewage stench gets, and then I picture Lauren's face in my mind.

I need to see her again.

What am I saying?

That lass is nothing but trouble, I remind myself.

I get out of the shower, dry off, and put the towel around me. Then I pace my bedroom, unsure why I'm so unsettled.

She's just a woman. I've had tons of them. I can go get anyone I want.

So why am I so obsessed with her?

I'm not obsessed.

I am.

The sun peeks through the clouds when I make another move that I know I shouldn't, but I can't help myself. I'm too far into this, even though I know I shouldn't be.

I pick up my phone and hit the call button.

Samuel, one of our men who's infiltrated the O'Learys, answers, "Devin, long time."

I skip the niceties, stating, "I need ya to do something, and it needs to stay between us."

Silence fills the air.

I add, "You understand?"

"Brody know? What about Alaina?" he questions.

I flat-out lie to him. "They do. And they don't want ya talking about this to anyone, including them. Do ya understand, or do I need to spell it out?"

The line goes quiet again. He finally asks, "Why do I get the feeling they don't know?"

I reply, "Ya know what? I'll find someone else to do this and report your insubordination to Alaina and Brody."

"No, don't be stupid!" he replies.

"They don't want ya to talk to them or anyone but me about it. This is a test. Can you pass it?" I lie again. But everybody knows Alaina and Brody have been testing many clansmen lately to see who's loyal and can follow orders.

"Of course you can trust me," he answers.

My heart races faster. "Good. There's a lass who runs The Confessional."

"Lauren," he interjects.

The hairs on my arms rise. "Aye, ya know her?"

"Sure, everyone does. She's Caleb's woman," he states.

The disgust I felt when Alaina first told me fills me again. My stomach flips until I feel nauseous.

"Hello," Samuel asks.

"Aye. I'm still here." I refrain from blurting out that she won't be Caleb's for long, even though I know there's no way I can be with her. Yet everything within me tells me I'll be damned if Caleb gets her, not me.

So against everything in my gut, I order, "I want ya to monitor her. If Caleb goes near her, I want to know immediately."

9

Lauren
Six Weeks Later

our men secure the mirror against the wall. It's the final piece of the rebuild. We had to special order the glass, which was supposed to take a few months. Yet it miraculously arrived today.

Pride fills me as I assess the pub. It makes me happy to see everything back in place and even better than it was before. And ever since I created the new rules, people have been on their best behavior.

There was only one incident where someone started getting out of hand, but Ronin stepped up. All he had to do was give one warning and, to my surprise, it stopped. My mum's even secretly happy, although she still won't admit it.

The head installation guy holds a clipboard in front of me and says, "I need you to sign here."

I scribble my name next to the X, stand back, and put my hand on my hip, staring at my reflection.

Mum states, "Looks beautiful, doesn't it?"

"It does," I confirm.

"I guess ya finally spent my money," Caleb's voice booms, and a chill runs down my spine.

I spin and snap, "What are ya talking about? This isn't due to your money."

My mum grabs my forearm and feigns a nervous smile, quietly chiding, "Lauren."

And all the anger I've ever felt toward Caleb resurfaces. It figures he'd come here and claim he gave us the money to fix the pub. I blurt out, "What? It's not his money. He shouldn't take credit for it."

Mum keeps her smile tight, pleading with me with her eyes to agree. She admits, "Lauren, I called Caleb to thank him for taking care of us. Now say thank you."

I jerk my head back, and the blood drains from my face. Betrayal fills me. How could she have done such a thing?

I shouldn't be surprised. Mum's always kissed Caleb's ass. It doesn't matter that she's seen his evil side.

She arches her eyebrows and nods toward him, demanding, "Express your gratitude for his generosity."

"But it wasn't him," I repeat, lowering my voice.

Caleb steps up next to us, narrowing his gaze, challenging, "No? If I didn't give ya the money, then who did?"

"It was an anonymous donor," I reply.

He grunts. "Stop being silly, Lauren. No one in this pub has more than their tab to part with, never mind the amount I left for ya."

I should drop it. I'm not in a winning situation. I need to shut my mouth and allow Caleb to take credit for it, but I can't. Maybe it's because I slept with Devin to get it.

I didn't. He tricked me and left it.

He used me as a prostitute.

This isn't the time for a trip down memory lane.

My stomach churns, and I push the thoughts to the back of my mind. I cross my arms over my chest and hurl out, "Why did ya leave it anonymously, then? If you're going to come in here and tell everybody it was you, what was the point?"

"I had more important things to do than be here. Who said I left it anonymously anyway?" he questions.

My gut sinks. "Well, there wasn't a name on it."

He scoffs. "Why would I leave my name on it? No one else has money like I do. I'm the only possible bloke who would give ya such a gift. Aren't I?"

My insides quiver. His sneer cuts into me, and even though I'm not his and free to do whatever I want with whomever, he doesn't think so. If he found out about Devin and the others coming in here, I'm scared to find out what would happen.

"Give the man credit," Paddy calls out.

I spin to face him. "Shut up and stay out of our business."

He gets up and strolls over to Caleb, giving me a dirty look. It's the same expression he's shot at me since I announced the new rules. He states, "It's about time ya showed up. Someone needs to put Miss High and Mighty in her place."

Here we go.

I knew this was going to happen eventually. I've spent the last few weeks wondering when Caleb would show up and knowing I'd have to fight him regarding this. In all reality, I'm shocked he hasn't appeared sooner.

I glare at him, but the quivering in my gut only grows. I straighten my shoulders and lift my chin, ready to stand up for myself and my pub. All I care about is ensuring that my mum's property stays respected and doesn't get destroyed. Yet I can't lie and say I'm not scared.

To my surprise, Caleb's eyes turn to slits. He directs them at Paddy and snarls, "Is there something I'm unaware of?"

Paddy gives me a smirk. "Aye. There is. This lass made new rules. Ones ya didn't approve. They go against the rules that have been in our clan for years...even decades." He glances at me in satisfaction, knowing he just put my head on the chopping block.

I attempt to not look intimidated, yet I assume I'm doing a horrible job. Paddy has me and knows it. Caleb will surely try to override my authority.

Caleb asks, "Who said I didn't approve the new rules?"

Shock fills me, and I try not to let it appear on my face. Then a new horror fills me. I don't like surprises where Caleb's concerned. He doesn't do anything without expecting something in return. There's no doubt he'll demand something for letting my new rules stand.

Paddy argues, "Surely ya didn't approve. Why would ya change perfectly good rules?"

"Perfectly good rules! Ya think destroying our pub and having no consequences is a good rule?" I shriek.

"Easy," Caleb warns.

I gape at him, still confused about what his motives are and if he's really going to enforce the new rules or not.

He refocuses on Paddy, adding, "And I approved them because I can."

Paddy's face hardens.

"Ya got a problem, Paddy?" Caleb questions.

Paddy starts to speak, then shuts his mouth when Caleb arches his eyebrows even higher. He replies, "No, Caleb, we're good."

"Tell ya what, Paddy," Caleb says, slinging his arm over his shoulder. "I'm going to put you in charge of something."

Paddy's body stiffens. "Oh? What's that?"

"You're going to be in charge of ensuring no fights happen here. So do ya know what that responsibility entails?"

Paddy's face drains of color. He clears his throat. "No."

"No, who?"

Paddy swallows hard. "No, boss. Please explain."

Caleb's lips twist. "It means that I'm holding you accountable if anybody fights here. And I won't only ban ya from the pub. I'll have to unleash real consequences on ya. Do ya understand?"

Paddy's hand holding his Guinness shakes, and liquid splashes onto the floor.

Caleb glances down. "Looks like ya made a mess, Paddy. Why don't ya go get a bar towel and clean it up?"

More shock fills Paddy's face.

As much as I enjoy seeing Paddy squirm, I don't understand why Caleb is acting like he has my back. The only time he ever had was to trick me into thinking he cared about me. I'm not about to be gullible and think he's changed.

"Why are ya standing here, Paddy? Are your legs broken?" Caleb questions.

Paddy recovers. "No, boss." He lunges toward the bar, grabs the towel, and steps near the puddle.

Caleb points to it. "What are ya waiting for? Clean it up."

Paddy's bald head and cheeks turn fire-engine red. He crouches, cleans it up, and rises.

Caleb points to the floor. "It's shiny, so it's still wet. Wouldn't want someone to slip. That would put Lauren and her mum in a bad position. Get another towel."

Mum puts her hand on my arm.

I quickly glance at her and roll my eyes.

She's got admiration in her expression and is giving me her *You need to marry Caleb* look.

My stomach churns. Of course she's buying into Caleb's game...whatever it is that he's playing.

What does he want from me?

Me.

Ugh! Gross!

My stomach flips faster.

Paddy grabs another towel and wipes the floor until the shine is gone. He rises. "How's that, boss?

Caleb glances at it. "It's good. From now on, if anyone spills anything on the floor, you're to scrub it up. Are we clear?"

Paddy's face hardens. Caleb waits until he answers, "Aye, boss."

Caleb slaps him on the back. "Good. Now go buy me a round."

Paddy clenches his jaw and steps in front of the bar. "Round for Caleb."

Emily sets a shot glass on the counter and pours whiskey into it. Then she fills a pint with Guinness. She chirps, "Should I put it on your tab, or would ya like to pay now?"

"Tab," he grumbles and picks the glasses up. He hands them to Caleb.

Caleb doesn't say thank you and tosses the whiskey back, then chases it with the Guinness.

Paddy returns to his table.

Caleb jumps on a chair and shouts, "Everyone listen up."

Deafening silence follows. Respect fills the patrons' faces, which is the opposite of when I demanded their attention.

It's another thing that disgusts me and only ignites more anger.

Caleb announces, "All of ya will follow the new rules and respect the pub. If ya can't, you will be banned for life. Understand?"

Shock ripples through the crowd of patrons.

Caleb threatens, "I asked if ya all understand me, and I expect an answer."

The room fills with affirmations, the opposite of the grief they gave me.

Caleb warns, "Ya won't just be banned though. You'll have to deal with me and my wrath. So either behave or you're not allowed to be here. And there will be other consequences if ya get banned."

Tension builds as he stares each of them down.

I should be full of gratitude, but it's impossible. I don't understand what's happening.

Before I can think about how to get out of it, Caleb slinks his arm around my shoulder and leans into my ear, muttering, "I think it's time we talked, don't you?"

Time to deal with it, I tell myself, wishing my skin wasn't crawling. I allow him to lead me into the kitchen. As soon as I step inside, I tell the cook, Bradan, "Go take a smoke break."

He glances at Caleb, nods, says, "Boss," and then grabs his pack of cigarettes and exits the building.

When the door closes, I glare at Caleb, accusing, "What do ya want?"

"Since when do ya make rules without my approval?"

I remain quiet, unsure how to answer him, even though I've thought about this moment more times than I can count over the last few weeks.

He adds, "Ya got lucky that I understand why ya did what ya did. Plus, I already planned on making the new rules. I don't like seeing the place destroyed either."

Unable to stop myself, I scoff. "Then why were you the one who was destroying it the other night?"

"Destroying it? I didn't destroy it," he claims.

"You were in the middle of the fight. Of course you destroyed it," I insist.

He arrogantly smiles. "I don't think accusing me of things is any way to thank me."

More rage fills me. "Thank you? I have nothing to thank ya for except busting up my pub and making us put it back together again."

He jerks his head backward. "Ya don't? I paid for this place to be rebuilt. I just made it clear that no one will destroy it ever again. Don't ya have any gratitude?"

I want to call him out on his lie and prove to him that he didn't give me the money. But then I'd have to tell him where I got it, and the guilt around that fills me once more.

Plus, Caleb would kill me if he knew I slept with an O'Connor.

"Cat got your tongue, Lauren? Looks like there's something ya want to say to me." He studies me closer.

I'm suddenly worried that he knows the O'Connors came into the pub. Is that why he's been gone? Did he go after them?

Is Devin dead?

My heart races faster and my palms turn clammy.

Why am I panicking over this? I don't care about that asshole.

Ugh! I wish that were the case!

"Well, whatever ya got to say, ya better say it now," Caleb offers.

I hold my tongue, glaring at him and not trusting myself to speak.

He grabs my chin. I try to move my head, but I can't. He's got too tight a hold on it. He leans closer, demanding, "Say thank you."

My pride won't let me. He grips my chin harder, once again ordering, "Say thank you, Lauren."

I decide it's not worth letting my ego win. I mumble, "Thank you."

"For what?" he pushes.

My pride hits a new low. He stares at me until I say, "Thank you for telling the patrons to support the new rules."

He cocks an eyebrow. "And what else, Lauren?"

My gut spins. "I don't know. There's nothing else to say."

He grips my chin even harder, and I wince. "Why don't ya thank me for giving ya my money?"

"It's not your money," I snap before I can think about it.

Disapproval washes over his expression. "No? Then who gave ya the money, Lauren?"

My entire body trembles. I claim, "We told ya. It was left at the door by an anonymous donor."

He shakes his head. "No, it wasn't."

My fear grows.

He knows.

He has to know.

I can't speak, for fear what I might say and what he'll do next.

Minutes pass as I try not to shrink under his scowl. Then his expression turns eerily calm as he states, "I'm not anonymous, Lauren. My money is not anonymous. The things I do for this community and you are not anonymous."

My insides quiver harder.

He adds, "Now, I'm going to release you. Kiss me and show me how grateful ya are for my generosity and support."

Bile crawls up my throat. "I'm not kissing ya, Caleb."

"So ya don't appreciate my gifts and support?" he challenges, stepping toward me.

I step back, and he continues to move forward until I'm against the wall. The smell of his cologne reminds me of the time he choked me so hard and scared the crap out of me.

Sickness fills me. I try to push him away, but he grabs my hands.

He seethes, "Are ya trying to play hard to get, Lauren?"

"Leave me alone, Caleb."

He takes his finger and drags it down the side of my cheek, over my jawbone, then down the front of my neck. His fingers lace around my throat.

My knees buckle from fear, but he pushes against me, holding me between the wall and him. He threatens, "I don't like ungrateful lasses."

I stay quiet.

He continues, "I'm going to go now, but ya better think about how you're acting. When I get back, ya better return to the woman who shows me how much ya want me."

"I don't want ya. I'm never going to want ya," I manage to get out.

Arrogance washes over him. He flicks his tongue on my lobe, making my skin crawl.

I try to get away from him, but I can't.

He declares, "You're mine, Lauren. You've always been mine. You're always going to be mine."

"I'm not!"

A sinister smile forms on his lips. He insists, "Oh, but ya are, lass. And the next time I step foot in this pub, ya better be packed and ready to leave with me."

"Never! I will never leave with ya!" I spout.

The calm look washes over him again. I'm not used to it, and it freaks me out further. Caleb usually doesn't know how to manage his emotions. This new sense of control is throwing me for another loop. My gut tells me it's more dangerous than him making his thoughts known.

More time passes, and all I can hear is my heart thumping against my chest and his breath coming out of his nostrils.

He finally releases me, stepping back. He goes to the door, turns back, then declares, "Pack up, my dear Lauren. I'm coming back for ya soon."

10

Devin

y phone buzzes. I yank it out of my pocket and glance down.

> Samuel: He's at the pub.

My pulse skyrockets. It's the first time Caleb's entered The Confessional since I told Samuel to monitor Lauren, except when he came in to claim that he'd paid for the pub destruction.

It didn't surprise me that he took credit. Samuel reported Lauren and the others were claiming an anonymous donor left it. I'm sure it's eating Caleb up, not knowing who left the money. And that thought satisfies me.

> Me: What's he doing?

> Samuel: He just pulled Lauren into the kitchen.

The hairs on my neck rise and my heart pounds harder.

> Me: Find out what they're doing in there.

> Samuel: That's a death sentence, and ya know it.

He's right, but that's not an excuse I'm willing to accept.

> Me: It's your job. Are you unable to do your job?

> Samuel: I'm not looking to die a painful death anytime soon.

> Me: Figure out how to get in there. I want to know what's happening. That's an order.

A moment passes as I watch the dots appear in the message. It finally comes across.

> Samuel: If you don't hear from me, it's because I'm dead from making a stupid move.

> Me: Then don't make stupid moves.

I rise, then down my Guinness faster than normal. I toss cash onto the counter and leave the pub, stepping into the chilly air.

Declan nods at me, declaring, "No one's been near your car."

I have no reason not to trust Declan, but since I had my fun with Lauren, I've been more cautious than normal. So I take out my pen and check the car, ensuring there are no bombs.

Declan grumbles, "I said there was nothing to worry about, boss."

I spin on him. "Good. Make sure it stays that way."

"Of course I will," he insists.

I pat him on the shoulder, get into the car, and pause for a brief second. My chest tightens as I turn the ignition.

Relief hits me when the engine revs. Even though there weren't any bombs that I detected, the anxiety never goes away.

Plus, since we went to Dublin and returned, Caleb's recruited a lot of new members over the last month. He's starting to push the boundaries of our territory lines. So everything in my gut says war is about to happen again.

And it's not just me who feels it. Brody and Alaina are on edge. I wish I knew what Caleb had planned. But what's bothering me more is that I don't know what his plans for Lauren are, and that's dangerous.

I shouldn't care, yet I'm obsessed over it.

The usual disgust fills me, gnawing in my gut. I dwell on the same thing that I never get the answers to.

Girlfriend.

How the fuck could she ever let that thug touch her?

I drive down the road, unaware of where I'm heading, until I realize it's toward Coolock.

I mutter, "What am I doing? I need to go back."

My awareness of the situation does nothing to deter me. I don't turn around. I continue moving past the border of our territory.

The sun's fully set, and the darkness and fog grow. My head-lights are the only source of light in front of me. I should move to the main road, but I stay off the beaten track.

I don't know why. It's slowing things down. And as much as I tell myself I'm not going to Coolock, I know I am.

An hour passes during my drive and my phone rings. I glance at it and debate whether to answer it. On the fourth ring, I face the music and finally pick up.

Brody demands, "Where are ya going, Devin?"

"Out. I need to clear my head," I lie.

He seethes, "Why are ya headed south?"

"I'm just going for a drive."

"Get back here, now."

"I'll be back when my head's clear," I state, then hang up and turn off my phone.

I don't know what my punishment will be this time if Brody finds out I went back to The Confessional. He promised it would be worse than the sewers, but I'll risk the consequences.

All I've done for the last month is wait for reports from Samuel. From time to time, I've made him send me pictures. I can only imagine what he's thinking about why I need him to report to me about Lauren. Still, I don't care. So far, he's stayed true to his word and not let it slip to anyone about my little job.

And I wish I knew what it was about Lauren that's made me so obsessed with her, but I never can figure it out.

She's the total package.

She's not.

I veer to the left and continue the debate.

Maybe it's because I know I can't have her again.

Yes, that has to be it. I want her because I'm not supposed to have her.

There's nothing special about this woman. She's just another lass, another barmaid, another willing woman who spread her legs for me.

That's a lie. Everything about her is special.

The petrol light dings and flashes. I groan, change directions toward the motorway, and exit when I see a sign for a station.

I reach behind the seat, grab a baseball cap off the floor, and put it on. Then I pull into the lot, fill the tank, and don't make eye contact with the bloke pumping petrol across from me.

When I get back into the car, I tell myself I really should turn back, but I don't. The closer I get to Coolock, the more my pulse races. I rack my brain about how to play this out, still unsure what I'm going to do once I get there.

It's close to midnight when I finally get to town. I park on the street where I can see the pub, staying in my car. I turn on my phone, knowing my brother will know exactly where I am.

> Me: What happened in the kitchen?

> Samuel: Not sure. I went in and acted like I needed to talk to the cook, but Caleb ordered, "Get the fuck out."

It isn't rational for me to be angry with Samuel. Of course Caleb wouldn't let him witness his interaction with Lauren.

But I am angry. I want information and expect to get it, even if it's impossible.

> Me: You need to step up your game.

I turn my phone off and sit back in the seat, tapping my fingers on the steering wheel.

I keep my eyes on the pub. Caleb and his brothers finally stumble outside, drunk and singing with their arms around each other. A car pulls up, and they get in.

I'm tempted to get out of my vehicle, but I wait, confident more people are inside. Over the next half hour, more patrons leave. It's another hour until Lauren's cousins step outside with the security guard and the lights turn off.

My heart thumps against my chest. I force myself to wait a little longer, then finally get out of my car. I stay in the shadows and creep into the alley. I take a deep breath and ring the bell.

What am I doing?

Having what's mine.

She's not mine.

She was and will be again tonight.

Nobody answers. A burst of wind picks up, slapping against my cheeks.

I ring the bell again. The door finally opens, and Lauren gapes at me.

"Miss me?" I question and drag my eyes over her body. My mouth instantly waters at the thought of what's underneath her jeans and T-shirt.

She nervously glances behind me and frets, "What are ya doing here? Ya know ya can't be here."

"Then I guess ya should let me in, angel. Standing out here isn't safe, and ya know it."

"I'm not your angel, and I'm not letting ya in!" she declares, lifting her chin in defiance and pinning her cold gaze on mine.

I step forward, and she retreats. It takes two steps, and I'm inside. I shut and bolt the door.

"Get out. I didn't tell ya to come in," she snarls.

My stomach flips. I proclaim, "Now, why would I get out? Ya know ya want me here."

Her voice shakes when she says, "Ya have a lot of nerve." She takes another step backward.

I lunge toward her, and she retreats into the main part of the pub until she's trapped between the bar counter and me. She gasps and glares, her soft breath coming out faster.

I study her, my cock aching as a flush fills her cheeks.

She snaps, "What do ya want, Devin? Tell me and go."

"You and Caleb, huh?" I accuse, my voice full of disgust and the gnawing in my gut growing.

Her eyes turn to slits, and she looks as disgusted as I feel. She asserts, "I am *not* with Caleb."

"But ya were?"

"It's none of your business, and why do ya care anyway?"

"Who said I care?"

She scoffs. "Ya just drove hours to ask me about him. You do the math."

"I was in the neighborhood."

"Bullshit."

I ignore the truth and push, "How long have ya been with Caleb?"

Her tone hardens as she repeats, "I am *not* with Caleb."

"He's the one who choked ya, isn't he?" I blurt out, unable to hide my curiosity and needing the answer to one of the questions I've obsessed over for too many hours on a daily basis.

She glares at me. "Whatever happened between ya and me will never happen again. Ya lied to me. Ya tricked me. Ya set me up. I have nothing to say to ya, and my business is not yours to meddle in. Now get out!" She points to the kitchen door.

I press closer, slide my hand over her cheek, and her jaw trembles. She blinks hard, and her eyes glisten. I quietly state, "I don't think ya want me to leave."

Silence and tension fill the air, mixing with her floral scent, heating my blood until it's scorching in my veins.

"Ya need to go, Devin," she softly repeats.

I ask, "Is that what ya really want? Me to go?"

She turns her head, and I see a tear fall. I swipe at it with my thumb. She slowly turns back to me and locks her blues on mine.

Instinct takes over. I press my lips against hers, sliding my tongue into her mouth before she can object. It only takes her a few seconds before she returns my kiss.

I tug her closer, but she suddenly pushes against my chest and jerks her head backward.

She orders, "Don't touch me."

My stomach flips, and my chest tightens. I demand, "Admit ya missed me."

"I didn't," she proclaims.

"So ya didn't miss me because you're with him?"

"Stop saying that! I'm not with Caleb."

I blurt out, "Aren't ya? My sources say you are."

Shock fills her face. "Sources? Are ya spying on me?"

I just stare at her silently.

She directs the same disgusted expression that she used for Caleb at me. She seethes, "Who do ya have watching me?"

I continue to maintain my silence, and the blood pounds between my ears.

Her voice turns louder. "Tell me!"

I lean closer to her face. "Do ya think I would tell ya my secrets?"

Horror replaces her disgust. "So O'Connors are in my pub?"

I reach for her cheek. "Ya don't need to worry about this. It's not to hurt ya."

She moves her face away from my hand, demanding, "Why would ya be watching me?"

I can't answer her. Anything I say would make me sound weak.

"What do ya want from me, Devin?"

"I don't want anything from ya. I thought I made that clear last time."

Anger overshadows the horror in her expression. "Ya made it clear? Ya did everything in your power to seduce me."

My stomach dives. "Is that how ya see it?"

"What other way is there to see it?" she snaps.

My arrogance takes over again. "From where I was standing, you were a willing participant."

Fire burns in her eyes. She scolds, "You're a pig. And I'll never forgive ya. Now get out of my pub."

Her words sting. It takes me a moment before I taunt, "How many times are ya going to tell me to leave before ya realize that's not what ya want?"

"It is what I want. I don't ever want to see ya again."

It's another knife to my chest. But I'm no quitter. Now she's in front of me, I'm not leaving until I've exhausted all my options to have her again. So I grab the back of her hair, tug, and slide my other hand over her throat.

Her eyes widen. I lean my face over hers and slowly grip my fingers around her neck.

She can still breathe; I've not cut the air supply off yet. And I see all her thoughts in her eyes.

Her hatred for me runs deep. The lust swirling beside it is a powerful aphrodisiac, tormenting me. It propels me to give her more than what I gave her the last time I was here.

She manages to get out, "Go."

I ignore her order, warning, "Let me be very clear. Caleb is not the man for ya." I squeeze my fingers a little bit tighter and kiss near her earlobe.

She shudders softly and whimpers.

Fuck, I've missed this.

I assess her, unable to take my eyes off her blues. "Do ya understand me, Lauren? I don't want ya with him." I release the pressure on her neck.

She chokes out, "I'm not with him. I can't stand him, just like I can't stand ya."

Her words continue to cut me. They shouldn't. Words never hurt, but how she looks at me and says it affects me. It's something I've not felt before and takes me by surprise.

After a moment, I recover. I stress, "I don't want him in here around ya. Do ya understand?" I step back, needing a minute to breathe and figure out my next move.

She sarcastically laughs, "Do ya actually think I have a choice to allow him in or not? Not that it's any of your business."

I insist, "I don't want him around ya."

Helplessness fills her expression. "Do ya think I have choices like you do? Let me assure ya, I don't."

Her statement's a slap in the face. Alaina pops into my mind, mad as hell, lecturing me about how O'Leary women don't have choices. For the first time, I understand she's right.

Still, I don't want Caleb anywhere around Lauren. And I'm not sure of the solution to keep him out of the pub, so I suddenly feel as helpless as she looks.

Another tear falls down her cheek, and she swipes at it, declaring, "There's no reason for ya to be here. All you're going to do is put me in danger. Is that what ya want, Devin? Do ya want Caleb to do something to hurt me and punish me for ya being here?"

"Of course not," I assert.

She softens her tone. "Then ya need to go."

She's right, but my body won't move now that I'm here. I can't leave. I've obsessed over her, thinking every moment about trying to reignite the feeling I had when I was with her. And I curse myself again for even going down the road of coming here in the first place. If I could do the night over and never have come here, I would. In my mission to quench my boredom, I created a new problem.

"So ya do want to hurt me," she accuses, stepping away from the counter and out of my grasp.

I shake my head, softening my tone. "No, I don't want to hurt ya. I've never wanted to hurt ya."

"Didn't ya? Isn't that why ya came here that night? To hurt me?" she insists, the pain in her voice digging into my heart.

"No, that wasn't my intention."

"Then what was your intention? Why did ya come into my pub?"

I blurt out, "It was just an itch I needed to scratch. Something I needed to do."

Her face turns slightly green. Horror lights up her features. Her lips and voice shake harder. "I was an itch?"

I scrub my hand over my face. "That came out wrong."

"Did it? It sounds like the truth to me. You're only backtracking since you didn't mean to admit it!"

I glance at the ceiling, frustrated by my stupid outburst and unable to keep my gaze on her pain-filled expression.

"Devin, get out. Ya don't belong here. You're not an O'Leary. This is an O'Leary pub. Get out," she repeats as tears fall down her face and she quickly tries to swipe at them.

In a quick move, I step forward and tug her into me. I don't know why I do it. I should leave. She's right. This is an O'Leary pub, and I'm not an O'Leary. But nothing about our situation can be rationalized.

I hold her closer, and she tries to push me away. But I wrap my arms around her tighter and press her head against my chest. I mutter, "I'm sorry, angel."

She slowly relaxes, her body going limp against mine and not fighting me. "You're not sorry," she declares in a muffled voice against my chest.

I kiss the top of her head. "I am. I didn't mean to hurt ya."

"Yea, ya did. Are ya happy that ya did? Does it make ya feel better that ya set me up and got what ya wanted?"

The reality sounds horrible coming from her. And I can't argue with her. It's exactly what I did. Still, I don't want to admit it to her. So I repeat, "I didn't mean to hurt ya."

She suddenly gets a burst of energy and pushes out of my arms. "Yea, ya did. And whoever ya have spying on me, ya better stop it. If Caleb finds out, there will be blood in this pub. Besides, ya have no right to watch me anyway."

I don't say anything. There's no way I'll take Samuel off her. He'll continue monitoring her until I work through whatever this obsession is that I have with her.

"I mean it, Devin. Nobody is to be watching me. Call it off. Caleb will find out. I can assure ya that he will."

I grunt. "Caleb's the last person I'm worrying about. He's a fucking moron if ya haven't noticed."

"Of course I've noticed. But he'll still find out. And you're a moron too. You're the one who came down here, and now ya have surveillance on me. What do ya think will happen when he finds out?" she hurls out.

I cross my arms. "There's one thing ya need to learn about me, Lauren."

Her eyes burn with heat. "What's that?"

I confess, "Nothing and no one scares me. That includes Caleb and all the other O'Learys."

She shoots me more daggers with her eyes. "Well, ya should be."

I grunt. "No, I shouldn't."

She shakes her head in anger, trying to stop fresh tears. "Then it's your funeral. Now get out. There's no reason for ya to be here."

11

Lauren

Tension builds between us. I can't tear my gaze off his. I've thought about him so many times since he left that night, unable to get his sharp features out of my mind, craving to have his hand on my throat as he just did it. But I never thought I'd see him again.

His body presses against me, and I mold right into it, hating myself for reacting to him. I should feel nothing but disgust toward him after what he's done, and now he admits he's spying on me.

I rack my brain, trying to figure out who he has watching me. But everyone I know in the pub is an O'Leary.

That means there's a traitor in the clan. It's my duty to tell Caleb so he can figure out who betrayed us. But how would I even do that? What would I tell him? I can't admit Devin told me.

And I don't know how many times I've told Devin to leave, even though I don't want him to. I hate that I'm conflicted about how I feel about him when there should be so much clarity around it.

He lunges toward me, and I back up until I'm against the staircase wall. He never takes his eyes off me. His warm, muscular frame pushes against mine. He puts his hand on my throat again and his other one on my cheek.

Blood pounds hard between my ears. My breath shortens. I'm fully aware of all the things I feel for him that I shouldn't. It's wrong on so many levels.

His eyes drift over my face, freezing on my lips, and all I want to do is kiss him. I wish we could go back to how we were that night, before I knew anything about him. I'd do anything to return to when I'd fully let go and wasn't worried about anything except being in the moment.

He quietly states, "I have every reason to be here."

"Ya have none," I insist.

"I do. You're my reason."

My pulse skyrockets. I blurt out, "Why are ya doing this?"

He calmly orders, "Let's go upstairs, Lauren."

My insides quiver harder. I don't say anything, scared of giving in to his request but also petrified of not.

He needs to leave.

No good can come of anything between us.

He leans closer. "Tell me you haven't thought about me, Lauren. Tell me you haven't, and I'll go if that's what you want."

My mind tells me to lie. I open my mouth, but nothing comes out.

He takes his thumb, traces my bottom lip, and curls his fingers tighter around my throat. His voice deepens as he asks, "Ya know what I remember?"

I can't understand why he's doing this to me and why I can't just push him out the door.

I need to fight harder.

I don't want to.

He needs to go.

I want him to stay.

He continues, "I remember your moans and your cries and the way your body gripped mine. I remember ya telling me to choke ya as ya came hard on my cock and how ya reacted with my lips around your pussy. Remember that, my little vixen?"

An explosion of endorphins fills my body, and I hate myself for it. Tingles race down my spine to my core and I squeeze my thighs tighter.

It's like Devin knows. He moves his hand off my mouth and slides it into my pants.

I gasp as his finger slides into me. He presses his thumb against my clit and starts circling it.

"What are ya doing?" I ask in a shaky whisper.

"Shh. Do ya remember me now? Do ya remember what we're like together?"

I swallow hard against the palm of his hand.

His lips twitch. He brings them to my ear. "I've thought about ya. Too many hours to count, I've thought about us and what we were like. Now tell me one more time to go, and I will. But I think ya want what only I can give ya." He presses his thumb harder against me, and my knees buckle, but his body is pressed against mine.

It's just like how I was pinned to the cold wall when Caleb was here. But unlike the disgust I felt earlier, only desire surges through me with Devin. And it shouldn't.

"Jesus, you're arrogant," I mumble.

Tell him to leave.

Order him to take his hands off me, leave, and never return.

I can't get the words out, no matter how hard I try. All I smell is his woodsy Meghann scent, and I feel his heart beating faster.

He continues, "I've gotten a bit obsessed about ya, lass. Does that not mean anything to ya?"

I'm happy he's thought about me. Lord knows I've thought enough about him, but I should only be angry he's here. So I scold myself again. Yet no amount of reprimanding can stop the thirst I have for a repeat of our previous encounter.

He licks my lobe, curls his finger inside me, and my body shudders. "That's my good lass. Such a good angel. Now, do ya want to go upstairs or stay down here?"

I don't move. I'm too scared.

He keeps working my body and heat flies to my cheeks. He kisses my neck, and shivers run down my spine at lightning speed, making me moan.

"Fuck, I've dreamt of your sounds. No matter how much I tried to relive it, nothing is as good as hearing ya in person. Now, upstairs or here?" he asks again.

I stay frozen, even though adrenaline lights up every cell in my body.

He nibbles on my lobe, working my clit harder. An orgasm hits me, filling me with endorphins. I whimper, shaking all over. My eyes roll, and my knees fully buckle.

The only things holding me up are the wall and his body. His grip around my throat gets tighter the longer he maintains my orgasm. He stops from fully cutting off my air supply, murmuring in my ear, "Ya get everything ya want when ya choose whether ya want it here or upstairs." He stops manipulating my lower body and loosens his grip on my neck so I can speak, ordering, "Tell me now, Lauren. Upstairs or here?"

I swallow hard.

He removes his hand from my body, shoves his finger in my mouth, and I automatically suck on it, tasting my arousal. It's just an aphrodisiac making me want more.

He demands, "Tell me. Tell me now, my vixen. Upstairs or here?"

I finally cave. I know what I want. It's the only thing I've wanted since he left. "Upstairs," comes out of my mouth, and I curse myself the moment it does, knowing I shouldn't be doing any of this.

He kisses me and pulls back.

I quickly blurt out, "Ya need to go."

His eyes narrow. "That's not what ya want. Ya just told me upstairs."

I close my eyes.

His fingertips caress the back of my neck. He demands, "What's it going to be, Lauren? Do ya really want me to walk out of here tonight, or do you want one more night together?"

I can't speak. I'm afraid of telling him to go and also telling him to stay.

It's like he knows. He reaches behind my body, palms my ass with both hands, and picks me up. He kisses me, and I wrap my limbs around him tighter than ever before, unable to stop myself from returning his affection with vigor.

Everything he does creates life within me. And I hate myself for the fact that this man, my enemy, the one who tricked me, who shouldn't be here, and who can cause a lot of damage to my life, feels like he's meant to be with me.

Before I know it, he's carrying me up the stairs effortlessly. He shuts my bedroom door. I barely hear the lock click.

He puts me on the bed, ripping my T-shirt off me before I can even get it over my head.

"Jesus," I cry out.

He shoves his tongue in my mouth, shutting me up, rolling it like a masterpiece against mine.

I sink into his body. He only takes a breather to tug his own shirt over his head. He tosses it on the floor. And when my skin hits his warm flesh, I whimper.

"Ah, ya feel good, angel. Just like before but better than I imagined. Isn't the real thing better than just the memory?" he asks.

I can't deny it. I nod and slide my hand into his hair, pulling him back to me. I don't know how he does it. But between his knee and his foot, he tugs my jeans off as well as his own, never taking his lips off mine.

And then he's in me, thrusting. Filling me, teasing me, and dominating me the way no one else does or ever has.

He mumbles, "Don't hold back, my vixen. I want to hear you."

He reaches again for my neck. The air begins to close off around me, and he thrusts harder and deeper, pushing my chin back until I'm staring at the headboard, unable to breathe.

Endorphins explode everywhere within me. I shake against him, my body spasming hard. My muffled cries grow louder, and never-ending.

He declares, "Aye. Fucking aye! This is what I missed. Right here. Let it out, angel. Let it out."

And everything feels way more intense than from what I remember. I don't know how that's possible, but it does.

The intensity seems to go on and on. And then he's suddenly kissing my breasts, my stomach, and above my pussy. He dips lower, making me so dizzy I can't see anything.

I gasp out a cry and grip him, not wanting him to let me go, even though I should, until it somehow shifts. It becomes just us.

The guilt vanishes. Before I know what's happening, he flips me over on my stomach, cages his body over mine, and tugs my hips up. He licks the back of my lobe, and I shake harder. His fingers curl around the back of my neck. He mumbles, "I want all of ya, Lauren. You're mine and meant to be mine. And there's something ya haven't given me."

I don't know what he's talking about, so I turn my head and ask, "What?"

But he doesn't let me see his face. He keeps his lips on my ear and orders, "Just relax."

He thrusts back inside me several times, and I moan, "Oh, Jesus, Devin."

"I want it all, my vixen," he says. He pulls back and then puts his cock against my forbidden zone.

The hairs on my arms rise. "What are ya doing?"

"Shh," he says and pushes past the hard ridge.

"Oh God!" I cry out.

"Shh," he coos again, holding himself still with only a little bit inside me. He restates, "I need you to relax, angel. Just relax. I promise ya it'll be good."

I don't know why I believe him, but I do. I can't trust him as far as I can throw him except when it comes to manipulating my body.

He orders, "Take a few deep breaths."

I do, and he slowly begins to inch in and out of me.

A new feeling fills me. To my surprise, I like it. Just like every-thing else he does to me. I whimper, "Jesus Christ."

He murmurs, "I told ya, my vixen. You and me...all of it." He continues thrusting slowly, and a new wave of adrenaline hits me, giving me sensations I've never felt before.

He takes his hand, sliding it around the front of my throat, and right as I start to see stars, he squeezes my neck. And the high is so intense I convulse harder than before, arching up, but there's nowhere to go.

It's just the mattress beneath me and Devin's torso over me. The point comes where I need air, and I start to gasp. He tightens his grip, and adrenaline shoots even higher in me. I think I'm going to black out.

And it's like he knows my breaking point. He comes inside me and releases his grip so I can breathe. He loudly groans and shudders on top of me.

We both try to catch our breath. A few minutes pass, and he mumbles against my neck, "Let's go shower. I want to make ya come under the water. Plus, time is running out. I should leave before the sun rises."

Reality hits me. All this will be is another experience that's going to haunt me.

12

Devin

*W*e finish taking a shower, and I turn the water off. I grab a towel and dry Lauren off. She steps out of the shower, and I wipe the droplets of water from my own body.

She lunges toward the toilet and kneels. She heaves and throws up.

I step out of the shower and grasp her hair. I bend over and rub her back, fretting, "Angel, what's wrong?"

She continues to get sick but barely anything comes out. When her gagging stops, she wipes her mouth and slowly looks at me. Her blue eyes water, and a few tears slide down her red cheeks.

"What just happened?" I question.

She shakes her head. "I don't know. I just felt sick."

I put my hand on her forehead. She's warm but doesn't feel like she's burning up. I inquire, "Have ya felt sick all day?"

She forces herself to her feet and shakes her head. "No. It just came on suddenly."

I put my hand on her forehead again. "Ya feel hot, but—"

"I'm fine," she claims, moving my hand off her.

"Ya might have the flu."

"I don't. I'm fine," she declares. She pushes past me and exits the bathroom, going to her closet. She grabs a robe and puts it on.

"Ya don't just puke out of nowhere and be fine," I state.

She shrugs. "The fish and chips I ate earlier didn't taste right. Maybe I got food poisoning."

"Ya would've been sick sooner than that," I claim.

"I'm sure it's from that."

I'm not buying it, but I don't think arguing with her will help. I point at the mattress. "Why don't ya go lie down."

She hesitates, then obeys.

I pull the covers back. She slides in, and I lie next to her. I tug her into my arms and kiss her forehead, asking, "So ya weren't feeling sick earlier?"

She says, "Can we stop talking about me being sick? I don't know what just happened, but now I feel fine. I just... I need to go to sleep."

I release a frustrated breath but agree. "Okay. Just close your eyes, then."

She does and then opens them and slowly looks up at me.

I stroke her cheek and ask, "What's up, angel?"

She licks her lips and then questions, "If I fall asleep and wake up, will you be gone?"

Silence fills the air. I glance out the window. The darkness of the night is fading into daylight. I'm pushing my luck still being here, so I answer, "Aye."

She blinks hard, then curls back into my chest. "Okay. It was nice knowing ya."

I softly chuckle.

"It wasn't meant to be funny," she asserts.

My face falls. "No, it's not. You're right. I can't come back anymore."

"Then don't," she says, but all I hear is hurt in her voice. She rolls away from me and curls into a ball around her pillow.

I reach for her.

She firmly orders, "Go now, Devin. There's nowhere this can go, and we both know it. And don't come back again."

I freeze for a moment.

"I mean it this time. I need ya to go," she says in a sterner voice.

I slowly slide out of bed, get dressed, then stare at her.

She warns, "This isn't the time to linger. You know what'll happen if someone sees you."

She's right. I know she's right, as much as I don't want to admit it. So, I lean down and give her a final kiss.

She keeps her eyes closed and won't open them.

"If things were different—"

"They're not," she interjects.

I open my mouth again and snap it shut. What am I saying anyway? She's right. They're not different, and they never will be.

I force myself to leave and sneak through the alley, looking around, but there's nobody on the street. I get to my vehicle, start the engine, and get down the street before I realize I didn't even check it for bombs.

I have to start being smarter.

When I get into O'Connor territory, I turn my phone on, expecting a ton of messages from my brother, but there's only one.

> Brody: You're playing with fire. It can't go anywhere with her.

What a fucking hypocrite. He and Alaina couldn't go anywhere and look at them now.

It doesn't matter. I'm not going to end up with an O'Leary woman.

Maybe I could.

How am I even thinking these thoughts? I'm done with Lauren now. My appetite for her is quenched. I just needed one more time.

Her face appears in my mind. I try to force it out, but it haunts me the entire ride. I get to my flat and message my brother.

> Me: I don't know what you're talking about.

It's a stupid message to send. After all, I had to turn my phone on when I was in Coolock. I'm sure he saw it.

> Brody: You went to see her.

I continue to lie.

> Me: No, I didn't. I just needed a night away to think.

> Brody: About what?

> Me: None of your business.

> Brody: You turned your phone off all night.

All night?

Does that mean he didn't know when I turned it on briefly in Coolock?

Maybe I did get away with it.

No, he knows.

He doesn't. He'd be ordering me to get to his house so he and Alaina can serve me another punishment.

I slide into my bed to sleep, but I can't stop thinking about Lauren. I'm worried she's sick, so I text her.

> Me: How are ya feeling?

> Lauren the Enemy: No more texts. We can't keep communicating. Delete my number.

I start to write her another message, then erase it.

She's right.

After a few hours of fitful sleep, I finally get out of bed and go to the gym. I do several rounds on the punching bag when Dante Marino, Boris Ivanov, and Killian O'Malley walk into the gym with my brothers. I stop punching the bag, and they approach me.

My sister, Bridget, is married to Dante, but she used to be married to Killian's brother, Sean, before he was murdered. And Boris is married to Killian's sister, Nora. All four of our families have been allies for decades.

"What are ya crazy fuckers doing here?" I slap all their hands.

Killian's eyes turn dark. "Had to take care of some business."

Chills run down my spine. "Meaning?"

"Caleb had the balls to send a crew over to Chicago."

My eyes widen. "Why would he do that? That's suicide."

Killian seethes, "Tried to overpower our men on the docks. Take over our territory."

Dante adds, "He sent another crew to New York, and they surprised us when we opened the containers at the shipping yard."

I jerk my head backward. "He's unable to hold his own territory in Ireland, and he's trying to expand in America? That makes zero sense. He needs all the men he can get here."

No one disagrees.

Tynan declares, "No one claimed Caleb was smart."

Dante's expression hardens. "We took those bastards out, so he wasn't successful. But we need to send him a clear message, and that's what we're going to do."

The hairs on my neck rise. I ask, "How are ya going to do that?"

Boris shifts on his feet and exchanges a glance with Killian.

My gut drops. I push, "Well?"

Killian glances around and steps closer. He admits, "We're taking out his men in Coolock tonight."

My stomach pitches. Lauren's face appears in my mind. I blurt out, "Coolock? Why there?"

Brody answers. "It's prime for the taking. Ya yourself said that. I thought ya'd be happy, bro." He gives me a knowing look, like I'm caught with my hand in the cookie jar.

My pulse skyrockets. I feel sick and wonder if I'm getting whatever Lauren had, but I also know it's not that. I demand, "How are ya doing it?"

Boris crosses his arms. In his Russian accent, he states, "We have over a hundred armed men positioned around the pub and the borders."

"What does the pub have to do with it?" I question, trying to stay calm and not give away my thoughts.

Brody states, "Caleb's got an event at the pub tonight. They'll all be there, making them an easy target to take out."

My mouth turns dry. I know the answer before I ask but hope I'm wrong. "You're going to shoot them in public when they exit the pub?"

Killian sniffs hard. He shakes his head. "No. That would give them time to notify those inside the pub. We'll only have a few minutes to do what needs to be done. Ya know how this works."

I swallow down bile.

Brody states, "Caleb should know better than to mess with American territory. But we'll send that message. He's going to get it loud and clear. He messed with the wrong families."

More panic fills me. "You're going to storm the pub?"

"Aye, by the time midnight hits, it'll be a blood bath everywhere in Coolock, including the pub."

My chest tightens so much I feel like I'm having a heart attack. I declare, "There are women and children in there."

"No, only strippers," Dante says.

I freeze. "What do you mean? It's not a strip club, it's a pub."

He adds, "Caleb's banned women and children from entering tonight. He's having his own private show."

More shock fills me. I blurt out, "In front of Lauren?"

Brody's eyes turn to slits. "So ya did go see her?"

I stand taller and continue to lie. "No, I didn't. Alaina said he was seeing her. If he's seeing her, then why would he take strippers in front of her?"

Aidan gives me a knowing look. "Caleb does what Caleb wants."

I argue, "The barmaids are women, and so are the strippers. Ya can't go in there and shoot up the place without taking them out too."

Boris claims, "Our men have been given orders not to shoot any of them."

"Ya know ya can't guarantee they won't get hurt or killed," I point out.

Tense silence fills the air. Everyone exchanges glances.

I accuse, "You're okay killing innocent women now? Women who've done nothing but their jobs?"

Dante replies, "Our men will do their best to ensure that none of the women get hurt." He pats me on the back and asks, "Where's the locker room?"

Aidan points to the door behind me.

Dante pushes past me.

Killian adds, "Who's first in the ring? I'm ready to do some damage."

"I'm ready for ya," Brody declares.

They all disperse, and the amount of horror that fills me is unheard of. The image of Lauren's body covered in blood fills my mind.

I have to get her out of there.

In a trance, I watch the others enter the locker room until it's only Tynan and me.

"We can't let the barmaids stay in the pub. They'll get hurt. They might die," I tell him.

He shakes his head with a solemn look on his face. "It's not what any of us want, but it's also not our call."

"Damn if it's not," I say.

"Ya can't do anything about it, bro. Let it go. It was one night. We don't owe these women anything. Besides, they're O'Learys."

My stomach flips and flips and flips. He continues assessing me. "Don't tell me you've fallen for her."

"I haven't," I claim.

He squints, studying me. "Ya sure? Because ya sure are acting pretty protective of her."

I argue, "They're women. Innocent ones. You heard Alaina. They don't have choices."

He grunts. "Since when do we listen to Alaina about stuff like that? I try to drown her out. I thought ya did too?"

I don't say anything.

He adds, "I'm going to get changed. I'm ready to get in the ring." He steps past me.

My heart beats harder. When everybody comes out of the locker room, I go in it. I grab my bag and keys and don't even change. I move toward the exit, and Tynan steps in front of me. He demands, "What are ya doing, Devin?"

"I'm leaving."

"Ya can't go warn her. Ya heard everyone. Our men are surrounding Coolock."

"I'm not doing anything of the sort," I say, pushing past him. I exit the building and start my car, once again not checking for bombs. I curse myself a few blocks down, realizing I need to stop doing that, or I'm going to get blown up one of these days.

I have to warn her.

I pull over and call Lauren, but she doesn't answer. I call several times, but it goes to voicemail.

I text.

> Me: I need to talk to you. It's important.

She doesn't respond.

I get to my flat and pace it, unsure of what to do. Tynan's right. I can't go past our border and into Coolock. There's no way. And even if I could, I can't go to the pub. Too many people would see me. So I try calling Lauren again.

She sends me to voicemail.

"Damn it," I shout and tug at my hair, staring out the window across Belfast.

I shoot her another text.

> Me: I need ya to call me right now.

I wait and wait and continue to try calling her. I finally get a text back a few hours later.

> Lauren the Enemy: Why are ya contacting me? We said this was over, and it is.

I call her.

She doesn't pick up.

> Lauren the Enemy: Don't contact me again. It's over. It's for the best.

> Me: I need you to pick up. This isn't about us.

> Lauren the Enemy: Then what's it about?

I text again.

> Me: Pick up when I call.

I call her again and she answers. The sound of her sweet voice makes my heart swell.

She demands, "What's going on, Devin?"

I think about what to say, but I'm suddenly tongue-tied.

She huffs. "Devin, what do ya want?"

I burst out, "Something's going to happen tonight."

Silence fills the line.

She finally asks, "What's going to happen?"

"I can't tell ya. But I need ya to listen to me and do what I say," I order.

She scoffs. "I'm not doing what ya say. Ya have no authority over me. This needs to end, Devin. Stop with the—"

"There's going to be a blood bath in the pub tonight," I blurt.

Deafening silence fills the air. The sound of her breath picks up.

I soften my voice. "Listen to me, angel. Get your cousins and your mum away from the pub. Go with them and stay with your mum."

Her voice is laced with worry. "What are ya talking about, Devin?"

"I can't tell ya what's happening except that ya need to listen to me."

"I can't just leave the pub unattended. You're going to need to tell me a little bit more than that," she declares.

I squeeze my eyes shut. "I can't," I admit.

"Devin, this isn't funny. You're scaring me."

"I'm sorry, angel. I'm not trying to scare ya."

"Stop calling me angel."

I blow out a breath of frustrated air. "Lauren, I need ya to listen to me and do what I say."

"Stop saying that. I already told ya, ya don't have authority over me."

"This isn't about that. This is about ya staying safe and not dying tonight."

Her voice shakes when she replies, "I will not let someone destroy my pub again. If your people are out there to hurt me and destroy my pub, then I should call Caleb right now."

I angrily warn, "Listen to me! It's not about ruining your pub. And this isn't in my hands. I'm telling ya, it won't be safe for ya, your mum, or your cousins. Do not stay in the pub tonight. Ya need to go somewhere else."

"I will not leave my pub to be destroyed," she claims.

I bang my head against the window. "Stop being stubborn."

"I need to tell Caleb. He'll protect the pub."

"He can't. Trust me."

There is silence on the other end of the line.

"I'm trying to protect ya," I admit.

"Who's coming after us if it's not you?"

"I can't tell ya that," I state.

"If you're lying—"

"I'm not lying. I need ya to make sure that you're safe. Ensure your cousins, your mum, and ya are safe before midnight."

"We can't just not show up to the pub. Caleb's supposed to be here. Do ya know what he'll do if he shows up and we aren't here?"

"Lauren, Caleb doesn't care about ya. He cares about himself."

"Ya don't think I know that?" she snarls.

I sigh.

"Around midnight, it's happening?"

"Aye."

"Then I'll figure something out before then."

I decide the best I can do is come to an agreement with her. I order, "Lauren, keep your phone on tonight. Ya need to prepare the others to listen to ya too."

"Devin—"

"I'm not playing, Lauren. I'm coming to get ya, risking my life to do so, or you can assure me that you'll listen to me. When I text ya, ya go into your flat, no matter what happens. Do ya understand me? Ya do what I say tonight," I interject.

Tension mixes with her silence.

I add, "Ya once told me ya don't have a choice as an O'Leary woman. Is that no longer true?"

She stays quiet.

"Answer me," I demand.

She finally does. "Yea, it's true."

"Okay, then I need ya to trust me."

"Why would I trust ya, Devin?"

"Because I'm going against my family right now. I'm going against our allies. I'm going behind their backs and trying to protect ya. Because I know that ya don't deserve what will happen. So please listen to me and do what I say tonight," I beg.

Her breath is the only thing I hear for several minutes.

"Just tell me you'll keep your phone on ya and follow my orders tonight."

"If ya get me in trouble with Caleb, where I get harmed—"

"I'm only trying to prevent ya from getting harmed. I swear!"

She finally agrees, her voice quivering. "Okay, I'll wait for your text. But...can't ya stop this? I just got the pub redone. I swore I wouldn't let it get destroyed again."

I sincerely tell her, "If I could stop it, I would. But I can't. No one can. And definitely not Caleb. But do not say anything to him, Lauren. I swear to God—"

"Do ya really think I'd say something to him? Do ya believe I want anything to do with him?"

It makes me happy that she said that, but I still hate that they have some sort of past. So I just reply, "I'm trusting ya, Lauren. And I'm trying to protect ya and keep ya safe. So keep your phone on. I'll be in contact later tonight."

13

Lauren

I can't help but wonder if Devin is telling the truth. I don't know what to make of his call. He was so insistent, yet he showed me the night we met that he knows how to play games.

He's an O'Connor.

Why would he go against his family to warn me?

My allegiance is with the O'Learys. It's my duty to tell Caleb.

What would I say? Devin O'Connor just called?

"Ugh!" I sit up and put a hand over my face and the other over my belly, warding off another round of queasiness.

Am I getting sick?

I rack my brain if anyone's had the flu around me, but nobody I know has been ill. I breathe for a few minutes, and it passes.

What am I going to do?

I pick up my phone. I text Devin.

> Me: Are you lying to me?

> Devin: No. I wish I were, but I'm not.

My stomach flips. I debate more about whether to trust him, but my gut screams that I need to.

But what exactly is going to happen?

The thought of something happening to my pub again makes me feel sicker. I rise and go to my kitchen cabinet. I pull out a box of crackers and try to eat a few. Then I get dressed. I make sure my phone is set to vibrate and toss it in my pocket.

I make my way downstairs. The pub is full of men, more jovial than normal, waiting for the strippers to arrive. It's not the first time Caleb's paraded them into our pub.

I glance at my watch. They'll be here in the next half hour. Time is of the essence if what Devin says is true.

My mum's talking to two regulars. I don't say anything to them and pull her aside.

"Lauren, what's going on?" she questions.

I glance behind her, then nod to go into the kitchen.

She follows me.

I order Bradan, "Go take a break."

"Aye," he replies, then grabs his cigarettes and steps outside.

Mum crosses her arms, demanding, "Lauren, what's the fuss about?"

"Take the night off, Mum."

Her eyes turn to slits. "Now, why would I do that?"

Butterflies replace my queasiness. I claim, "Ya don't need to be here to witness Caleb's debauchery tonight."

Mum's disapproval shows on her face. She states, "Neither do you. Why don't you be the one to take it off, dear?"

And that's just like Mum. Bury whatever Caleb wants to parade around me under the rug and act like he can't do any wrong. It angers me that she thinks I should accept that behavior.

Stay on task, I remind myself. *This isn't the time to think about Caleb and my mum's disregard for his actions.*

I firmly assert, "No, I'm working tonight. Go home. Ya look tired, Mum."

"I'm not," she claims.

"Mum, I have it covered. Go home."

She tilts her head, peering at me closer. "Why are ya trying so hard to get rid of me, Lauren?"

"I just want ya to rest tonight," I lie.

"I'm not buying that. What's really going on? You're hiding something."

I insist, "I'm not hiding anything, Mum. Ya look exhausted. I have it covered. Go home. Get some rest. Tomorrow ya can give me a night off."

She arches her eyebrows. "You're going to take a night off?"

My chest tightens. I force a smile. "Yea, I am, but only if ya go home and rest up tonight so ya can cover for me tomorrow."

She narrows her eyes, and I do everything I can not to shift on my feet or look guilty.

"Ya don't want me to take a night off?" I accuse, knowing that she does. She's always telling me to, but I never do. I don't like the thought of her here working her butt off while I'm out having a good time.

She inquires, "What are ya going to do if ya take a night off?"

I think quickly on my feet. "I'm just going to go to a movie."

She wrinkles her nose. "Since when do ya go to movies?"

"Never. That's why I'm going to go to one," I state.

"But why would ya suddenly want to go to the movie theater?" she pushes.

I lie, "I'm trying to expand my horizons."

"By going to the movie theater?"

I shrug. "It's something new. But it sounds like ya don't want me to take tomorrow night off. So I guess I won't," I declare and step past her.

She grabs my arm. "All right. I'll take tonight off and leave a little bit later."

"No, ya can leave now, or I'm not taking tomorrow night off," I assert.

She stares at me harder. "Are ya sure nothing else is going on?"

I sigh, claiming, "Yea, Mum. I just want to take tomorrow night off. But if ya don't go home now and get some rest, I'll feel bad and end up working."

A quick moment passes, and she finally nods and hugs me. "Okay, sweetheart. I'm glad you're finally going to take a night off. Ya work too hard in this place." Then she leans back and stares at me again, but sadness has replaced the suspicion.

"What?" I question, suddenly more anxious.

"I wish I could have given you a different life. And that's why ya need to marry Caleb. Ya could have the whole world at your fingertips."

Rage fills me. "Mum, we're not talking about this right now. Go home and text me when ya get there so I know you're safe."

"Why would I not be safe?" she questions.

"You're my mum. I worry about ya."

She declares, "I'm the parent. I should worry about ya. Ya shouldn't be worrying about me."

"Well, that's not how things work around here." I go over and grab her purse out of the cabinet. Then I put my arm around her back and move her through the pub, announcing, "Time to go."

Ronin arches his eyebrows when we get near him.

"Make sure Mum gets in her car safely," I order him.

"You're leaving so soon?" he questions.

She glances at me again, admitting, "Lauren's insisting I take the night off."

I chirp, "Because I'm going to take tomorrow night off. Now, have a nice night, Mum. Rest up so ya can take care of this place tomorrow."

She gives me another look, then finally caves and kisses me on the cheek. She says, "Okay, text me if things get too crazy and ya need extra help."

"I won't," I practically sing, beaming at her. But it's not false enthusiasm. Knowing she won't be here is one less worry for me. I point to the door, demanding, "Now go."

She hesitates one last time and then leaves.

I sigh in relief, then resume my pub duties. I run around filling drinks, checking my phone occasionally, and watching my cousins, debating about what to do next.

Fifteen minutes pass and Mum texts me.

> Mum: I'm home.

> Me: Let me see a selfie.

> Mum: Selfie? Since when do I take selfies?

> Me: Just humor me.

> Mum: Lauren, is something going on that you're not telling me? This is a weird request, even from ya.

I close my eyes and take a deep breath. Then I reply.

> Me: No. I just want to see your beautiful face.

She sends me a picture of her in the kitchen, and I relax.

> Me: Looking good, Mum. Rest up for tomorrow night.

Mum: Okay, but I'm here if ya need me to come back in and help.

Me: I won't. Enjoy your night.

I put my phone back in my pocket and decide my next move. I order my cousins into the kitchen and tell Bradan again, "Go take a smoke break."

He wrinkles his forehead. "Another one?"

I question, "Do ya suddenly not like your cigarettes?"

He chuckles. "Nope. Still love them."

"Then ya better go now before we're too busy for ya to have one."

He nods. "Aye. You're right. I shouldn't complain, should I?"

"No, ya shouldn't."

He grabs his pack of cigarettes and disappears out the door.

Emily cocks her head. "What's going on?"

"Emily, you and I can handle things tonight, right?" I ask.

"By ourselves? Ya know how packed this place is going to be."

"More tips," I state.

Jessica moans, "I need to make money. Tonight's going to be a great night."

"Not really. The money will all go to the strippers. Or did ya forget about last time?" I point out.

Her face falls.

Before she can reply, I command, "Alison, you and Jessica take the night off. Emily and I are going to handle it."

"We're going to have to work extra hard," Emily declares.

I arch my eyebrows. "I thought ya needed to make good money to help your da pay his rent?"

"I do."

I nod. "For either of us to make good money tonight, only two of us need to be on the floor. It'll be more work but worth it in the end."

"I need to make money too," Jessica whines.

"Emily's da is more important to take care of, unless you have something ya need to spend your earnings on that's more important?" I suggest.

She snaps her mouth shut. Guilt fills her expression. Emily's da's been sick with cancer for a few years, and she's helped him stay in his house.

"Jessica, Alison, you two go," I order. "You won't miss out because if there are four of us here, we're not making shit tonight. So go."

"Are ya being serious right now?" Jessica asks, putting her hand on my forehead. "Or are ya ill?"

I shrug off her touch. "Ha, ha, funny. But seriously, you two go home. Now."

"I guess we can go out on the town, then," Alison declares, turning to Jessica.

Her face lights up. "Yea! Let's go have some fun."

Panic hits me. I sternly state, "No! You're to both go right home."

They freeze, staring at me with the same suspicious look my mum gave me.

Jessica asks, "Why do we have to go home?"

My heart races faster. I haven't thought about this or what I would say.

Emily has my back, like always, even though she doesn't know what's happening. She interjects, "Because if Lauren says ya need to go home, then ya need to go home."

Alison peers at me. "What's really going on?"

"I just need both of ya to go home. Do ya understand me? Ya go directly home, ya don't stop anywhere, and ya text me when ya get home so I know you're safe."

"Why wouldn't we be safe?" Jessica asks.

I groan and rub my hand over my face. "Jessica, for once, can ya just do what I say and not question it?"

"Well, you're not making any sense."

Emily orders, "Jessica, go home. Do what Lauren says. Text her when ya get there. Do not leave your house. Do ya understand?"

"You know something's going on too, and you're keeping us in the dark," Jessica asserts.

I groan. "Nothing is going on. I need ya both to go home and stay there. Better yet, choose one of your places, and both of ya stay there together. I don't care whose house you're at but pick one. Do ya understand my orders?"

Jessica opens her mouth, and I glare at her in warning. She snaps it shut.

Alison puts her arm around Jessica. "Ya can come to my place. I just subscribed to that new movie channel."

She glances at her. "I'd rather go to a club."

"You're not going to a club," I insist, my voice rising.

Tense silence builds.

Alison caves. "Okay. We'll see ya later."

Relief hits me. I remind them, "Make sure you text when you get to Alison's. I want selfies throughout the night."

Jessica and Alison give me more uneasy glances but finally grab their stuff and go.

When they're gone, Emily takes me aside. "Do ya want to tell me what's going on?"

I debate but realize I have to. "Ya can't say anything to anybody."

Emily's face falls. She nods. "Ya have my word."

My stomach flips as I admit, "Devin warned me that something is happening tonight. He'll text me later and says I must go into my flat to stay safe."

Emily's eyes turn to slits. "Devin? The O'Connor?"

"Shh," I reprimand, glancing around us, but nobody's in the room.

Her voice turns stern. She asks, "Lauren, why are ya in contact with Devin?"

I realize she didn't know I have his number. I shouldn't tell her anything, but I blurt out, "He was here last night."

She gapes at me.

"Well, say something. Don't just look at me like that," I state.

Disproval fills her face. "Lauren, tell me you're not seeing him? It can't go anywhere."

"I know. Don't worry about that. I just... Look, he told me that something's going to happen tonight. It's not going to be good."

Panic overtakes her features. "What does that mean?"

"I don't know."

"And ya trust him that he's telling the truth?"

I hesitate but admit, "Yea, I do. And I need to make sure that ya and I are okay tonight. That's why I got the others out of here. I can't watch everybody, but you'll do what I say, right?"

She stares at me for a moment in confusion.

I beg, "Please tell me you'll go into my flat when I tell ya."

Minutes pass.

"Please!" I beg.

"Shouldn't we tell Caleb?"

My face hardens.

"Lauren?"

"What would I say?" I ask.

She stays quiet. Sympathy and confusion mix in her expression.

I plead, "Please tell me you'll do what I need ya to do."

She straightens her shoulders. "Okay, I will. When is all this happening?"

I shrug. "I don't know, but try to stay in eye contact with me at all times, okay?"

She nods. "Okay, Lauren." She briefly studies me, then asks, "Are ya feeling okay?"

I'm actually not. I'm nauseous again but swallow the bile and convince her, "Yea, I'm fine. I just want to make sure you're okay tonight."

She takes a deep breath. "As many bar fights as we've been in, we can handle anything, can't we?" She gives me a smile.

I softly laugh. "Yea, we can."

She puts her arm around me. "Okay then, it's ya and me, huh?"

I smile for the first time all day. "Yea, ya and me. Thank ya."

"Sure." She gives my shoulder a squeeze, then says, "Shall I let Bradan back in?"

"Yea."

I return to the pub, and within minutes she's back as well. For the next few hours, we serve drinks and food. We work our butts off serving Caleb, his brothers, and all the rest of the men in the pub with too much alcohol.

Six strippers work the crowd, and the men get drunker and drunker, getting handsier with the women as the night progresses.

It's near midnight when my phone finally vibrates. I glance at it.

Devin: Get into your flat now.

Panic erupts inside me.

I glance at Emily, and she freezes across the pub. I nod toward my flat. She sets a pint on the table and rushes toward me. I grab her arm, and we shove through the crowd, ignoring the men ordering us to get them more drinks. I open the staircase door, and we both step inside.

Someone tries to follow us.

I push him out of the way, tug the door shut, and lock it. We hurry up the steps, enter my flat, and I lock that door as well.

"Lauren, what's going to happen?" she frets.

"I don't know."

She goes to the window, staring through my curtains.

Another text comes in.

> Devin: Go into your bathroom and sit on the floor. Do not go near the window. Lock all the doors, and do not leave until I tell ya it's safe.

> Me: You're scaring me.

> Devin: Just do as I say, and you'll stay safe.

"What did he say?" Emily asks.

"He said to go into the bathroom and stay there."

Her eyes widen. "Bathroom? Why?"

"I don't know. Let's just do what he says."

We go into the bathroom. I shut and lock the door. We sit on the floor, taking up the entire space.

"What's going to happen?" she frets again.

I still have no answers, so I only shrug, feeling helpless and panicky.

Within minutes, gunshots ring through the air.

My heart races faster.

Emily looks at me in horror.

We clutch each other, both of us shaking.

The gunshots continue and it sounds as if we're in the middle of a war. Shouts, screams, and more gunfire seem to go on forever.

But it's not. In all reality, it's only a short time span before the shouting grows quieter and the gunshots lessen. Suddenly, there's deafening silence.

Emily and I stare at each other in fear, unsure about our safety.

My phone vibrates.

> Devin: Tell me you're still in the bathroom.

> Me: We are.

> Devin: Who's we?

> Me: Emily and me.

> Devin: What about the others?

> Me: I sent all of them home hours ago.

> Devin: That's my smart angel.

My heart swells, but I'm still shaking as I text.

> Me: What just happened down there? There were gunshots.

> Devin: Delete this text chain. Someone will be up there soon. Ya don't have to be afraid of them. They have strict instructions not to hurt ya. I won't be contacting ya anymore.

My heart sinks. No more contact from him. Of course, that's for the best, yet why do I feel so sad about it?

> Me: Why did ya warn me?

> Devin: I told ya to delete this chain. No more messages. It's for your safety.

I almost text him back, and Emily grabs my hand. She orders, "Delete the chain, Lauren."

I glance up at her. My lips tremble, and my voice cracks. I admit, "I don't want to."

I don't know why I want to hold on to these messages. Most of them are the two of us fighting and accusing each other of things.

Emily takes my phone and does it for me. Then she turns my phone off. She says, "We need to wait," just as there's a bang on the door.

A man's voice shouts, "Anybody in there? Answer or I'll have to shoot through the door."

Emily shouts, "There're two of us! We're just barmaids!"

"Unlock the door with your hands in the air," the voice orders.

We do as we're told.

The door opens, and a man I've never seen asks, "Are ya lasses okay?"

"Yes," we both state.

"Is anyone else in this flat?" he asks.

I answer, "No, just us. My place is small, as ya can see."

He nods. "I'm glad to see ya lasses are safe. Ya were smart to hide up here."

"What happened to everybody in the pub?" I question, but my gut already knows the answer.

His face darkens with hatred. He sniffs hard and relays, "We killed all of them. And I suggest ya stay up here for a while. I'll let ya know when we've disposed of the bodies and what's going to happen next."

"Happen next?" I fret.

His nods. "Aye. This pub is now property of the O'Connors."

14

Devin

I 've never felt so anxious before.

Thank God she's alive.

I stare at the messages for another moment, then do exactly what I told Lauren to do. I delete the chain, put my phone back into my pocket, and leave the bathroom. I return to the game room where all my brothers, Boris, Killian, and Dante have set up camp.

Alaina's not been present the entire night, and her absence strikes me for the first time. I ask Brody, "Where's your wife? She's missed the show."

His face hardens. "She's been doing other things." He turns and tosses his dart at the board.

Bullshit, I think.

I barely listen to the conversation for another half hour, then decide to go find Alaina. I'm pissed that she put Lauren and the others in that position when she runs around claiming how O'Leary women don't have choices or rights. Yet when push comes to shove, she does nothing to protect them.

I enter her office and find her staring at her TV screens, watching our men in the sewers, on the docks, and in different parts of the city.

I hurl out, "So ya don't like to think about the O'Leary women dying, but ya do nothing to stop it, do ya?"

She spins and gapes at me.

I add, "Ya hide up here when ya know the danger you've put them in."

She recovers, and her eyes turn to slits. "Ya don't have a right to judge me."

"Don't I?"

She tilts her head. "Ya better watch your mouth, Devin."

"Or what, Alaina? Ya can always speak your mind, but I can't speak mine since you'd have to look at the truth of what you've allowed to happen?"

Tension builds between us, then she sighs. Calm replaces her glare. She sits down at the desk and points across from her. "Sit down. Get whatever ya want to say off your chest."

I don't take the seat. I just cross my arms and shake my head. "It's pretty sad to me. Ya want to make all these claims about O'Leary women and what they will and won't do or the choices they have or don't have, but ya did nothing to protect them tonight."

"Brody told me they're fine. There were no barmaids killed. They're all fine, including Lauren," she claims.

I push. "Is that how ya sleep at night? They're fine, so it's okay that ya put them at risk?"

She purses her lips and presses her fingers together. Then she asks, "Why do ya care so much, Devin? Lauren get under your skin? Do ya think there's a future for the two of ya?"

I don't tell her that she's hypocritical. That would be admitting that I think about it. Hell, I'd have to admit to myself that I think about it. So I continue to scowl and say, "I hope you're proud of yourself." I turn and exit the room, returning to the game room.

When I walk in, Dante's phone rings. He answers it. "Aye?"

The room goes silent. He squeezes his eyes shut. "You've got to be kidding me. They escaped? How the hell did you let that happen?"

The hairs on my neck rise. One thing that I was looking forward to was Caleb, along with all the O'Leary men, dying. My gut tells me the phone call is about Caleb.

Dante blurts out, "You better find them," and hangs up.

"Who escaped?" Brody questions.

Dante relays, "Caleb and his brothers."

"Ya got to be fucking kidding me. How the fuck did those bastards get away with that?" Tynan blurts out.

Anger fills the room. It figures that Caleb got away. I'm sure he didn't even look to protect Lauren.

Brody picks up the phone, hits a button, then orders, "Take out the authorities. Make sure it's a ghost town."

Another rush of panic fills me. I go into the bathroom again and pull out my phone. I send Lauren a text.

> Me: Whatever ya do, stay in your flat. Get back into the bathroom.

> Lauren the Enemy: What are ya talking about? Your guy just said we could stay anywhere in the flat.

> Me: Just do it. And delete these messages again.

A long time passes. I pace the game room, try not to pull my hair, and Brody confirms we've taken over the garda station.

I text Lauren.

> Me: Are ya still in the bathroom?

> Lauren the Enemy: Yea.

> Me: Good. Ya can roam around the flat. Delete this chain.

Only a bit of relief hits me. Until this night's over, and I feel her in my arms again, I won't rest.

What am I thinking?

I can never see her again.

She needs to be mine.

I need sleep. I'm not being rational now.

More time passes, and Brody's phone rings. He listens, then hangs up. He orders Aidan, "Send our officers in."

Aidan picks up his phone and walks out of the room.

My stomach flips. All I want to do is see Lauren with my own eyes, yet my hands are tied. And while it's confirmed that the O'Learys are no longer in charge in Coolock, nothing is guaranteed. I don't trust all of our men not to hold it over Lauren's head that she has an allegiance to the O'Learys.

Plus, Caleb escaped. He's going to try and come back for her.

That thought creates an intense gnawing in my gut.

It's early morning when everything is finally settled. Brody receives another call to assure him no more O'Leary men are roaming the streets of Coolock.

Our authorities have taken over their garda and their headquarters in the town. Our men are now in place, and pictures arrive of the pub.

Bodies lay scattered. The tables and chairs are broken. The mirror behind the bar is shattered. Pools of blood mix with Guinness on the floor.

The gnawing in my stomach doesn't go away. I get in my car, and as soon as I get several blocks away, I pull over and call Lauren.

Her voice shakes as she answers, "D-Devin."

"Are ya okay?"

She admits, "We're still in the bathroom."

I ask, "No one's gone up there to come get ya?"

"Not yet."

"Okay. Stay there until we talk again." I hang up.

Rage fills me. I return to Brody's. I step through the door and shout, "Brody!"

Alaina comes down the stairs, announcing, "He went to bed. What are ya doing back here?"

I don't want to hate Alaina, but I'm starting to. She put Lauren in danger tonight. And while I shouldn't feel anything for Lauren, I can no longer deny that there is something between us.

I size Alaina up and decide I no longer care what she thinks or knows about my feelings toward Lauren. I tell her, "Lauren and Emily are in her bathroom in the flat. Someone needs to go up there and tell them it's okay to come out."

Alaina's eyes widen. "How do ya know that?"

I just stare silently at her.

She sighs. "Jesus Christ. If Caleb finds out you communicate with Lauren, he'll kill you. And she'll pay the price too."

"What are you going to do about Lauren?" I say, ignoring her warning. I'm so tired of hearing about Caleb killing me. He will never kill me, but I will take him out. Now more than ever, I'm committed to it.

Alaina puts her hand through her hair and her other hand on her stomach. She closes her eyes for a minute, shaking her head.

I demand, "What are ya going to do to keep them safe?"

She opens her eyes, pinning them on me. "I'll take care of it."

"Will ya?" I question.

Anger flares across her features. "Of course I will. I just told ya I will. Have I ever not done what I said I was going to do?"

I wish I could tell her she had, but she hasn't. She always follows through. So I finally admit, "No."

She nods. "Okay then, I'll take care of it."

I spin to leave.

"Devin," she calls out.

My insides squeeze tight as I turn back. "What?"

She warns, "Don't go near Lauren again. I will take care of this. But you're not to go near her. It's an order. Do ya understand?"

Instead of telling her I do, I state, "Don't take her pub away from her. It's all she cares about."

Alaina's face falls. "Aye, but they can't keep working there. It's an O'Connor pub now. That's the way these things work, and ya know it."

"She lives in that pub," I argue.

Alaina takes a deep breath. Sadness fills her expression. Yet she keeps her voice firm and asserts, "She'll have to go live with her mum or somewhere else."

Anger fills me. I curl my fists at my sides.

Alaina glances at them, then back at me. "Devin, ya know how these things work. She's going to have to move on. She and her mum will both have to move on, and there's nothing ya or I can do about it."

"Sure ya can. You're head of the clan," I point out.

She looks at me closer. "Do ya think that I don't want to help them?"

"Sounds like ya don't."

"Of course I would help them if I could."

"Ya can," I insist.

She shakes her head. "No, Devin, I cannot. I'm an ex-O'Leary who took an oath to uphold the O'Connor laws. As are ya—if I need to remind ya. They are O'Learys, and unfortunately, there will be no more O'Learys in The Confessional."

I scowl at her, suddenly hating this life I'm in, which I've never hated before. And it makes zero sense.

Lauren's just another lass I've shagged.

She's not.

She is.

I curse myself. I shouldn't even care about her, but I do. This will break her. I know what that pub means to her.

Alaina orders, "Go home, Devin. Stay away from Lauren. Get some sleep. When you wake up, it'll be a new day."

I grunt. "Is that how ya do it? Ya just tell yourself tomorrow's a new day, so what ya did today doesn't matter?"

She gives me a disappointed look. "Of course not. Ya know how these things work though. And let me remind ya that I didn't make the O'Connor rules."

"But ya can change them."

She squeezes her eyes shut and releases a long breath, shaking her head. She opens her emerald eyes and insists, "No. I can't."

"Bullshit."

Silent tension fills the air, with both of us staring the other down.

I finally give up and turn to leave. I get to the door and turn around one last time, adding, "I want a text message when she's safe."

Alaina nods. "That's the smartest thing you've actually said tonight."

"Aye, why is that?" I question.

"Because it means ya aren't going to be texting her. So make sure ya don't ever again, Devin. It's not safe, and ya know it. Caleb will find her. He's obsessed with her, and he will have her. So get it out of your head, whatever's in there. Nothing can ever happen again between ya two."

I clench my jaw.

She adds, "And those are orders."

I debate about arguing with her but decide it's pointless.

I leave and slam the door. I get in my car and go directly to my flat, forcing myself not to go to Coolock, knowing that if I do, it'll make things worse.

I shower, then I pace my flat, naked, staring out the window. I keep glancing at my phone, wanting to text Lauren but knowing that Alaina's right in some ways.

I need to resist messaging her.

But I want to.

There's no future for us.

Caleb is going to have her.

Over my dead body, he will.

I can't get Alaina's voice out of my head with her warning, but I figure that right now, Caleb and his brothers have retreated. There's no way they're in Coolock knowing that the town's been taken over. At least for today, Lauren will be safe from him.

I don't go to bed. I go to the gym, get in the boxing ring, and start fighting whatever man will join me.

Hours pass, and it's only when I'm bloody and exhausted that I stop. I get out of the ring, and Killian calls out, "You're stopping now that I came in, huh? I knew I intimidated you."

I glance at him and grunt. I'm not in the mood for his antics or jokes. I normally appreciate them, but not today. No matter how much I fought, I couldn't get Lauren off my mind.

He steps toward me and points at my face. "Ya got a good shiner there. Can guarantee ya I would've given ya a better one."

I can't hold myself back. I have too much anger and frustration, and Killian becomes my target. I slam my fist in his face, catching him by surprise.

Killian flies to the ground and then slowly looks up. A wild animal lights up his eyes, and he shakes his head.

Killian's one of the meanest fighters I've ever seen, and I've never provoked him before, yet there's no rationale left in me. I'm pissed at the world, and he's going to see my wrath because he was part of what happened tonight, whether rightly or wrongly.

He quickly jumps to his feet and comes after me, landing a hard punch to my cheek, but I recover quickly and go after him.

The gym erupts in shouts. Several men try to separate us, but they can't. Killian's a wild animal, as am I.

We both get in too many punches to count before we're separated. Three men hold me back, and three hold Killian. We're both out of breath, bleeding, and glaring at each other.

"What the fuck is your problem?" he barks.

I say nothing and shrug out of the grasp of the three men. I head into the locker room and pick up my bag.

Killian follows me. "What the fuck was that about, Devin?"

"Mind your own business, Killian," I order.

"Ya just punched me when we weren't in the ring. What the fuck is going on?" he repeats.

I don't answer him.

He grabs my shoulder and spins me, taking me by surprise. I slam into the locker. "Answer me!"

I push his chest. "Get off me."

He steps back and holds his hands in the air. "I deserve an answer!"

Killian's always been one of my favorite O'Malleys. We've been friends ever since Bridget met his brother. But how do I explain what I'm feeling right now?

He scowls. "Has to do with that bird in Coolock, doesn't it?"

"No," I lie.

He looks me over. "Sure seems like it."

"It doesn't," I declare.

He stares at me for another minute, and I shove past him. I get to the door and he calls out, "Devin."

I spin. "I don't need a lecture."

He warns, "Don't do anything stupid. Stay out of Coolock. If ya go there, it won't be good for anyone, including her."

I hear his warning, but I don't acknowledge it. I leave the gym and step outside. The cold air hits my bloody, swollen face, adding additional stinging sensations. I get to my car, almost start it, then realize I have to stop being risky.

I get out, take my laser pen, and check for bombs. When I'm satisfied I won't blow up, I slide into the seat and turn on the engine.

I drive toward Coolock and get to the edge of the territory line that used to separate us from the O'Learys. Now, the line no longer exists.

I'm tempted to keep going, but Killian's warning won't go away, and I know he's right. The last thing I want is to make it worse for Lauren.

So I pull over. I sit there for hours, debating about what to do. I finally receive a text.

> Alaina: She's safe. They escorted her to her mum's. We'll make sure her property is boxed up and taken there. Now come back to Belfast, Devin.

I don't reply. I almost disobey her and go on to Coolock but decide now is not the time.

Nothing makes sense anymore. I don't understand my pull toward Lauren, but I can't deny it. So I make a new resolution.

Caleb will feel my wrath. After that, I'll figure out how to make this up to Lauren.

15

Lauren

*L*ight streams onto my face. I snuggle into the pillow, but it grows brighter, so I open my eyes.

Where am I?

Mum's guest room comes into focus and my gut drops. *The pub.*

How could they have done that to the pub?

Monsters!

Is it really no longer ours?

My heart races, and I sit up in bed, recalling the events of the prior evening. My gut drops.

Mum had already heard what happened when they dropped me off at her house. I didn't know the man's name who escorted me. I only knew he was an O'Connor. And I'll never forget her devastated look when she opened the door.

A muffled yet gruff voice fills the air. I force myself to get out of bed and stare down at the dressing gown Mum gave me to sleep in. I toss my hoodie over it, step outside the bedroom, then freeze.

Three boxes are piled near the door. A scary-looking man stands next to them. He asks, "What do ya want us to do with the furniture?"

Mum opens her mouth, then shuts it. She glares at him.

"What's in the boxes?" I question.

Mum spins. "Your personal items from your flat."

My insides quiver. I seethe, "Ya have no right. That pub's been in our family forever, and that's my home." I blink hard, willing myself not to cry but swipe at the tear that escapes my eye.

The man shows no remorse. In a neutral tone, he states, "I don't make the rules. Now, what do ya want us to do with the furniture? If ya don't tell us, we'll donate it."

Mum looks around, but her place is small. It's bigger than my flat, but there's no extra room. She has her own furniture. She stares at me helplessly and says, "Lauren, I don't know what to do."

I want to tell the man to get Devin on the phone, but I can't say that. So instead, I tell him, "Don't go anywhere. Hold on." I go into the bedroom and shut the door. I pick up my phone off the table, find Devin's number, and call him.

He doesn't answer.

I send a text.

> Me: I need to talk to ya now.

> Devin: I can't talk right now, angel, but ya shouldn't be texting me. It's too dangerous.

I swallow more of my pride.

> Me: They cleaned out my flat. They want to know what to do with my furniture. Your thugs threatened to donate it. My mum doesn't have room in her place. Please, help me.

Minutes pass. My phone finally rings. I go to the window, and my entire body shakes.

Devin's voice comes out low, as if he's trying to stay quiet. "I can't talk long."

I beg, "This is all I have. Please, don't have them get rid of my stuff."

"I'll make sure it gets stored," he states.

I can't hold back my tears. I sob. "Don't let them take our pub, please. That's all my mum and I have."

The line goes quiet.

I sniffle, trying to control my outburst.

Devin says, "This isn't my decision, angel. I've tried."

"Then try harder," I snap and hang up. I toss the phone on the bed and grab the windowsill, looking out and taking deep breaths.

My phone rings again. I go over to it and pick it up, answering, "Are ya going to help me?"

"I'm sending a message to put your furniture in storage. Don't do anything stupid, Lauren," Devin warns.

I sarcastically laugh. "Now what could I possibly do that's stupid?"

He sighs. "I don't know, but don't." He hangs up.

I feel as lost as ever. I try to pull myself together and go back into the other room.

His thug has his phone to his ear. "All right, boss." He hangs up and looks at me. "I have to put your furniture in storage."

"Storage? What storage?" Mum demands.

The man shrugs. "Whatever storage unit the O'Connors tell me to put it in." He spins and leaves, shutting the door.

Mum turns on me. "What just happened in the bedroom?"

"Nothing. Why?"

"What did ya do in there?" she questions.

I shake my head. "Nothing. I just needed a minute. I didn't want to cry in front of him."

She narrows her eyes, and the same look she gave me the night before returns. "I want to know how ya knew to keep me out of the pub last night, Lauren."

I fib, "I didn't. Stop asking me about this."

She steps closer. "Since when do ya lie to me, Lauren?"

"I'm not," I insist.

She puts her hand on my cheek. "It can't be a coincidence ya sent me and the others home."

"That was so Emily and I could make better tips," I declare.

Her face falls. "After everything that's happened, losing the pub and now being under the O'Connor's control, you're going to stand there and say these untruths to me."

Guilt eats me. I start to speak, but a wave of nausea hits me so hard I put my hand over my mouth and run to the bathroom. I throw up in the toilet, then sit back against the wall and grab a towel. I wipe my mouth.

Mum stares at me in the doorway. "How long have ya been sick, Lauren?"

I shake my head. "I'm not. I've just... I had some nausea the last few days. I'm sure it's due to stress. But I'm fine," I insist.

Mum steps closer and crouches down. She grabs my chin and stares at me.

Anxiety fills me. "Why are ya staring at me like that?"

Horror fills her face. "Oh, sweet Jesus. Tell me you're not pregnant."

A wave of shock crashes through me.

Pregnant? What is she talking about?

I blurt out, "Of course I'm not pregnant."

"When did ya last have sex with Caleb?" Mum questions.

"Mum!"

"Tell me!"

"Before we broke up! I haven't touched him, nor would I, even though ya want me to," I accuse, taking my anger over the entire situation and hurling it at her.

She sighs, rises, then leans against the sink. "Are ya sure you're not pregnant?"

"Yea," I affirm, trying to sound as confident as possible, but a new fear swallows me.

She arches her eyebrows. "So, you've taken a pregnancy test?"

My heart beats faster, and my pulse skyrockets to the ceiling. "Why would I take a pregnancy test? I've not had sex."

Mum doesn't look convinced.

Goddammit, how could I be so stupid?

Devin and I never used condoms, and I stopped taking the pill when Caleb and I broke up, not seeing the need for it.

Mum snaps her fingers and points at me. "You've had sex, haven't ya? Who was it with?"

"No one." I continue to lie.

"Then why are ya running in here throwing up if you're not sick?"

"I don't know. Maybe I'm just nervous after everything that happened," I claim.

"Lauren, whatever's going on, this is the time for ya to tell me and be truthful. We've just lost everything. The O'Connors killed almost all the men we know in our town."

"They didn't kill Caleb, unfortunately," I sneer.

"Watch your mouth!" Mum scolds.

"Why? Who cares about Caleb and his brothers?" I bark.

Her face darkens. "Caleb and his brothers protected us."

"They did not protect us. Look at what just happened, Mum. They didn't protect the pub, did they? If they had, then we wouldn't have lost everything. My items wouldn't be in boxes in your front living area."

Disappointment fills her face. "We are O'Learys. This is exactly the reason that ya should marry Caleb. Now, I have nothing to offer ya upon my death."

"Stop saying that."

She shakes her head, looking defeated. She softens her voice. "Lauren, there's no other choice now. We have to have some way to survive. Without the pub, I..." She looks the other way, swallows hard, and blinks fast.

I close my eyes and bang my head against the wall. How did all this happen? How could we have something one minute and not the next? How could Devin have not stopped this?

What am I talking about? Devin owes me nothing. He only used me for sex.

Then why did he protect me?

Did he?

The pub was still taken away.

But I'm alive. I could be dead.

Mum sighs and steps out of the bathroom. She spins and states, "I'll be right back."

"Where ya going?' I ask.

"To the store."

Curiosity gets me. "Why are ya going there?"

"Because I need to get some things. Take a shower, clean yourself up, and put some fresh clothes on. I'll be back soon," she orders, then leaves before I can say anything else.

I decide to do what she says, and I take a long shower. I dig into the top box, feeling sick again as the few items I own stare back at me. I take out a pair of sweatpants and a sweatshirt and get dressed.

What are we going to do?

I can't live with Mum.

What if I'm pregnant?

No! I can't be!

It's possible.

No, no, no!

I sit on the sofa, wondering how we'll make ends meet. My mum has no other skills. I don't have any either. The only other thing I know how to do is ride horses, and that's not going to pay the bills. I continue getting lost in my thoughts when my phone rings. I glance at it and pick it up. "Emily, are ya all right?"

She replies, "Yea... But I need to ask ya something."

"What?"

She hesitates, then informs me, "We just got an envelope dropped off at our house. Did you get one?"

"An envelope?" I question, confused.

"Yea," she replies.

"What's in the envelope?" I ask.

"So ya didn't get one?"

Confused, I say, "No. Why should I have gotten one?"

The line goes silent.

"Emily, what's going on?" I question.

She reveals, "An envelope with €10,000 was dropped off at our house."

"€10,000?" I shriek.

"Ow. Not so loud in my ear."

"Sorry."

She adds, "Yea, the guy just dropped it off."

"What guy?"

"Some...some guy."

"Well, what did he say?" I ask.

"He told me our allegiance is to be with the O'Connors now and we'll be taken care of. I don't need to worry about my da losing his house or being unable to pay his bills or get his treatments."

Shock fills me. Several minutes pass.

"Lauren, ya still there?"

"Yea," I say, but I don't know what to think about it.

Emily clears her throat. "Why would the O'Connors give me money? Do ya think it's from Alaina?"

My stomach twists. I have mixed feelings about Alaina, as do my cousins. I always wanted her to rule the O'Learys instead of Caleb. She's tough, but I assume she would've at least tried to care for us women better than Caleb. Maybe things would've changed, but she went over to the O'Connor side, and that was a shocker. The idea of aligning with the O'Connors after being so loyal to the O'Learys all these years feels wrong.

"Well, do ya think it's from her?" Emily asks again.

"I don't know."

"What if it is?"

"Does it matter?" I question, suddenly wondering what does matter anymore.

"Well, if it's not from her, do ya think it's from the guys?"

I rise and go to the window, staring out at the road. "Why would the guys give us money?"

"Well, Devin warned ya. He must care something about ya," she asserts.

My heart hurts. I don't know what to think about Devin. I curse the day he came to my pub that's no longer mine. Yet, I'd probably be dead if it wasn't for him.

Emily blurts out, "Maybe they're going to take care of us. Maybe... I don't know. Maybe this is a good thing?"

I jerk my head back. Never in a million years did I think we would be having this conversation. I turn and stare at the boxes and shake my head. "No. They've taken everything away from us. There's no way this is a good thing."

"Then what are we going to do?" she asks.

"Well, you have your €10,000. You've got some time to figure it out," I say.

"I'll give ya some. Don't worry. I won't let your mum and ya suffer," she assures me.

I can't help but smile. I soften my tone. "Thanks, Emily, but Mum and I'll figure it out."

"How? They took the pub," she says, as if I don't know it.

I take a deep breath. "I'm not sure, but we'll figure something out. Go take care of your da."

She hesitates.

I add, "It's okay. Do what ya got to do, girl."

The door opens, and Mum walks back in.

I say, "I have to go now. We'll talk later."

"Okay, bye," Emily says and hangs up.

I put my phone in my pocket.

Mum looks at me suspiciously. "Who was that?"

"It was Emily."

"What did she want?" Mum asks.

I shrug, not ready to reveal what Emily told me. "She just wanted to know if we were okay."

"Okay? I don't think we'll ever be okay again," Mum declares, and my heart sinks further.

She sets a bag on the table, takes a box out, and holds it in front of me.

I glance at it and a cold sweat breaks out over my skin. "Why did ya buy that?"

She shakes it, demanding, "Go into the bathroom and pee on it. Then we'll know for sure if you're pregnant or not."

"Mum, I'm not pregnant," I insist.

She shakes the box again. "Then prove it to me. Go. Now."

I stay frozen, unable to move. I can't be pregnant. I can't. I can't. I can't. But it is possible. Even so, if I am, I don't want to know. So I continue staring at the box.

Mum steps closer, takes my hand, and curls my fingers around it. She declares, "I can't pee on it for ya, Lauren. Ya got to do it yourself."

"There's no reason to!"

Her eyes narrow. "The way you're acting, it tells me that ya did have sex with someone. Look, I'm not here—"

"Mum." I put my hands over my face.

She continues, "I'm not here to shame ya for having sex. I just need ya to go find out if you're pregnant or not. If ya are, we got to take care of this baby."

Baby.

Oh my God, I'm not ready for a baby.

Mum puts her hand around my waist and leads me to the bathroom. When we get there, she takes the test out of the box and puts it on the counter. "I'll be waiting outside." She shuts the door, leaving me alone inside the bathroom.

I stare at the stick, and fresh tears fall. This can't be happening to me. I swipe at my tears and straighten my shoulders, looking at my reflection in the mirror.

I just need to take this test. I'm not pregnant, and I'll prove it to Mum. Then she can shut up about this, I try to convince myself, but my gut is telling me my life is about to change forever.

I sit down and unwrap the stick from the foil package. It takes me a few minutes, but I finally pee on it. I cover the end and set it on the counter. I finish on the toilet, wash my hands, and open the door.

Mum's standing there. She states, "We have to wait two minutes." She sets a timer on her phone.

I glance back at the stick. "Mum, I'm not pregnant."

She nods. "Okay. If you're not, then no harm, no foul. But if ya are—"

"I'm not," I say and brush past her, going into the bedroom, but I'm not sure why I'm in there. I leave, return to the main room, then go over to my boxes. I ask, "What should I do with all my stuff?"

"Unpack it and put it in your bedroom. The kitchen stuff put in the kitchen. Don't worry. It'll be fine," Mum assures me.

I lock eyes with her, suddenly unable to control anything. My entire body and voice shake, and I break down, crying, "What if I'm pregnant? What are we going to do then? There's no room in this house for a baby, and I don't know anything about having a kid."

She comes over and puts her arms around me, cradling my head into her shoulder. She coos, "Shh, Lauren. Everything will be okay."

"It won't. It won't, Mum. It's never going to be okay again. Nothing's ever going to be the same," I declare.

She continues trying to soothe me, shushing and holding me close.

I just continue to cry.

The timer buzzes, and I tense. I slowly pull away from her and whisper, "Don't go get it."

Sympathy fills her expression. "We can't sweep this under the rug, Lauren."

"I don't want to know," I say.

She silently goes into the bathroom. When she returns with the stick, she doesn't need to say anything. Her expression says it all.

16

Devin

I groan. "What do ya mean they wouldn't accept the pub back?"

Alaina crosses her arms. "Lauren's mum refuses to pledge her allegiance to the O'Connors."

My gut flips. Of course her mum wouldn't. She's as stubborn as a mule, from what I hear. Still, I ask, "Did ya talk to Lauren?"

Alaina nods. "She won't go against her mum."

"So they don't want the pub back?"

"No, I didn't say that," Alaina states.

I wait.

She leans against her desk and relays, "They want the pub, but they don't want to make an allegiance to the O'Connors. And I can't give it to them if they don't. Ya know this."

I know the laws and the rules. My dad made most of them. Still, Alaina can break whatever rule she wants if she really wants to. I try to stay calm. It was a lot for me to convince her to go to Coolock and offer the pub back to Lauren and her mum. So I suggest, "Maybe there's a way around it."

She arches her eyebrows. "And what would that be? Ya know that we can't take over territory and let people stay in their positions without making an allegiance to the O'Connors. It doesn't work like that, Devin, and you're not naive."

I don't argue with her. I head toward the door.

She calls out, "Devin, don't go to Coolock. You're still to stay away from Lauren."

I spin. "I'm going to convince them to take it. That's all."

"Don't," she warns.

I scowl, arguing, "Why? What's the big deal, Alaina? It's been over a month. We have the territory. There's no risk, and we have nothing to worry about being there. So let me go talk to Lauren and her mum."

Alaina tilts her head. "And what are ya going to admit to her mum?"

My heart beats faster. "I'm not admitting anything to her mum. I'm just going to go talk to them."

Alaina scoffs. "Ya think she's going to listen to you over me? I used to be one of them. I have a previous relationship with them."

I shrug. "I don't know. All I do know is I have to try. And you're not going to stop me." I open the door and walk out, slamming it. I get in my car, not checking it for bombs, and turn it on. I leave Alaina in Brody's mansion and drive for hours toward Coolock.

The closer I get, the more my nerves take over.

I haven't seen Lauren since the night before the pub massacre happened. She's ignored my calls and texts, driving me crazy. As much as I've tried to forget about her and stay away, I can't.

When I'm not thinking about her, all I'm doing is trying to find Caleb. I'm on a mission to take him down, and I will. It's become an obsession for me, even interfering with my work and daily life, but I can't stop it.

I cross the border into the city, and everything about the town feels different. It looks the same though. If you didn't know what happened, you wouldn't be any wiser. But I do, and I see our men everywhere where O'Learys used to stand guard.

It doesn't take long to get to the pub. I pull up and go inside, then I freeze.

I shouldn't be surprised. Alaina told me there were new barmaids—women who have sworn allegiance to the O'Connors. Yet, it just feels wrong.

One looks at me, beams, and chirps, "Guinness? Whiskey? Something else?" She gives me a suggestive look.

I ignore her. I go over to the staircase and open the door.

"Where are ya going? That's private, and ya can't go up there!" she calls out.

I spin. "I'm Devin O'Connor. Learn your manners."

She gapes at me. "Oh. I'm sorry. Please forgive me."

"Aye. Mind your own business, lass," I bark. I shut the door, go up the stairs, and enter the flat.

I had our men put Lauren's furniture back in place. In some ways, it feels good to have something familiar. But her scent's no longer here, nor are her clothes or personal items. It's just bare bones.

I shake my head, still pissed that I couldn't protect her from all of this. But I'm also determined to make sure that she and her mum take the pub back.

I go down the stairs and leave, ignoring everyone. I return to my car, once again starting it without checking for bombs. I program Lauren's mum's address into my GPS and drive a few blocks over to their house.

I park on the street, get out, and stare at the front door, my heart beating faster and my chest tightening.

I have to play it cool. I don't want her mum to realize we know each other or have been together. It won't be good for Lauren. But it's going to be hard to resist pulling her into me. I know it is.

All I can do is dream about her lips, hands, and how she looks at me, even when she's pissed off or being defiant.

I climb the three steps. I knock on the door. It's quiet, so I knock again.

The door slowly opens. Her mum glares at me, seething, "What are ya doing here? I already told your boss we're not pledging any allegiance to the O'Connors."

"May I come in?" I question.

Her hatred for me swirls around her. She answers, "No, ya can't. Now go away." She goes to shut the door, but I stick my foot between it and the frame so it can't shut.

"Lauren!" I call out.

Her mum opens the door again. "Go away. This is my home. Or are ya going to take that too?"

I state, "I'm not here to hurt ya, but I need to speak to Lauren."

"Why would ya need to speak to my daughter?" she demands.

I ignore her and call out again, "Lauren!"

"Ya have a lot of nerve."

Lauren exclaims, "Mum! Devin, what are ya doing here?"

I gaze at her, my pulse skyrocketing and butterflies filling my stomach.

"Well?" she asks.

Her mum spins. "How do you two know each other?"

Lauren opens her mouth.

I quickly say, "I came to the pub a while back. Lauren kicked me out."

Her mum glances between us. I can tell she's not buying my lie.

"It's true," I insist.

Her mum refocuses on me. "Why are ya here?"

"I need to talk to your daughter. And you, for that matter."

"Why?" her mum asks again.

I lower my voice and say, "These things are better discussed privately. Ya mind if I come in?"

"Actually, I do," her mum replies.

"Mum, let him in," Lauren asserts.

Her mum glances at her, questioning, "Now, why would I do that?"

Lauren comes over and opens the door wider. She firmly insists, "Mum, let him in."

Her mum shakes her head at me and finally steps back.

I come in and shut the door. I point to the table. "Let's go sit down."

"You aren't in charge of anyone in my house," her mum states.

I hold my hands in the air. "I come in peace. I'm not trying to be in charge of your house. I promise ya that."

Her mum scoffs. "Sure ya aren't," she says, then sits down.

Lauren gives me a curious look, then follows her mum.

I sit between them.

Her mum says, "I'd offer ya a cuppa, but I don't offer my enemies anything."

I have to give it to this woman. She has a lot of strength to go up against me. So I once again try to reassure her. "I'm not here to fight, nor am I here to harm ya. I just want to talk."

"Talk about what?" her mum asks.

"Mum, could ya tone it down a bit?" Lauren reprimands.

Surprise fills her mum's expression before she hardens it again. She asks, "And why would I do that?"

Lauren darts her eyes at me, then back to her mum. "Let's just hear what he has to say and then he can go. Right? You'll go as soon as ya say whatever ya need to?" she asks, turning to me.

Nothing in my body wants to leave her, but I agree. "Aye. Let's have a conversation."

Her mum sits back and crosses her arms, her glare only intensifying, hatred swirling in the air around us.

Lauren gives me a confused, fearful expression.

I take a deep breath. "I spoke with Alaina before I came here."

"Traitor," her mum mutters.

"Mum, stop," Lauren orders.

I hold in a laugh. Her mum's growing on me. She's a moody old bitch, but I like it. Lauren has a lot of her mum's traits. And I had heard she was a tough bird. Still, I need to win her over. So I start again. "Alaina told me she offered ya the pub. Ya need to take it back."

Her mum snarls, "We aren't O'Connors. We never have been and never will be."

Lauren stays quiet.

I turn toward her. "Your furniture's in your flat. It's ready for ya to return whenever you're ready to take back the pub."

She gapes at me.

Her mum narrows her eyes at me. "What do ya know about her flat?"

The hairs on my neck rise.

Her mum inspects me closer, and her face drains of color. She turns to Lauren. "Tell me that that's not... Oh God. Sweet Jesus,

Lauren, please tell me that's not him."

Goose bumps break out on my skin.

Lauren opens her mouth, but nothing comes out.

"Oh my God, ya didn't. Not with him!" her mum cries out, covering her mouth, tears forming in her eyes.

How the hell does her mum know we slept together?

Her mum snaps her head toward me. "Get out of my house, and don't ya ever touch my daughter again."

I hold my hands in the air, claiming, "I'm not touching your daughter."

She seethes, "But ya did, didn't ya?"

I open my mouth, but I, too, am speechless.

Lauren states, "Mum, you're jumping to conclusions."

"Am I, now?" Her mum turns toward her.

Lauren once again goes quiet.

Her mum rises. She steps beside me and stares down, warning, "If ya ever come near my daughter again, I'll kill ya. I don't care what the consequences are or who you're related to. Do ya understand me, Devin O'Connor?"

"This isn't going how I wanted it to go," I blurt out.

She sarcastically laughs. "Oh, and how did ya want it to go? Did ya come here to try to get with my daughter again?"

"Mum!" Lauren reprimands.

"No, ma'am," I say, rising. "I came to talk some sense into ya. Ya need to take the pub back. Alaina's not going to offer it forever. She already has new barmaids in there. So ya need to get your pub back, and there's only going to be a short amount of time before the offer's off the table."

"Liar! Ya came to shag my daughter again!"

"Mum!"

I sigh, adding, "I know, Alaina. She learned her ways because she was an O'Leary, and there are certain things, even when you take an oath to the O'Connors, that ya don't lose. And I know how she operates, so I suggest ya take the pub while ya can."

Her mum's eyes light with fire. She declares, "Ya have no right to suggest anything to me. Nor did ya have any right to touch my daughter."

"Mum!" Lauren yells again.

I glance at Lauren. "It's fine. But ya need to take the pub back. Listen to me, Lauren."

"Don't you tell my daughter to listen to you!"

I ignore her mum and say, "Lauren, ya need to do what's right here, and what's right is getting your pub back. Do not ignore Alaina's offer. Do not turn it down. Tell her that ya will make the allegiance and take back what's yours."

Her mum insists, "We are never making any allegiance to the O'Connors. Tell Alaina to shove her offer up her tight little ass!"

"Mum! Jesus!"

I sigh and shake my head. "You're making this harder than it has to be."

She straightens her shoulders and lifts her chin. "Am I? Would ya give up your allegiance to the O'Connors for the O'Learys?"

"Hell no," I blurt out.

Her mum's glare deepens, her hatred spewing from her eyes as if it could cut right into my soul. She snarls, "Then ya shouldn't expect us to. Unlike ya, we know who we are."

"I don't know who I am?" I question, confused.

"Get out of my house. Just get out of my house!" she orders.

I decide it's best to diffuse this situation. I reply, "Fine, I'll go." I turn back to Lauren. "Ya need to talk some sense into her. This is your future."

"What do ya care about my daughter's future?" her mum accuses, her voice growing higher.

This is not going how I wanted this conversation to go.

I shake my head. "I'm very sorry I interrupted your day. Please think about what I said. The offer won't last long. Don't make a decision based on being hardheaded."

Her mom huffs. "My loyalty is not hardheaded."

I almost laugh again. I have to give it to her, so I admit, "I respect loyalty. But sometimes, the wind changes, and ya can either be blown away, fight the wind, or embrace it. This is one of those times ya should embrace it."

"Oh, aren't you poetic," her mum snaps.

I glance at Lauren one more time. "Take care. Make sure ya get the pub back." I ignore her mum's evil look, shooting me more daggers, and leave the house.

I get into my car and sit in it for a few minutes, staring at the house, willing Lauren to come out, but she never does.

At one point, she comes to the window, but her mum steps next to her and pulls the drapes shut.

I don't go back to Belfast. I stay in Coolock for the night in the flat. The next day I text Lauren.

> Me: I'm in the flat. Come see me.

For the first time in a month, she replies.

> Lauren the Enemy: No.

> Me: It wasn't a request. We need to talk— without your mum present.

> Lauren the Enemy: There's nothing to talk about.

> Me: There is, and ya know it.

> Lauren the Enemy: No, there isn't. It's over between us. Ya don't need to contact me anymore, Devin.

> Me: Lauren. We need to talk.

> Lauren the Enemy: Like I said, there's nothing to talk about. Don't message me anymore, or I'll get a different number.

I stare at the message, then toss my phone against the wall. I cry out, "Ugh!"

I spend a few hours pacing the flat and finally decide I need to leave. There's nothing here for me. If Lauren and her mum aren't going to listen, I can't do anything about it. And if Lauren's not going to see me, and doesn't want to talk to me, then there's really nothing in Coolock for me.

Right now, I only need to focus on finding Caleb and burying him deep in the ground.

17

Lauren
The Next Day

*M*um ranted for over an hour after Devin left and wouldn't stop questioning me if I slept with him.

I finally couldn't take it anymore. No matter how much I denied it, she wouldn't drop her suspicion that Devin's the father of my baby.

Because he is.

Still, I didn't want to admit it yesterday, and nothing has changed. After Mum's rant, I went into my bedroom, shut the door, and told her to stop talking to me.

I stayed in my room the rest of the day, even when she told me to come out for dinner. I refused, so she brought a tray into the bedroom, sat it down, and looked at me, stating, "This is a mess, Lauren."

As if I didn't know it.

My silence told her everything, but I was too tired to deny it anymore.

She sighed, and disappointment crossed her face, as well as worry. She patted me on the shoulder, then left the room, closing the door.

The doctor told me I needed to make sure I ate, and my mum's fed me like clockwork. I wasn't hungry but forced myself to eat so she wouldn't lecture me.

Sleep didn't help me feel any less stressed. I hoped the shower would but it's doing nothing.

I rinse the conditioner out of my hair, step out of the tub, dry off, and put on my clothes. I brush my hair and my teeth, then exit the bathroom.

Mum's waiting for me. She has her arms crossed, sitting at the table. She orders, "Lauren, sit down."

My gut drops. "I don't want to fight anymore. What's done is done."

She points to the chair, claiming, "We're not going to fight, but we need to talk. Sit down."

I groan, wishing I could return to living in my flat. There's no way to avoid my mum. Living with her is something I didn't want to do again. I loved my independence, but now I'm back in her house and have to obey her rules. And it sucks. I have no other options.

I should be grateful we're not homeless yet, especially with a baby on the way.

A baby.

Oh Jesus. I'm screwed.

The never-ending worry about being pregnant and not having an income flares within me. Who knows how long we'll be able to keep the house. And a kid definitely won't help our financial problems. Now, I'll be solely responsible for another life, and I'm still trying to wrap my head around it.

Maybe if Devin knew...

Stop. I have to stop these thoughts. Devin can never know.

I begrudgingly take the seat across from my mum. She puts a piece of Irish bread on my plate and says, "Ya need to eat."

I roll my eyes. "I'm not going to waste away, Mum."

She frets, "Ya haven't had breakfast yet."

I bite the corner of the soda bread to appease her, then swallow some water.

Mum announces, "I know what we're going to do."

My pulse picks up, and I arch my eyebrows, asking, "What do ya mean what we're going to do? About what?"

"About the baby."

My stomach flips. I cautiously ask, "And what's that?"

She looks at me for a moment, making me more nervous. My anxiety grows and grows until I finally say, "Mum, whatever it is, spit it out."

For the millionth time, she warns, "Ya can't ever let the O'Connors know."

I huff. "Yea, ya said that several times last night." I take another bite of bread.

She blurts out, "They'll take the baby from ya."

I freeze, and my breath catches. This is a new statement from her.

"They will," she insists.

I finish chewing, swallow, then shake my head declaring, "No, they wouldn't do that."

"Of course they would! Ya don't know them," she snaps.

I mutter, "Devin's not Caleb."

She jerks her head back and her voice rises when she says, "Why are ya taking the side of the O'Connors? We're O'Learys. Or have ya forgotten?"

I shove more bread in my mouth, tired of her constant bashing of the O'Connors. Maybe I should feel more loyalty toward the O'Learys, but right now, I can't. It doesn't mean I'm on team O'Connor, but her constant declarations about them are getting old.

She adds, "Your uncle Tommy would roll over in his grave."

I smirk. "He can't roll over in his grave. They burned him, remember?"

Anger flares on Mum's face. My uncle Tommy was a mean bastard. He wasn't even nice to her most of the time. I don't understand why she sticks up for him or any of the O'Learys.

And I know my loyalty is supposed to lie with them and it always has been, but the more time passes, the more I question why. When have they really protected us? I can't think of an instance. But Mum always claims that they're there protecting us, keeping us safe from the world. From what, though, I'm not sure.

She puts her hand on mine and softens her voice. "Ya need to find Caleb and convince him the baby is his. He won't—"

"Are ya crazy?" I interject, horrified at the thought.

"Absolutely not. Caleb can support ya and the baby. You'll both have a great life. It'll be his child. He won't know any different. Ya can give your baby everything I couldn't give ya and more."

Absolute disgust fills me. I gape at her, shaking my head.

She continues, "Think about it, Lauren. What are ya going to do when ya have the baby? We have no money coming in."

I point out, "We need to take the pub back. We're able to right now. All we have to do is make some stupid oath."

Disapproval flares on her expression. She exclaims, "Stupid oath! Shut your mouth, child! And we aren't doing any such thing!"

I scoff. "You're being ridiculous. It's always been our pub, and Devin's right. Alaina won't offer it forever."

Mum insists, "We are not taking an O'Connor oath. I don't care what they attach to it!"

"You're acting like a petulant child."

Mum snaps, "Don't ya dare talk to me in my home like that!" She glares at me as if I've just committed a sin by even suggesting it.

I sigh, calming my voice, admitting, "I don't understand ya. Your entire life, ya worked in the pub. You've busted your butt to keep it alive. And the only skill I have is running it. The smart thing to do is take Alaina's offer."

She seethes, "And give them the opportunity to own us? I don't think so."

I tilt my head, asking, "But it's okay for the O'Learys to own us? The ones who come in and destroy our place and have no remorse? The ones who have never protected us?"

She warns, "Ya better be careful what you say. Your uncle Tommy would—"

"Stop talking about Uncle Tommy. He was a horrible person. He was a vengeful and nasty man. He was cruel to ya too many times to count."

"He wasn't."

"He was! And I don't understand why ya are obsessed with accepting whatever the O'Learys do and not pointing out their flaws."

Her eyes narrow. She claims, "Ya don't know what it was like growing up in the era I did."

"No, I don't, but ya don't have to accept it anymore," I insist.

She closes her eyes briefly, then opens them. "Lauren, I know in today's age, women are more outspoken, and ya all think ya have more choices than I did, but we're clan members born and bred. It doesn't work that way. Ya are a woman. Ya need to understand what that means."

"I do understand what it means, but I'm not going to let them dictate my life and push me around," I declare.

"No. That's why you're going to find Caleb and marry him. He won't let anyone hurt ya," she proclaims.

I cry out, "Caleb will hurt me! He'll probably hurt my baby too. What about that do ya not get, Mum?"

"He won't," she insists.

"He will, and you're just throwing me into the lion's den."

"I'm doing no such thing. I'm telling ya to do what's right so your baby has a future."

"A horrible one if Caleb is involved!"

She glances around the house and frets, "We could end up on the street. What are we going to do then?"

My chest tightens so much I can barely breathe. I don't want Mum to lose her house. I want her to take back the pub and regain her independence and control of her life, but she's so stubborn.

She swallows hard. "We weren't born into an easy life. We have choices. They're not always fun to make, but ya have to look at the best solution. Caleb is it."

"He's not," I firmly assert.

Frustration fills her expression.

I quickly point out, "Even if he was, we don't even know where he's at."

"I already put the feelers out," she announces.

New anxiety plagues me. I mumble, "Mum, ya didn't."

She nods. "I did. Don't worry. I will find him, and when I do—"

"Mum, no! Ya will not tell him I'm pregnant. Ya will not try to arrange anything for me. Do ya understand? If ya do, I'll never talk to ya again," I declare with a tear falling down my cheek. I swipe at it, pissed that I'm so emotional these days, probably because of my hormones, but still.

She insists, "Lauren, it's for the best."

"Mum, no!" I rise and the chair tips over behind me.

"Lauren—"

"Mum, I mean it. I will never talk to ya again. I will run away, and ya will never see me. Do ya understand?"

"I'm trying to do what's best for ya. You're not thinking clearly. You're just emotional right now."

"No, I'm not. I'm never going back to Caleb. I don't want him. He's a horrible, mean, nasty person. He will end up killing me someday if I do. Do ya not get that?"

Silence fills the air. Mum's expression is full of pity. She can't seem to see the truth about Caleb.

But I know deep down in my gut what will happen if I go to him. Besides, I don't want him touching me.

I want Devin.

Maybe I need to tell him.

No, I can't.

"Don't go to the O'Connors. They will take the baby from ya," Mum asserts again, as if she can read what's on my mind.

Is she right?

No, they wouldn't.

I can't be sure.

"They wouldn't, but don't worry, Mum. I'm not going to anyone," I say, then spin on my heel and leave the room. I go into the bedroom and shut the door. I pick up the phone and stare at the text exchange I had with Devin earlier on, tempted to go to the flat.

Mum will find out if I meet him.

Who cares at this point? I need to see him.

I decide that Devin's right. We do need to talk, and I don't know if I should tell him about the baby, but at least I can feel him out.

Feel him out how? What am I even going to say?

I shove my insecurities down and grab my wallet. I walk out of the bedroom.

"Where are ya going?" Mum asks.

"I need some air."

"You're going to see him, aren't ya?"

"I don't know what you're talking about. I'm sure he's left town by now," I lie.

She gives me a knowing look.

"I'm going for a walk. I need to cool off. Do not do anything you'll regret regarding Caleb and me, Mum. Promise me."

She repeats, "I already put my feelers out, Lauren."

My gut drops further. I beg, "Mum, do not tell him when ya find him. Do not."

She releases an anxious breath. "I won't say anything until ya agree, but eventually, ya will agree, Lauren."

"I won't," I firmly insist.

Pity crosses her face again. I hate it, and she claims, "But you will."

"No, I won't. I'm going for a walk. I'll see ya later," I state and leave the house.

I take a deep breath of the cold air, welcoming the wind slapping my face and fight it at the same time as I walk several blocks to the pub.

When I walk in, I freeze.

The shattered mirror has been replaced. And everything I thought would be stained up isn't.

New flooring and wallpaper have been installed. A few of the booths have new leather on the seats.

It all looks beautiful, but it's already different. It's another slap in the face that the pub is no longer mine. Then I see the new barmaids.

They're women who've taken oaths for the O'Connors to be here. They're the same people who used to come in here, get drunk, and not respect the place.

One of the barmaids, Rebecca, gapes at me. Satisfaction and arrogance then fill her expression. She chirps, "Well, Lauren Byrne. I didn't expect to see you here."

"Shut up," I say, then go to the staircase door.

She shouts, "Ya can't go up there."

"I can do whatever I want," I declare. I open the door, then shut and lock it behind me. I walk up the steps, feeling nostalgic, and get to the landing. I take a deep breath and open the door.

When I step inside, my heart beats faster. I glance around the tiny space, staring at my empty apartment, except for the furniture.

My gut drops. Devin is nowhere to be seen.

I go into the bathroom, and he's not there either. Every hope that I have fades. It withers and dies, and I feel more hopeless than ever.

That's when I realize I had false hope thinking I could talk to Devin and he would make everything better. It was foolish to think he would protect and take care of the baby and me.

What was I thinking?

He's gone, and my mum's right. He needs to stay away, but I can't go with Caleb either.

I sit on the bed and start sobbing, scared, unsure what to do, knowing that my mum will find Caleb. She can always find anyone in the O'Leary clan. She has connections because of my uncle Tommy. Once she finds him, I don't trust that she's not going to convince me in a moment of weakness to let Caleb take care of us. Or she might just tell him behind my back because she thinks she knows best.

My fear hits a new high. I feel like there are no decisions to be made. I turn over on the bed, crying into the pillow, and fall asleep for a few hours. Then I wake up to my phone buzzing.

I glance at it and see several missed calls from my mum. I open my text messages.

> Mum: Where are ya, Lauren?

> Mum: Ya need to respond to me, Lauren. I'm going to put feelers out for ya.

Mum: Last warning.

Me: I'm fine, Mum. My phone was in my wallet. I'll be home shortly.

Mum: Where are ya?

Me: Nowhere exciting.

Mum: You're with him, aren't ya?

Me: No. I've not seen him since our house, and I'm not lying. Don't ask me again about it.

Mum: I have good news for ya.

The hairs on my arms rise. A sinking feeling fills me.

Me: About what?

Mum: I found out where Caleb is hiding.

Panic fills me to the point I feel crippled. I can't let her bring Caleb around me.

What am I going to do?

A new pressure fills me. I glance around my flat, but no answers come. I get up and start to pace. I get another text.

Mum: We'll leave tonight to go to him. We don't have to tell him about the baby immediately, but it'll be good for you two to see each other.

I stare at the text message, unable to comprehend that she did this after I've insisted I want nothing to do with him.

And she knows how he treated me. Well, not everything, but enough. I don't get it. Why would she want me to return to someone I'm scared of?

I stare at the phone and decide there's only one solution. I leave the pub, ignoring the barmaid on the way out and whatever snotty comment she has to say. I walk down the street and go directly to the train station.

The man behind the ticket counter looks up. "Miss. Where ya going?"

I glance at the screen, looking for the farthest place from here and Dublin I can afford. I answer, "Clifden."

"Round trip?" he questions.

The oxygen in my lungs turns stale. I have never known anywhere besides Coolock. I shake my head and then clear my throat. "No, just one way."

He states the price.

I reach into my wallet and pull out cash, realizing I have barely any left.

What am I going to do for money?

It doesn't matter. The first step is to get away from here. I cannot let my mum take me to Caleb.

I slap the cash on the counter.

He takes it and hands me a ticket. "Have a nice journey."

"Thank you," I say, then go over to a seat and wait until my boarding time comes.

I get another text.

Mum: Lauren, where are ya?

My pulse skyrockets. I glance at the clock. There are only a few more minutes before boarding.

Me: I'm picking up some groceries. I'll be home soon.

My heart hurts lying to her. I wonder if I'll ever see her again.

Tears well, and I swipe at them, but they fly down my face uncontrollably.

How could my life have changed so much in so little time?

How could I have been so irresponsible to have sex without a condom or being on birth control?

I didn't even think about it. It never once crossed my mind.

I put my hand on my belly, feeling nauseous, and I close my eyes. I rest my head against the wall, swallowing bile and breathing through it.

When the nausea passes, there's an announcement on the microphone. A woman's voice declares, "Gate thirteen to Clifden is now boarding."

My butterflies take off.

Is this really the only solution?

Yea, it is.

I glance around the station, not recognizing anyone, and board the train. I find my seat and sit. It doesn't take long before the train starts moving, and a strange feeling hits me. It's a mix of dread and sadness but also hope. No matter what, I need to figure out how to make it work on my own.

I'll get a job. I can work in a pub. I'll find something, I tell myself.

I look at my wallet again and count my change. Barely over twenty euros.

My stomach growls. I curse myself for not eating more than the Irish soda bread this morning.

I put my head against the window and close my eyes, trying to sleep, but I can't. I never stop worrying. I almost text Devin several times but stop myself.

What if my mum's telling the truth? What if the O'Connors take the baby from me? Or what if Devin gets mad that I'm pregnant?

I expect Caleb would enjoy it because he would know he had me and I was his to control.

And Devin doesn't seem like the settling-down type. I'm sure he wouldn't like it if I showed up and told him I was pregnant. Maybe Alaina would insist they keep the baby.

I debate over and over what the O'Connors would do until the train finally stops.

I glance out the window at the station. It looks a lot like the one in Coolock. I take a deep breath and follow the crowd, exiting the train. I walk through the station, then step outside.

It's drizzling. I stare down the street, unable to move.

"Ya need directions, lass?" someone says next to me.

I glance at an older man with wrinkles all over his face.

His shamrock-green beret is tattered and worn. He removes it and adds, "Ya look like you're lost."

I stare straight ahead, unsure what to do or where to go.

He offers, "Ma'am, where are ya going? I can help direct ya if ya need help."

"I'm fine," I lie, walking away from him, unsure where I'm going or what my options are.

18

Devin
Two Weeks Later

*T*ynan and I pull out of the warehouse. He claims, "It's time to take over the territory to the border of Donnycarney."

"Brody said not yet," I remind him.

He grunts. "Brody's being too cautious."

I open my mouth to reply, but my phone vibrates.

> Alaina: Get over here now.

> Me: Don't be so snippy.

> Alaina: It's an emergency.

Goose bumps pop out on my skin. I glance at my brother. "It's Alaina."

"What does she want?"

"She says it's an emergency," I inform him, veering to the other side of the road and making a U-turn.

Tynan glances at his cell. "I didn't get a text."

Alaina rarely says there's an emergency, and normally if there is, all of my brothers get notified.

"She must have found Caleb," I state.

"I would have gotten notified too. Something else is going on. Drop me off at my place first."

I scowl at him. "No. It's an emergency."

He grumbles, "Come on, bro. I got a lot of stuff to do today."

"Tough shit. Deal with it," I mutter and turn down the road leading to Brody and Alaina's mansion.

It only takes a little while to get there. I ignore the rest of my brother's whines, pull through the gate, and get out of the car.

Tynan slides down, pulling his hoodie over his head. He orders, "Try to hurry up."

I don't reply. I go into the house and run into Brody, asking, "Where's your wife?"

His face hardens. He nods toward his office.

"Why is Alaina in your office, but you're out here?" I question.

He admits, "She asked me to step outside."

"Why?"

"There's a visitor," he declares.

More uneasiness fills me. I peer closer at him. "What visitor?"

Disapproval fills his expression. "Tommy's sister."

I blurt out, "Lauren's mum's here?"

"Aye. And that woman might just be worse than Tommy."

I push past him and go into his office. Alaina rises, and Lauren's mum turns in her chair. She gives me the same look of hatred she did at her house.

"Is something wrong with Lauren?" I ask, concerned.

Her mum bolts out of her chair and comes at me, jabbing my chest. "What have you done with her?"

Confusion fills me. "What do ya mean, what have I done with her?"

She jabs me harder.

I grab her hand, warning, "Don't do that."

She gives me such a dirty look that I can practically see fumes coming from her skull. Her voice shakes angrily, demanding, "Whatever you've done with my daughter, give her back to me."

My pulse skyrockets. "I don't know what you're talking about."

Alaina interjects, "Lauren's been missing for two weeks."

My eyes widen. "Missing? And you're just telling us now?"

"Ya know where she is! It's not a coincidence ya were in town. So what did ya do with her?" her mum accuses.

I shake my head. "I don't know anything about this, but ya need to calm down so we can figure this out."

"Calm down? My daughter is missing! And ya know where she is!" she insists.

Alaina asserts, "Kathleen, Devin's right. Ya need to calm down."

She spins on Alaina. She points at her, hurling, "Ya would stick up for him, wouldn't ya, ya traitor?"

Alaina's face hardens, but she holds her hands in the air. "Please. We all want to find Lauren."

"Do ya now?"

"Yes, we do. We didn't know she was missing. I can assure ya that Devin is telling the truth."

"How do ya know he's telling the truth?" Kathleen questions.

Alaina lifts her chin, squaring her shoulders. "Because Devin always tells the truth."

Alaina's caught me in many lies before. However, she's very convincing, and I don't know why she's sticking up for me right now, but it's not the first time she's surprised me. Then again, Alaina knows how to play her cards well.

Kathleen surprises me. Her hard exterior breaks and she crumples, sobbing.

Alaina comes around the desk and puts her arm around her.

She shrugs out of it, sniffling. "Ya need to find my daughter. Even Caleb can't find her!"

"Caleb?" I narrow my gaze on Kathleen. A shiver travels over my skin. I ask, "Ya know where he is?"

Kathleen tightens her lips, glaring at me.

"Where is he?" I push.

She seethes, "None of your business."

"Like hell, it's not!"

Alaina scolds, "Enough! Let's focus on Lauren."

Tense silence fills the air.

Alaina breaks it, stating, "Lauren's a smart, capable woman. Let's think about where she could be hiding."

Her mum shrieks, "Hiding? She wouldn't hide from me! Especially in the condition she's in!"

"Condition? What condition?" I question.

Kathleen's expression changes to frantic, then returns to angry. She closes her lips into a tight line, trying to gather her emotions, and looks away.

I glance at Alaina.

She gives me her *I don't know* expression.

Something tells me that I need to find out what Kathleen is referring to, so I step in front of her. "Tell me what ya meant."

"Nothing. But I want my daughter back!"

"I promise ya, I don't know where she is. However, now that I know she's missing, I will find her."

"How? How will you find her if you don't know where she's at?" she demands.

Alaina interjects once more. "Let's go have some tea and calm down."

"I don't want any tea. I just want my daughter."

"And I'll find her," I vow, walking toward the door.

"Wait," her mum calls out.

I spin, arching my eyebrows. "Aye?"

"Promise me when ya find her, you'll bring her back to me."

I nod. "I won't keep her from ya, I promise."

"Ya swear on your mother's and father's lives, and anyone else who means anything to ya?" her mum questions.

I hold my hand over my heart. "I do. I will find her, and ya will see her again," I insist, then walk out the door.

I exit the house, trot down the stairs, and slide into the car.

Tynan sits up. "Thank fuck that was fast."

"Shut up," I say.

He groans. "Uh-oh, Alaina on the warpath?"

"No." I start the car and pull toward the gate. I admit, "Lauren's missing."

Tynan grunts. "Missing?"

"Aye. She's been missing since I went to Coolock. Her mum hasn't seen her in two weeks."

"Two weeks? Where would she have gone? Coolock's not that big."

"I don't know. But there's something else. Something her mum won't tell me."

Tynan waits.

"She said something about Lauren that she wouldn't elaborate on. She's holding something important back. We need to go to Coolock."

He scoffs. "We? I'm not going to Coolock."

I glance over at him. "Lauren's missing. You're going to help me find her."

"Are ya being serious right now? I have a million things to do. Coolock is not on my agenda, and I don't care about your missing lass. It was just one night anyway. What do ya care? Why are ya holding on to this bird?"

"Shut up. Go back to sleep," I order. I pull out past the gate and speed up down the street.

My mind races the entire way to Coolock. Something is going on with Lauren, and I need to find out the specifics. The way Kathleen went tightlipped doesn't sit well with me. My gut tells me that I'll only find Lauren if I know the details.

The Coolock sign appears, and I veer away from the main drag toward Emily's house. It takes several minutes, and I pull onto the curb.

"Where are we?" Tynan asks, opening his eyes and looking out the window.

"Emily's"

He groans. "Why are we at that lass's house? Unlike ya, I don't need a trip down memory lane."

I remind him, "Ya didn't seem to have any complaints the night of."

He huffs. "Aye, the night of. I prefer not to see my one-night stands again. Unlike you, apparently."

"Get out of the car," I order, not into his antics. I step out and shut the door.

He begrudgingly follows me, and we hoof it up to the house.

I ring the bell. A few seconds pass and the door creaks open. An old man wrinkles his forehead and asks, "Can I help ya?"

"Aye, I'm looking for Emily."

He looks a bit sick, frail, but I'm not sure. He narrows his eyes. "Why are ya asking for my daughter? I don't know ya. I've never seen ya."

"My name's Devin O'Connor and this is my brother, Tynan."

Her da's eyes widen. "Then what do ya want with my Emily?"

I hold my hands in the air. "We come in peace. I just need to ask her some questions about Lauren." My statement doesn't help the situation.

Anger flares on his face, and strength takes over the weakness. He declares, "Ya should leave my niece alone as well. Ya have no business knowing anything about any of these lasses."

Tynan barks, "Listen, old man, we don't have much time."

"Shut up," I firmly tell my brother. He snaps his mouth shut and looks bored.

Emily's da sneers at both of us.

I try again. "Sir, we need to speak with Emily. Now, I'm not here to make your life hard or to do anything bad. I promise ya that. I just need to talk to your daughter."

"She's not here," he declares.

"Then where is she?"

"She's at her new job," he admits.

"Where's that?"

"The meat plant."

"Why is she working there?" Tynan questions.

Red rage fills her da's face. He seethes, "Because you lot took over the pub. Ya stole it from them."

"They were offered it back," Tynan states.

"Shut up," I say to him.

Shock fills the old man's face. "What do you mean they were offered it back?"

I give my brother a dirty look, warning him that he better shut his mouth going forward.

"Well, what did ya mean by that?" her da presses.

"Alaina offered Lauren and her mum the pub back."

"Under what terms?" he questions.

I confess, "They had to make an oath to the O'Connors."

"Just had to make an oath to the O'Connors? Just that easy, isn't it?" he asks.

Jesus, is everybody in this family pigheaded like Kathleen?

I sigh and scrub my face. "Time's of the essence here. How long is Emily's shift?"

He shakes his head. "None of your business."

I step closer. He takes a step back, and I'm happy. Intimidation can be good. I put my hand on the doorframe, holding myself from stepping inside, declaring, "I'm not here to cause trouble. However, if I don't speak to your daughter, there will be. Again. All I want to do is speak to her. So I suggest ya tell me when her shift's over, or I will go in there right now and make a scene. I don't want to get her fired after all."

More hatred spews from his expression, but he finally caves. He glances at his watch. "She's off in an hour."

"Aye, thank ya. Have a good day," I say and nod. I turn and go back to the car.

Tynan and I get in and take off toward the meat packing plant.

"Jesus. He's a fun one," Tynan sarcastically mutters.

"Shut up. Ya need to stop talking. Ya weren't helping matters back there."

"Well, he wasn't really giving anything to us, was he?"

I threaten, "I'm warning ya. You're on my last nerve right now."

"You're the one who said I had to come," Tynan reminds me and slinks down in his seat.

It takes ten minutes to get there. Then I wait another fifteen. Five minutes before Emily's off her shift, I go into the plant.

The foul smell of blood and innards reminds me of when we have body disposal duty.

"Jesus, she really picked the job of all jobs," Tynan comments.

I shake my head and make a fist at my side, threatening, "Ya really are pushing it today."

He gives me another bored glance.

I decide to ignore him and move forward.

A woman with a clipboard approaches us and asks, "Can I help ya with something?"

I answer, "I'm waiting for Emily to finish her shift."

She glances behind her at the row of workers. They all have hair nets and gloves on. Their backs are toward us, so I don't know which one is Emily.

The supervisor refocuses on me. "You're going to have to wait outside."

"Can ya tell her we're here and need to talk to her?" I question.

"I'll tell her when she's off," the lady states.

I decide not to press my luck or make a scene. "Aye, thank ya." I nod and return outside, standing right by the door.

Tynan whines, "Do I really need to be here?"

"Aye, ya do."

"Why?"

"Because she might talk to ya more than she'll talk to me," I admit.

Tynan rolls his eyes. "I told ya my one-night stands are one-night stands. I'm not looking for another go-around. She's a great lass and good in the sack, but I'm not one to string things along. Ya know that."

I groan. "I'm not asking ya to take her to bed. You're only here to help get her to talk."

"Fine," he grumbles.

Another minute passes, and a bell rings through the air. Shortly after, the door opens and a stream of workers exit the factory.

I step aside and wait. As soon as Emily steps through the door, I call out, "Emily."

She snaps her face toward me with a look of confusion. She hesitates, then leaves the crowd.

I guide her to the other side of the building.

She asks, "What are ya doing here?"

I announce, "I need to talk to ya about Lauren."

"Why?"

"Where is she?" I question.

"How would I know? Besides, Auntie Kathleen said she's with ya... That ya took her." She narrows her eyes.

I firmly assert, "I didn't take her."

Emily glances at both of us.

Tynan winks at her. "How ya doing, lass?"

Her cheeks slightly heat.

Now he's going to be like this?

She replies, "I'm okay. How have ya been?"

"Good. So ya got a new job."

She glances back at the door and shrugs. "It pays the bills."

He declares, "Would've been nicer if ya got your pub job back."

Her face hardens. "Well, that wasn't really my choice, was it?"

He slinks closer and puts his arm around her.

She looks up at him, then freezes as if unsure what to do.

He leans closer. "What would ya say if I said I could get your job back for ya?"

She scrunches her face and then pushes him away. She warns him, "Don't touch me." She refocuses on me.

Tynan's eyes widen, and I withhold my chuckle. Women never turn him down. It might be the first time he's had that happen in his entire life.

Emily refocuses on me and states, "I don't know where Lauren is. I haven't heard from her since the day before you showed up in town."

The hairs on my arms rise. It didn't take much to see that Emily was probably the closest person to Lauren. I was hoping she knew something and hadn't told Kathleen. I state, "Okay, let's assume I believe ya."

Emily huffs. "Believe me? Believe me if ya want or don't, but that's the truth."

"Okay, lass. What's her mum hiding?"

Something passes in Emily's expression, but she quickly turns her face neutral. "Her mum's not hiding anything."

"Bullshit. She said Lauren had a condition going on. What does that mean?"

Emily's lips form a tight line. I glance around us, making sure no one's near. Then I lean closer to Emily. "Listen to me, lass. Lauren's missing. I want to go find her, but I need information. Caleb is out there, and ya know how obsessed he is with her. So if there's something ya know, whatever it is, I don't care how minute ya think the detail is, I need to know."

She opens her mouth and shuts it, hesitating.

"Emily, I need to find Lauren. Time's of the essence. If I don't find her, Caleb will. Her mum admitted he's looking for her."

Emily shuts her eyes and bites her lip.

"Tell me," I demand.

She slowly opens her eyes and shakes her head. "I shouldn't tell ya anything."

"Ya should," I insist.

"Lauren will kill me."

"It's better than Lauren ending up in a body bag, isn't it?" I warn, but it's not a false warning. Who knows where Lauren is or what's happening. Especially if Caleb is involved.

Emily sighs. "I really don't know where she's at, but she's pregnant."

"Preg—pregnant?"

"Pregnant?" Tynan exclaims.

Pregnant.

We didn't use anything.

Oh shit.

I blink a few times.

Emily never takes her gaze off mine.

My gut flips. I ask Emily, "How far along is she?"

Emily stays quiet, continuing to give me the same expression.

My heart races faster. "It's mine?"

Tynan whistles.

I shoot him a dirty look, barking, "You're such a motherfucker."

"Dude, ya should have wrapped your shit," he claims.

"Ya really are an asshole," Emily accuses.

"Aye. He is," I agree.

She refocuses on me. "Ya need to find her. I was hoping she was with ya and ya were taking care of her."

I shake my head. "She's not. But I'll take care of her when I find her."

"Ya—" Emily snaps her mouth closed and exhales through her nose.

"What?"

She swallows hard then asks, "Ya won't take the baby from her, will ya?"

I furrow my eyebrows. "Why would I take the baby from her?"

Emily confesses, "Her mum swore the O'Connors would take the baby from her if she told ya. I thought maybe she had and ya were hiding her for a bit before telling her mum."

I groan. "Her mum has some warped ideas. We wouldn't take the baby from her. That would be really fucked-up."

"Would it?" Emily asks, peering at me closer.

I sigh. "We don't do things like the O'Learys do."

Emily sadly shakes her head, restating, "I don't know where she is. I really did think she was with ya, but now..." She bites her lip and blinks hard.

"Don't worry. I'll find her," I promise.

"How?" Emily asks.

"I don't know, but I will. Is there anything else that ya need to tell me?"

Emily ponders my question for a moment, then shakes her head. "No, that's all I know. She was upset about the pub. She found out she was pregnant and was living at her mum's. That's all I know. Oh, and it's not Caleb's, even though her mum wants her to tell Caleb it is."

"Over my dead body," I burst out.

Emily releases another anxious breath. "Well, ya better get to her before Caleb does, because her mum is adamant that she tells him it's his."

Rage fills me. I declare, "Ya don't know me very well, Emily, but there's no way in hell that bastard is ever touching my kid." I spin and leave, more determined than ever to find Lauren. I get in the car and curse myself for ever letting her out of my sight. Then I try to process the fact that I'm going to be a father.

19

Lauren

The first two nights in Clifden, I spent on the streets. Then I saw a line of women on the street outside a church. My curiosity got the best of me, and I learned it serves as a women's shelter. So I swallowed my pride and got in line.

There are barely any beds. You have to be one of the first people in line to get one, but I've managed to get a spot every day.

Some faces are becoming familiar, yet I barely talk to anyone. I found out within the first day on the street that you couldn't trust anyone when my wallet got stolen.

"Here you go, love," Annie beams, handing me the number to my bed. She's a nice older woman, probably my mum's age, with just as many wrinkles. Yet unlike my mum, she doesn't look hardened. She's always cheerful and radiates joy.

I trusted her immediately, and she's the only person I dare to let my guard down around. I return her smile. "Thank you, Annie."

She pats me on the shoulder.

"There's my love," a man's voice shouts.

I turn and freeze. The man looks familiar.

Where have I seen him?

"Dominick, what are you doing here?" Annie questions.

He pulls flowers from behind his back and walks over to her. "Wanted to give ya your anniversary flowers."

Her face lights up. "You remembered."

"Have I ever not remembered?" he asks, his eyes twinkling.

Her face blushes slightly. She lifts onto her tiptoes and reaches for his face, giving him a quick peck.

"No, you haven't," she replies.

They stare at each other for a moment and then she turns. "These are beautiful." She smells them, pulls one out, and hands one to me, offering, "Here ya go, love."

I take it and breathe deeply, imagining I'm somewhere else besides the shelter. There's been so many times I've questioned whether I should have left Coolock or not. But deep down, I know this has to be better than getting in the grasp of Caleb or having the O'Connors take my baby.

Yet I can't shake the anxiety over my pregnancy and the reality that this lifestyle isn't healthy for the baby or me. But I don't know what my other options are.

I remember my manners and offer, "Thank you."

Dominick peers at me and snaps, "I know where I've seen ya."

"Oh?" I question.

He nods. "At the train station a couple of weeks ago. It was nighttime. Ya seemed a little bit lost."

I don't say anything, a little embarrassed as I recall the event.

His face falls. He glances around, then refocuses on me. "What's a lass like you doing in here?"

"Dominick," Annie reprimands.

He slides his hand behind my waist, and to my surprise, I don't flinch. He moves me over into a corner, and Annie follows. He claims, "Lass, you're too sweet of a girl to be in this place. Why are ya homeless?"

"Dominick, ya can't ask things like that," Annie scolds, following us.

"It's okay," I state. I shrug. "I just am."

He looks at me and then at Annie. She smiles bigger, and he refocuses on me, squinting. He asserts, "I reckon you're a good worker."

"Yea, I am. I've been trying to find a job, but it's hard when you don't have an address to put down on applications."

He continues assessing me and I try not to shrink back. Then he announces, "We've been saying we need someone to help out." He glances at Annie.

"What do ya mean by help out?" I ask.

Annie nods at him.

He turns back to me. "We own a bed-and-breakfast. We can't offer a lot above room and board. And it's not much of a room.

It used to be a storage closet, but it's big enough for a bed and a couple of personal items. We can make sure you're fed and have a roof over your head in exchange for your employment. You'd help keep the bedrooms tidy and the guests happy, as well as help Annie out in the kitchen. Is this something you'd be interested in?"

I gape at him.

Is he really offering me shelter and a job?

Annie chirps, "I think ya surprised her."

I turn toward her. "Are ya really offering me a job?"

She softly laughs. "Let me introduce ya to my husband, Dominick. He can be overwhelming, but his heart is always in the right place."

I blurt out, "Do ya always take strays off the street?"

He grunts. "Ah, but ya aren't a stray, are ya? We've already met. We go way back to the train station." His eyes light up, and he winks.

A warmth I've not felt in a very long time fills me. I blink hard and get teary-eyed.

"Now, now, lass. No need for that," Annie says, putting her arm around me.

I sniffle. "Thank ya for your kindness. I would love to take the job if you're serious about it. Please."

"Okay, but like I said, lass, we don't have much money to pay ya."

"It's okay. Room and board are fine."

"Well, no, we'll pay ya as well."

"No. Really. Room and board are fine," I insist.

Dominick shakes his head. "No, we will pay ya as well. Now, Annie has another half hour here. Do ya want to wait in the car with me?"

"Sure," I say and hand the number back to Annie. "Ya can give this to somebody else."

She beams. "Sounds good, dear." She pats me on the shoulder. "I'll see ya in a little bit."

I follow Dominick to the car in a daze, practically skipping.

Is this really happening? Has my luck changed?

I get into the back seat of his car, and he turns on the engine. "Let's get this thing warmed up. It's getting colder."

"Yea," I agree.

He looks at me in the rearview mirror. "Have ya been on the street often, or have ya gotten a room at the shelter every night?"

I take a deep breath, trying to avoid the shame that fills me for being homeless. Mum always instilled that we would work hard and never be in this situation. But it's given me a new understanding of homeless people and how lucky I always was to have a roof over my head.

I realize Dominick's still staring at me, waiting for an answer. I swallow hard. "I've gotten a room since I found the shelter."

He squints and cautiously asks, "But ya had to spend some nights on the street?"

"Only two," I admit.

"Were ya safe out there?" he questions with a bit of protectiveness in his tone.

"Yea, I was fine," I assure him.

"Good," he says in relief.

We continue our small talk until Annie finally appears. She gets in the car, and Dominick leans over and kisses her cheek.

He drives off, and it takes about twenty minutes to get to the bed-and-breakfast. He pulls up to a small house with a wrap-around porch.

"This is beautiful," I say.

Annie turns and beams. "Dominick has done everything to the place. He's quite handy."

"Aw, you're going to make me blush," he teases, then exits the car. He goes around the hood and opens her door. I get out, as does she.

"Let's show ya around," Annie says.

We split off from Dominick, and she gives me a tour of their private quarters compared to the ones the guests use, the common areas, then she opens a door. She states, "Like we said, it's not much. It used to be a storage closet, but the bedding is fresh and dry."

I peek past her.

She orders, "Well, go on. Ya can check it out more than that."

I step inside.

She flips a switch. It is a small space, but I don't need anything more. She pulls a curtain back, revealing a wall with empty shelves. She declares, "You can put your clothes here."

I stare at her, my stomach flipping. I confess, "I don't have any clothes."

She smiles. "Ya will after tonight."

"What do ya mean?"

"We have lots of clothes around here. I'll grab something for ya, and ya can look at all the options later. I assume you'll want a nice hot shower? What are ya, a medium?" She glances at my body. "Large?"

My face heats. Does she know I'm pregnant? "Um, it depends. Probably either."

"Alrighty, then. So if these living quarters are okay for ya—"

"It's perfect," I affirm.

"And you're okay with the workload?"

"Yea. Thank you so much."

"Okay, the bathroom's over here." She steps out, and I follow her. She points to another door. "There are all sorts of toiletries in there. Help yourself. We'll have dinner in an hour."

"Thank ya," I say, then blink hard, feeling emotional again.

She steps toward me and hugs me. It's a grandmotherly embrace, and it makes me cry harder.

I blurt out, "I'm sorry. I don't mean to be crying."

"Shh, it's okay, lass. It's all good. We're happy to have ya. We've needed someone we can trust here."

"How do ya trust me? Ya don't know me," I point out, hating how my voice shakes but unable to control it.

She continues patting my head and shushing me. "We can tell. We know good people when we see them, and ya, Lauren, are a good person."

It's the nicest thing anyone has said to me in a long time. I've felt so alone lately. I sniffle and straighten up. "Thank ya."

"No, thank *ya*. See ya in the kitchen after your shower." She turns and disappears.

I go into the room and sit on the bed, tapping my fingers on my thigh, wondering how I got into this situation. Then I promise myself I'll do a great job for Annie and Dominick, so they're happy they hired me.

I go into the bathroom and take a long shower. It's the first decent one I've had since leaving Coolock. I dry off and wrap the towel around me, and when I go into the bedroom, there are clothes on the bed.

I slide the yoga pants and the T-shirt on and then put the cardigan over me. I put on the socks and then make my way through the house.

My stomach growls as I step into the kitchen and the smell of roasted lamb hits me.

Annie looks up. "There ya are. I'm just putting the final touches on everything."

I state, "I can eat in here. I don't want to interrupt Dominick's and your anniversary dinner."

"Oh, nonsense," she says, waving her hand before her. "Don't be silly. We're excited to have company."

"Don't ya always have company since this is a bed-and-breakfast?"

"Yea, but not company we're excited about like ya."

I laugh. "Okay, well, thank ya."

"Come on, dear," she says, carrying a bread basket.

I follow her and go into the other room.

Dominick's already sitting at the table. There's a rack of lamb, potatoes, and cooked vegetables.

I declare, "Everything smells so good."

"Sit down so ya can eat," Dominick offers, pointing to the chair.

I obey.

Annie fills a plate for me, then she grabs my hand. She says, "It's time to say grace."

Dominick holds his hand out, and I take it, feeling slightly uncomfortable since I didn't grow up religious.

Annie says softly, "Just close your eyes, dear. Say whatever ya want to the Lord."

I obey her as well.

She says, "Thank ya, Jesus, for bringing Lauren into our life. We appreciate this food and all the good things you've bestowed upon us. Amen."

"Amen," Dominick says.

"Amen," I say and open my eyes.

They both squeeze my hands, then release them. I wait, not sure what to do next.

Annie motions toward my plate. "Eat."

I don't hesitate. I'm starving. We eat in silence for a while and then I realize my manners. I've been chowing down the food, and nearly half my plate's gone. I look up and see Dominick's twinkling eyes staring at me. I wince. "Sorry."

He chuckles. "What are ya sorry for, lass? This is good food. I'm glad you're enjoying it."

"I am," I state, then take a long drink of water.

"Have another piece of bread," Annie orders, putting a buttered slice on my plate.

"Thank ya," I say. I take a bite, wanting to groan at how delicious it tastes. I finish chewing, swallow, take another sip of water, then ask, "So what time should I be awake tomorrow?"

She answers, "We normally get up around six in the morning. We have a couple guests checking in later tonight."

I glance at the clock on the wall. It says it's six thirty.

"Oh, do ya always have people check in late at night?"

She shakes her head. "Not always, but these people are coming from far away."

The hairs on my neck rise. *What if it's Caleb and he knows where I'm at?*

What if it's Devin?

There's a small twinge of hope at the last thought, but I squash it.

The O'Connors will take my baby.

"Are ya okay, Lauren?" Dominick asks.

"Oh, yea, sorry. I'm fine."

"Are ya sure? Ya looked a little scared for a moment there." He studies me closer.

I make a note to myself to start figuring out how to control my expressions. I smile at him. "No, not at all. I was just wondering where they're coming from?"

"Somewhere in Dublin."

Dublin. Oh God, maybe it is Caleb.

"Dear, are ya sure you're okay?" Annie asks, putting her hand over mine.

"Yea. What time will the guests be here?"

She answers, "Probably not until ten o'clock. We normally shut the pub around then, but we'll keep it open. I'm sure they'll want a drink."

"It'd be good for ya to stay beside Annie tonight. That way, ya can see how we like to serve our guests. It's an experience when they come here," Dominick asserts.

"Sure, that'd be great," I agree. I look down at my plate, but suddenly, I'm too scared to eat.

"Don't tell me you're full. It'd be a shame to waste this food. It's delicious. Ya really outdid yourself this time, Annie," Dominick compliments.

"Yea. It's very good," I say, then force myself to continue to eat, trying to push the thought from my mind that it could be Caleb.

That's silly. He doesn't know I'm in Clifden, and he definitely doesn't know I'm at this bed-and-breakfast, I remind myself.

When we finish eating, Annie rises.

I stand too.

She says, "Sit down, dear. I have dessert for us."

"Oh, of course." I sit back down and look at Dominick.

He shrugs. "It'll be amazing. She's always making special things."

Annie disappears and quickly reappears carrying a huge Bailey's cheesecake.

"I love cheesecake. That looks incredible," I blurt out.

"It is," she assures me. She takes a knife, cuts three pieces, and sets them on plates. She hands Dominick and me each one.

I cut through the rich dessert and put a bite in my mouth. The flavors burst on my tongue, and I groan. "This is so good."

Dominick chuckles. "I told you she's great at what she does."

"Ya really are a good cook," I compliment.

She smiles. "Well, thank ya."

We finish eating, and I help Annie clean the table and do the dishes.

When we're done, she says, "Follow me." She takes me to a hall closet and opens it. "Here's all the clothes I was talking about."

"Wow. Where did ya get those?" I ask, gaping at the huge selection.

She answers, "Guests leave them. We always call and tell them, but they often don't want us to mail the item and don't want to come back because it's too far."

"This is nice stuff," I say, pulling out a piece of fabric, and when it falls open, I discover it's a pretty dress.

"Yea, it is. That would fit ya really well," she claims.

I stare at it. I don't remember the last time I put a dress on. I question, "How should I dress when the guests come?"

"However ya want. We usually wear jeans. Sometimes we get more dressed up. It just depends. Why don't ya try that on and wear it tonight if it fits?" she suggests.

I go into the other room and shut the door. I put the dress on and look at my reflection in the mirror. It fits perfectly, but my stomach is rounder than before.

How long will I be able to hide my pregnancy?

Annie knocks on the door. "Dear, how does it fit?"

I open the door.

Annie's expression lights up. She chirps, "Ya look amazing in that. How does it feel?"

"Good," I admit.

"Well, keep it on. I'm going to put something nicer on for our anniversary."

"Okay," I say, feeling guilty again that I'm interrupting their anniversary. But they don't seem to mind.

They're probably just being nice to me.

Regardless, I'm grateful for it. I've been on my own, by myself, for too many days to count.

"All right, dear. I think these are all things in your size." Annie pulls a bunch of clothes out until there's a huge pile on the floor.

"That's a lot of clothes," I say.

"It is, but it's good to have options, right?"

"I suppose it is."

She picks up half the pile and says, "Grab the rest. We'll take these down to your room and organize them."

I don't argue with her. We get into my tiny room and refold the clothes until they're neatly on the shelf.

She beams at me and says, "I think you've got everything ya need now."

"I do. Thank ya so much."

"You're welcome. We're really glad to have ya here."

"I'm really grateful to be here," I say and get teary-eyed again.

"Now, dear, you're going to make me cry if ya keep that up," she claims.

I softly laugh and wipe my eyes. "Okay. I'll try to stop."

"Good. Get some rest for a while. I'll have ya come to the pub fifteen minutes before ten. That way, we're there when the guests arrive."

"Sure. Sounds good."

"Okay then, make yourself at home," she orders, then leaves, shutting the door.

I stare at the clothes on the shelf for several minutes, then sit on the bed.

My new home.

For now.

I shake off the anxiety about the future. Right now, I just need to take one day at a time.

20

Devin
One Month Later

"You've got to stop this," Brody demands.

I cross my arms and clench my jaw, giving him the same expression I'd given him the last time he lectured me.

He points at me. "I mean it. You've been shirking your duties. Ya have to stop this obsession ya have with this girl."

I stay silent.

He steps closer. "Ya have responsibilities. Do I need to remind ya of them?"

"No, ya don't," I state, walking away. I slam his office door and leave the house.

Alaina calls out, "Devin."

I ignore her. I'm tired of Brody and Alaina telling me what to do. And while my brother may be right that I've slacked a bit, nothing's falling apart. There's no way I'll ever stop looking for Lauren, so he can kiss my ass.

I get into my car and peel down their driveway, beeping the horn so the gate opens and I don't have to stop. I drive through town, and my phone rings. I glance at the screen and my heart races faster. I answer, "Samuel."

He says in an emotionless voice, "Caleb and I are heading out to the mountains."

"She's up there?" I say, my pulse beating faster.

"She's been spotted. A tall woman matching her description, with strawberry-blonde hair and blue eyes."

"Where?" I demand.

"She's working at a pub, and she's pregnant, so it's got to be her," Samuel relays.

"Send me the coordinates," I order, then hang up and debate about who I want to take with me. If Caleb and Samuel are going to be up there, I might run into trouble. It's best if I don't go alone.

I could take Brogan or Cathal, but they're both on the other side of town. So I call Tynan.

He asserts, "Don't give me anything to do today. It's my day off."

"I'm picking ya up in two minutes. I'm right down the street."

He groans. "Not today, Devin. I've been working the last two weeks without any time off."

"I don't care. I need ya to come with me. Now, I'll meet ya outside." I hang up before he can say anything else, and I speed the rest of the way there. When I get there, I text him.

> Me: Here.

> Tynan: You're a bastard.

> Me: Tell me something I don't know. Now get your ass down here.

It takes another few minutes until he appears, stepping out of the building. He begrudgingly walks over to the car and gets in, snapping, "What the fuck is the urgency? I left a lass up there who's dying for it."

"I don't give a shit about your lass," I answer and take off before his door's shut.

"Devin, where are we going?" he questions.

"Lauren's been spotted," I announce.

He groans. "Not again. How many of these little scenic tours are we going to do?"

I angrily spout, "As many as we have to until we find her, but we're going to find her today. She's been spotted in a pub."

"Just like the last few pubs," he mutters.

I ignore him. "Why don't ya take a nap? We have a decent drive ahead of us."

"Of course we do," he gripes, pulling his hoodie over his head and leaning back. "Ya owe me big-time."

"I don't owe ya shit."

"We'll see about that," he warns.

I turn the radio up, feeling anxious but hopeful. It happens every time I go to find Lauren.

It's got to be her this time.

The description fits her, but there have been four other times that Samuel has called. I've been lucky so far. I've yet to encounter Caleb, but I want to get there before he does. So, I drive faster, cutting off cars.

A lorry blares its horn, and Tynan barks, "Jesus, that was close."

I swerve.

He grumbles, "Why don't ya get us there in one piece."

"Since when are ya a pussy?" I ask.

He grunts. "I'm not a pussy, but it would've been nice if ya let me finish with my lass before dragging me out here."

"She'll be waiting when ya get back," I assert, having no doubt that she will be.

"Bastard," he mutters.

I continue driving for another two hours, and the roads become more and more desolate until it's nothing but mountain roads. Then a small town comes into view. I slow down and pull over a few doors down from the pub. I nudge my brother.

He wakes up groggily, rubs his fists over his eyes, and looks out. "Not much happening in this town."

"Yea, it's a good place to hide," I acknowledge and glance around. I don't see Caleb or anyone anywhere. I would text Samuel, but it's too risky. I decide it's safe, grab my baseball cap, get out, and order, "Let's go." I lower the cap onto my head, and Tynan does the same. We walk down the street and enter the pub.

It's midday. The pub has who I assume are a few regulars drinking. They turn and stare at us as if we're aliens.

A redheaded woman beams, chirping, "Can I get ya anything?"

I glance around the pub again.

"Guinness and a shot of whiskey for both of us," Tynan states.

I give him a dirty look, and he gives me one back. The last thing I'm going to do is start drinking while I'm looking for Lauren.

The woman turns and grabs the bottle of whiskey.

Tynan whispers, "We're in a fucking pub. Act like it."

I take a breather. He's right. Still, I comment, "Ya didn't need to order shots."

He shrugs. "Got to have a little bit of fun. It is my day off after all."

"Go cry some more," I taunt.

He takes the barstool at the end of the counter, positioned so we can see the entire pub.

I grab the seat next to him.

The barmaid comes back and puts our drinks down. She pries, "Where are ya from?"

Tynan gives her his dazzling smile. "Oh, couple hours south, nowhere interesting. What's in this town besides your pretty face?"

I groan inside. My brother's the cheesiest person at times.

Still, she takes the bait like most lasses, and her face brightens. She bats her eyes, replying, "Well, thanks. What's your name?"

"Tyler," he says.

"Tyler. That's a nice name. I don't hear that much. And yours?" she asks.

"That's Danny boy," my brother states.

I refrain from smacking him. I hate that name. He does it to get under my skin. I state, "It's Danny only." Then I look around again. "Ya working here on your own, lass?"

Her eyes widen. "No, our cook's in the back."

"Oh, are ya the only barmaid?"

Her eyes turn to slits. "Why do ya want to know that?"

Tynan interjects, "He's just wondering how a beautiful lass like yourself manages to keep all the men off of ya if you're in here alone. That's all."

She relaxes, and her face blushes. "Oh, you're very sweet to say that."

"Well, you're a stunner. Definitely an eleven out of ten," he praises.

Her cheeks turn even redder. "Well, thank ya."

My brother's lines are old, yet they always work.

He glances at the pub staircase door. "Ya live above here?"

She shakes her head. "No, I still live with my parents."

He leans closer, lowers his voice, and puts his hand over hers.

She inhales slightly and glances at their hands.

He states, "Shame. I'd love to see your place."

"Who else works here?" I inquire, tired of his antics.

She looks back at me again. "There's a couple other barmaids."

"But you're here on your own?" I repeat.

She hesitates then announces, "You're the second person to ask that today."

Alarm bells ring in my head, and the hairs on my arms rise. "Am I?"

She steps back, and her eyes dart between Tynan and me. "Why would two different groups of men ask me that same question?"

I take a sip of my Guinness, swallow it, and answer, "I'll be honest with ya, lass. I'm looking for a girl."

Her face darkens. "So were they."

"Okay, and what did ya tell them?"

She crosses her arms. "Why is that your business?" She glances back at the kitchen door. I assume she's trying to decipher if she needs to get the cook to help her, in case we're dangerous.

Tynan puts his hands in the air. "No need to worry, lass. We're just looking for a girl. She's pregnant. Strawberry-blonde hair. Tall. Blue eyes."

I add, "Her mum's looking for her. She's sick."

The barmaid continues giving us the same look, as if she doesn't believe us.

"It's true," I lie.

Tynan adds, "We came to tell her that her mum's sick. That's it. Her mum wants to see her before she dies."

The barmaid's eyes widen just a tad. "She really gonna die?"

"Yea, she is," I reiterate.

She scrunches her face. "Well, Meghann's the only one who's pregnant."

"Okay, and where's Meghann?"

"She's home, I assume. She doesn't work until later tonight," she relays.

"Okay, and where is home?"

She bites her lip.

"Listen, lass, her mum's only got maybe a few days. This is important," Tynan states.

"Why don't I call her and see if she can come to the pub? I don't feel comfortable giving ya her address," the barmaid states.

"Well, I'd rather we talk to her in person since this is a delicate matter," I declare.

Tynan blurts out, "Who were these other men that came in?"

I want to smack him for asking that question. My brother never knows when to shut up.

The barmaid turns suspicious again. "This doesn't make sense."

"What doesn't make sense?" I question.

"Why two different sets of men would be looking for Meghann."

So she's calling herself Meghann.

I fib, "Well, I told ya Meghann's mum is really sick. But we were sent to inform her. Just wondering why someone else would be here."

The barmaid swallows hard, looking at both of us.

Tynan interjects, "Listen, lass, we just want to ensure that her mum and her can talk before she passes. Unless Meghann doesn't want to. But at least it would be her choice. Think about if it was your mum."

She keeps her suspicious look on us. "Ya both are making me nervous."

I attempt to reassure her. "Don't be. We told ya why we're here."

Another tense moment passes.

I lean forward. "Times ticking. If her mum dies and she doesn't know—"

The barmaid shakes her head. "Why don't I call her and tell her to come in...that you need to talk to her?"

My pulse skyrockets. "No, don't do that. If ya do that, she might not come in. Look, we know why she left, and we understand."

"You do?" the barmaid questions with a doubtful expression.

I nod. "Aye, we do. We know all about it, and we understand. We just want to let her know."

"And the other men who came in? You're aware of who they are?" she questions.

I lower my voice. "Aye, we are, and they're not good men. So we should warn her about them too."

The barmaid puts a hand on her hip. "How do I know that ya two aren't the bad men and the other ones are good?"

Her questions make me realize that it has to be Lauren. Why else would someone with her description be hiding in this pub with a co-worker who seems to be keen on protecting her? This barmaid must know Lauren's secrets.

I state, "Lass, do ya really think we're dangerous compared to those men who visited earlier?"

She continues assessing us.

I push, "What did ya tell them? What did they say before they left?"

She admits, "I told them that she'd be in, in..." She glances back at a clock. "Well, twenty minutes."

A chill skates down my spine. "She's coming in, in twenty minutes?"

"Yea," she states, nodding.

"And the men are coming back?"

"Yea. Was that bad of me?" she frets.

I try to reassure her. "No, it's fine. We'll take care of it. But ya can't tell them that we're here. Okay?"

More fear fills her face. "So I did the wrong thing, and I shouldn't have told them to come back?"

I try to stay calm. "It's okay. I told ya we'll take care of it. Just make sure they don't know we're here."

"What are ya going to do? Maybe I should call her and tell her not to come in if it's dangerous?"

"No, it's not. Don't worry, lass. We'll take care of it," Tynan restates, standing up. He downs his shot and then points at the kitchen door. "I assume it's okay if we go in there so that when they come in, they don't see us? After all"—he glances at the clock—"we're getting close, aren't we?"

Anxiety fills her expression.

Tynan adds, "Look, we just want to tell her about her mum, and we don't want the other men to do anything drastic."

"Who are they?" she questions.

I answer, "The men she's been running from. And I don't want to disclose her business. I don't know what she's told ya."

The barmaid sighs. "Okay, ya can go in the kitchen. Let me tell Franco that it's okay you're in there."

"Good lass," Tynan says.

We follow her into the kitchen. The cook looks up. "Why are ya blokes in my kitchen?"

The barmaid explains, "They need to stay back here for a minute. Some men are coming in. We need to ensure they don't hurt Meghann."

Franco puts his spatula down and his hand on his hip. "And why would they hurt Meghann?"

I put my hands in the air. "Look, it's no secret Meghann's not from these parts. Let us do our job and make sure she's safe. We just need to get a message to her about her mum."

"She's on her deathbed!" the barmaid states.

Franco eyes us suspiciously,

I claim, "It's true. And we're not looking for trouble. We just want to make sure she's safe. We know the men who have come up here asking about her."

He continues to give us a dirty look, and the door opens. A woman enters, blurting out, "What's going on?"

I glance at her, and my heart falls. "Please tell me that's not Meghann," I say to the barmaid, then glance back at her strawberry-blonde hair, long legs, and blue eyes. My gaze falls to her pregnant belly.

The woman puts her hands across her stomach. "Why do ya know my name?"

"Ya don't know these guys?" the barmaid questions.

Meghann shakes her head. "No, I've never seen them in my life."

"Then it's not her mum that's dying?"

Meghann's eyes widen. "My mum's dying?"

Another false lead. I'm going to kill Samuel.

Tynan steps between us as my heart drops. "No, lass, there's been a mistake. We thought ya were somebody else."

"Ya sure? My mum's okay?" she frets.

"Aye. Your mum's okay. We're looking for someone else," I say, shoving past them into the bar, then stopping in my tracks.

Caleb and Samuel stand ten feet in front of me.

Tynan follows and bumps into me.

Caleb blurts out, "What the fuck are ya doing here?"

"None of your business. And I should ask ya the same thing," I state, my fists curling at my sides.

Franco appears, ordering, "All of ya get out of the pub, now."

Caleb turns to him and gives him an arrogant look. "I don't know who ya are, but ya have no right to order us around."

"I said to get out," Franco repeats.

Caleb comes closer, and I step in front of Franco, not wanting the man to get hurt. I don't blame him for wanting to protect the place. And Caleb will surely hurt him. Franco's not a strong man, and he's got some balls to step in between us.

Caleb warns, "I'm not leaving without her."

"She's not who you're looking for," the cook states.

"Oh, and how do ya know who I'm looking for?" Caleb asks.

My heart pounds faster. I try to play dumb, asking, "Who are ya looking for?"

"Like ya don't know. Ya were looking for the same lass," Franco blurts out.

Idiot.

I spin on him and grab his shirt. "I don't know what the hell you're talking about."

Fear fills his face, but he maintains, "Ya were looking for Meghann, but it's not who you're looking for. Just like he is."

I shove the cook backward so hard he flies against the wall and then I spin before Caleb can do anything.

He snarls, "Why would ya be looking for her?"

"I don't know who you're looking for."

"Bullshit."

Samuel steps next to Caleb, as does Tynan next to me. Tynan warns, "Let's not have any trouble in here."

"I want to know why you're looking for her," Caleb barks.

I seethe, "My business isn't yours. If ya want, we can take this outside. No need to hurt people who have nothing to do with our business."

"Your business? She's not your business," he snarls, then glances at Samuel.

I take advantage of the brief moment when his focus isn't on me, slamming my fist against his cheek. It knocks him backward, and he falls to the ground. Blood spurts everywhere.

My brother and I dart past him and out of the pub, but not before Tynan gives Samuel a punch to the face since he's not supposed to be on our side. We slide into the car and take off as fast as possible.

Anger fills me. Another false lead. How is this possible? How can she hide so well when so many eyes are out looking for her?

I speed up, and we veer onto a few back mountain roads to ensure Caleb and Samuel aren't on our trail. After a half hour, when we're deep into the woods, I pull over and slam my hand on the steering wheel, shouting, "Goddammit!"

My brother just looks at me.

I stare out the windshield, wondering what my next move is and where Lauren could be.

Tynan quietly states, "Ya got to give this up, bro. It's not worth it."

I bark, "Don't you tell me what's worth it! She's carrying my baby."

Tynan points out, "She could be anywhere. She could have left the country."

More panic hits me. It's not like that thought's never crossed my mind before, but I don't like thinking about it. "Just shut up," I order, and veer back onto the road, making my way down the mountain, more determined than ever to find her.

21

Lauren
Two Months Later

"*L*auren, can I talk to ya when you get a minute?"

I don't know why, but the hairs on my arms rise. I spin toward Annie. "Sure. Is everything okay?"

She smiles. "Yea, everything's fine. Please come into the kitchen when ya finish."

"Okay," I agree and pour the remainder of the whiskey into the glass. I open another bottle, finish making the drink, then say to the patron, "Enjoy. I'll be right back."

"Sure," he nods. He's an old guy who arrived at the bed-and-breakfast a day ago. He seems nice enough.

I walk into the kitchen, wondering what Annie wants. When I step inside, Dominick's sitting at the table. I freeze, once again getting nervous. "What's going on?"

They both smile. Dominick points to the chair. "Have a seat, Lauren."

Suddenly I feel like I'm a schoolgirl in trouble. I sit at the table and stare at them as my anxiety builds. I don't speak, waiting for them to tell me what's happening.

Annie takes the seat next to me and puts her hand on mine. "We want to talk to ya about something, dear."

"Am I in trouble?" I blurt out.

"No, not at all," Dominick assures. He leans closer. "We just want to make sure that you're okay."

"I'm fine. Why wouldn't I be?"

Annie and Dominick exchange a glance, and my nerves heighten. Annie softens her voice and puts her hand on my stomach. "Lauren, it's obvious you're pregnant."

I gape at them and then stare at her hand. My stomach's gotten huge, so I knew I was showing but thought I was hiding it well. I look away in shame.

"Oh, honey, we didn't mean to upset ya," Annie states, scooting her chair closer.

"There's nothing to be ashamed of," Dominick says.

I look at them through blurry eyes, asking a stupid question. "How did ya know?"

Annie softly laughs. "Dear, what are ya, five, six months pregnant?"

I glance at my stomach again and squeeze my eyes tighter, admitting, "No, I'm seven."

"Seven? Wow. Well, ya did hide it quite a while," Dominick declares.

I open my mouth, but nothing comes out. What is there to say?

Annie squeezes my hand tighter. "Lauren, is that why ya ran away? Why ya were homeless? Did ya not want your family to know?"

I get choked up thinking about my mum and how she must be so worried about me. And then Devin's face flashes in my mind. I never stopped thinking about him or wishing he was with me, but that's impossible. And then I think about Caleb and what he would do if my mum had her way and he knew I was pregnant and thought I was carrying his child.

"Whatever it is, you can tell us. We'll protect ya," Dominick assures me.

I almost laugh, and before I can stop myself, I blurt out, "Protect me? Against the O'Learys or the O'Connors?" Then I slap my hand over my mouth. "Oh God, I shouldn't have said that."

Tense silence fills the air.

I open my eyes, and Annie and Dominick gape at me.

"I didn't mean that," I lie.

Dominick gets up and takes a seat next to me. "Lauren, no one mentions the O'Learys or the O'Connors as a mistake. What's going on? Are they after ya? Both families?"

Annie's expression is as confused and alarmed as Dominick's. She declares, "Yea, what would those men want with ya?"

I blink hard again, but I can't control my emotions. Tears drip down my chin onto my pants.

Dominick asserts in a stern voice, "Lauren, ya need to tell us what's going on."

I swallow hard. "I appreciate everything ya both have done for me. I should probably go now." I put my hands on the table to rise.

"What? No," Annie states, pushing me back into my seat as I try to get up.

Dominick orders, "Lauren, you're not going anywhere. Ya need to tell us what's going on. Ya can trust us."

"Yes, dear. We won't judge ya," Annie declares.

I take a deep breath, trying to control my emotions, staring at my lap and twisting my fingers together. They give me time, and I try to formulate my words, but it's hard. I finally confess, "My last name's Byrne and my mum was an Ahern, and..." I release an anxious breath.

"Tommy Ahern? That Ahern?" Dominick blurts out.

"Shush," Annie scolds.

I swallow harder. "He was my uncle, but I'm not like him. I swear," I state, knowing his reputation was cruel and destructive.

Annie squeezes my hand again. "It's okay, Lauren. We know you're not a bad person. Just tell us what's going on."

It takes me a few more minutes to collect my thoughts and debate what to tell them. But once I start talking, it all rolls out. "My mum is Tommy's sister. I'm sure ya heard he's dead, yet I can't escape the fact I have his blood, which links my family to the O'Learys."

They listen intently.

I continue, "One night, after the big game, there was a horrible fight in the pub that my mum owns. I sent her home, and the girls and I cleaned up the mess. Four blokes knocked on the pub door."

Dominick's eyes narrow. He demands, "What did they do?"

"We didn't know who they were. I swear we didn't know. But they were O'Connors, and well..." I look away in embarrassment.

"Lauren, it's okay. We're not going to judge ya, no matter what. What happened when the O'Connors showed up? Did they hurt ya?" Annie keeps her voice calm and reassuring.

I shake my head. "No. They just... Oh Jesus." I put my hand over my face, wishing I could have made different choices that night.

"Please tell us," Annie says, interrupting my thoughts.

I force myself to look at her. After all, she and Dominick have been nothing but nice to me, kind and caring. They took me in and saved me, as far as I'm concerned. They deserve the truth if anybody does. Plus, now that they know I'm pregnant and I've already started telling them my truth, I need to finish it. So, I cautiously admit, "I ended up... Well, the O'Connors wanted to play a game. My cousins, who work at the pub with me, and I were drinking and playing cards with them. Then Devin suggested we make a bet. It was stupid for me to agree to it, and I lost. And the crazy thing is, I never lose at cards, but I did that night. So, I ended up sleeping with Devin." I swallow hard and admit, "We didn't use protection, and I was off my birth control, and..." A fresh burst of tears falls down my face.

Annie puts her arm around me and pulls me close. "Shush, dear. It's okay. He took advantage of ya."

"No, it's not like he forced himself on me," I state.

Dominick's disapproving expression matches his voice. "Still. Devin O'Connor's how old? In his thirties? Forties? He knows better than to take advantage of a young lass like you. He knew exactly what he was doing."

I don't know why I stick up for Devin, but I do. I declare, "But I wanted it as much as he did." Heat fills my face the moment my admission comes out. I bite my lip and stare at my hands, muttering, "It doesn't matter anyway. The point is I'm pregnant and I can't let anybody know. I briefly dated Caleb O'Leary. He wants me, and he's a horrible person. My mum wants me to marry him and tell him it's his baby."

Hate fills Dominick's features, which is the first time I've seen that emotion on him.

Annie wears the same expression. She says, "Dear, we've heard about Caleb, what he does, and who he is, so it's understandable why you're hiding out. Your mum shouldn't be pushing ya to marry him!"

"Well, she will always be loyal to the O'Learys. It's who she is, but she means well. I begged her not to tell Caleb anything about my baby. I can't imagine what would happen if he thought I was carrying his child. And Devin... Well, if Devin finds out, my mum says the O'Connors will take my baby from me." I start sobbing.

Annie once again pulls me into her. She lets me cry until her blouse is soaked from my tears. She finally states, "Lauren, everything will be fine. We understand why you're here, and we will ensure ya and your baby have everything ya need."

I slowly look up. "But it's not your responsibility."

"Shush, dear. You're family. Besides, Dominick and I always wanted children. We couldn't have any of our own. You've become like our daughter, so we'll treat your baby like our grandbaby."

Emotions choke me up further. I take a few shaky inhales, shocked at their kindness.

Dominick adds, "Aye, we will. But now that we know the baby's coming, we must prepare. There's a lot to do before the baby arrives."

I glance at him, then back at Annie, still stunned, asking, "Are ya two being for real right now?"

She softly chuckles. "Of course, dear. Don't ya worry. We'll turn one of the bedrooms into your room, so ya and the baby have more space. That closet's not going to do much for ya."

"No. That's part of your income. The baby and I'll be fine in my current room."

Dominick insists in a firm voice, "No, ya won't. Besides, Annie and I have done just fine. We don't need to fill all the bedrooms to survive."

I argue, "That's too kind of you. But truly, if ya can just let me stay in my room, I'll be totally happy. I promise. And a baby doesn't take up that much space."

Dominick rises. "Don't be silly. We'll start today. Annie, ya take Lauren into town tomorrow. Start looking at cribs and other things."

More shock fills me. "What?"

Annie softly laughs. "We're going to need stuff. Besides, this will be fun. You're having a baby!"

The doorbell rings, signaling that a new guest has arrived.

I rise, overwhelmed by their generosity and support. They still barely know me compared to someone who has been in their life forever. I add, "I don't know what to say."

"Ya don't have to say anything, dear. Like we said, we've always wanted a child, and now we'll get to experience a grandchild," Annie chirps, beaming at me.

The doorbell rings again. "Thank ya. I'm beyond grateful. Let me greet our guests."

"I'll get it," Dominick says, patting me on the shoulder. "You go wash your face and take a moment." He disappears before I can say anything.

Annie gives me another hug. "Oh, a baby. This is so exciting."

"Annie, I don't know how to thank ya both," I confess.

She hugs me again. "Ya don't need to thank us anymore. Like I told ya, this'll be great for us. We're excited. We'll go shopping tomorrow. Okay?"

"But really, I don't need a lot. I don't want ya spending money on me."

"Oh, shush. We have savings. We'll be happy to spoil a baby. Now, I think it's time we schedule a doctor's appointment. I'm assuming ya haven't been to one in a while? Or have ya gone to one at all?"

Guilt hits me. I should be seeing a doctor, but I didn't know how. I shake my head. "I saw one once when my mum found out. I've been taking vitamins. I bought some at the store and doubled up on them, but..."

"Okay, dear." She pats my hand again. "I'll make an appointment."

"Do ya think I've hurt the baby by not going?" I ask worriedly.

She studies me closer. "No. Ya look healthy to me. Ya haven't been having pains or anything, right?"

"No."

"Great. I'm sure everything's fine, but it's time to see a doctor. Okay?"

I nod. "Okay. Thank ya."

"All right. Well, why don't ya go take a breather for a few minutes? Then ya can introduce yourself to the new guest when you're ready," she suggests.

"Okay."

She goes to the stove and starts attending to the pot of soup.

I stare at her back, still a bit in shock and overwhelmed with gratitude.

She doesn't look at me and calls out, "Everything's good, Lauren. I can feel ya staring at me."

I start to laugh. "Okay, I'm leaving now."

"Good. Everything will be fine," she assures me but still doesn't look at me.

I leave the room and go to my bathroom. I stare at my reflection, pull my shirt up, and assess my stomach. I put my hand over it.

Is this really happening?

Are they really accepting me and my baby and happy about it?

I whisper, "Annie and Dominick are taking us in as theirs. Everything's going to be okay. I promise ya, I'll give ya a good life."

I stare at my reflection some more, still overwhelmed by Annie and Dominick's kindness and love. Then I splash some water on my face, brush my hair, even though it doesn't need anything done to it, and go into my room.

I put on a fresh dress and make my way to the main room to say hi to the new guest. I turn the corner and bump into a woman, then I freeze. I grab the wall, shaking, not knowing what to do.

"Lauren Byrne! Is this where you've been hiding out?" Maeve, a girl from my town who's nineteen, maybe twenty, and whose father works for the O'Learys, cries out.

I beg, "Please don't tell anyone I'm here!"

Her face falls. "Okay. But everyone's wondering where ya went. The entire town is wondering if you're dead or alive. And your mum claims that Caleb got ya pregnant?" She glances at my belly.

My inside's quiver. I put my hand over my mouth. "Oh God. My mum actually told him that?"

She slowly nods. "Yea. He has his army of clansmen looking for ya."

I grab her arm, pleading, "Please, Maeve. Whatever ya do, do not tell him. Please. I'll give ya money. Well, I don't have a lot, but whatever ya want, I'll try to make happen. Just don't tell him!"

She puts her hands in the air. "Calm down, Lauren. I'm not going to tell him. I don't hold any loyalty toward Caleb."

My head jerks back. Besides my cousins, who privately admit they don't like Caleb any more than I do, I've never heard anybody say anything bad about him. No one would dare. I ask, "Ya don't?"

"No, he's a dickhead," she says.

I breathe a sigh of relief.

"But he's going to keep looking for ya. You're carrying his baby," she points out.

My gut dives again. "It's not his baby. My mum shouldn't have told him anything. It's a lie!"

Surprise fills her face. "It's not?"

"No. God, no," I repeat.

"Then whose is it?" she questions.

I swallow hard, my entire body quivering.

She steps closer and looks behind her. She lowers her voice. "Lauren, why would your mum tell him it's his if it's not?"

"Because she wants him to take care of me. She wants me to marry him, but that would be horrendous. Ya know how he is."

Sympathy fills her expression. She nods. "Yea. That would be a nightmare. But who's the baby's father?"

I open my mouth, but nothing comes out.

She adds, "I've never heard of ya with anyone besides Caleb recently."

I stay quiet.

She claims, "I won't say anything. Just like I won't tell Caleb."

"I can't tell ya. But please don't tell him. Don't tell anyone that you've seen me here."

She looks upset that I won't answer her question.

I ask, "Why are ya here anyway?"

Her face falls. "Well, I was online, and I met a guy. I thought he was amazing, so I came to meet him, and guess what?"

"What?"

She smirks. "I got catfished."

"Ya got catfished? Like, he wasn't who he said he was?" I inquire.

She nods. "Yea. He was an ugly old man. His name's not even what he said. And then he tried to kiss me. I kicked him in the nuts and then ran."

"Oh my God. Are ya okay?"

She huffs. "Yea. It is what it is. At least I didn't tell him where I was staying. I'll leave tomorrow to go back. I was going to stay the weekend, but it's pointless now."

"I'm sorry that happened," I offer.

She scoffs. "I don't even know why I thought something great could happen to me. Love sucks."

I don't know why, but her statement makes me laugh. "Yea, you're right. It does."

She tilts her head and studies me.

It makes me nervous. "Why are ya looking at me like that?"

She asks, "Do ya love the father of your child?"

"No," I say, but a funny feeling fills me.

She softly laughs. "You're such a liar."

"I'm not," I insist.

She keeps studying me.

"I don't love him. It was a mistake, so he can't know."

"Wouldn't it be better if he knows than Caleb thinking it's his?"

"Not when he's Devin O'Connor," I blurt out, then put my hand over my mouth.

Her eyes widen.

What the heck is wrong with me?

Panic fills me. I beg, "Maeve, I shouldn't have said that. Please. Promise you're not going to say anything to anyone. No one can know I'm here. Not my mum, not Caleb. No one."

A few moments of tense silence grow between us.

She asks, "What about Emily? She's worried about ya, as are your other cousins."

"No one, Maeve. I miss them, and I love them, but nobody can know. Please," I plead.

Something passes in her expression that I don't trust, but what can I do? My fate's in her hands.

She assures me, "Okay, Lauren, don't worry. Nobody will know."

"Ya swear?"

"I swear," she promises.

Relief hits me. "Thank you."

22

Devin
One Month Later

"Ya better tell me where he's at," I threaten, taking the knife and holding it next to Odhran O'Leary's balls.

He cries out, "I don't know! I keep telling ya I know nothing."

"Ya do," I declare just as my phone rings with the unique tone I gave to Samuel.

Normally, I hate to leave in the middle of a torture session. But I immediately hand the knife to Tynan.

"Keep going," I order.

His eyes narrow, and he steps closer to Odhran.

Aidan pushes Tynan out of the way and flicks his lighter, threatening, "I think we could have more fun than with that knife alone."

"Do whatever ya want. Just make the bastard talk," I assert and leave the room. I pull my phone out and answer, "Samuel, tell me ya have good news for me."

His voice is low as he states, "I know where she's at."

Goose bumps break out along my limbs. I demand, "Where is she?"

"At a bed-and-breakfast in Clifden. I'll send ya the coordinates."

"How do ya know it's her?" I question, tired of feeling hopeful yet knowing I'll follow up on any lead he gives me.

This game of cat and mouse that I seem to be in is driving me insane. There have been a dozen sightings in the last month. Lauren's about eight months pregnant. Every day that goes by scares me more. I must find her before she has the baby so I can ensure they're both safe. If Caleb gets to her before I do, who knows what he'll do.

Samuel's voice turns darker. He adds, "One of the men who work for the O'Learys got behind in his debt."

"And?" I anxiously ask, tapping my hand against my thigh.

Samuel announces, "Caleb was about to kill him, and his daughter, Maeve, showed up. She offered information in exchange for her to clear her father's debt."

I ask, "Who's Maeve?"

"She's a young lass, barely twenty, maybe only nineteen, I don't know. But she claims she was on a seaside trip. She stayed at a bed-and-breakfast, and Lauren's working there."

I run my hand through my hair. "How do ya know it's true?"

"Caleb's holding her captive with her da until he gets back. My gut says she's telling the truth."

I grumble, "I'm tired of these trips that lead nowhere." Over the last month, all these trips have ended with most of the lasses being similar in appearance to Lauren but not actually her. A few barely resembled her. And the longer it takes for me to find her, the more insane I feel.

Samuel relays, "Caleb was clear that if Maeve's lying, he's going to make both their deaths ten times worse. But Maeve insisted that Lauren was there. She said the bed-and-breakfast owners are an older couple. They seem to have taken Lauren in. She also confirmed she's pregnant."

I walk toward the door and grab my keys out of my pocket, stepping out into the daylight. I grimace from the sunlight. I've been in the warehouse for at least a few days, torturing one man after another for information. Yet all it's done is created a pile of dead O'Learys for my brothers and me to clean up.

I point out, "The other lasses were pregnant too."

"It's her. She was insistent no matter how much Caleb threatened her," Samuel insists.

"Send me the coordinates," I order and hang up, getting into my car. I start the engine and drive to the motorway. I veer toward Clifden, determined to retrieve Lauren, letting the hope fill me, even though I know I shouldn't allow it.

Eight months. She's at least eight months pregnant.

I need to get to her before Caleb does.

All I've obsessed over since she went missing is finding her and ensuring she and my baby are safe. Every day, the clock in my head continues ticking louder.

I'm an hour into the trip and glance at my phone, but there aren't any messages. I want to text Samuel, but that would put him in danger. And I can't lose my inside guy.

The last few months haven't been great for our spies inside the O'Leary clan. Several of our men were outed, and Caleb showed them no mercy. One by one, their heads showed up in Belfast in boxes.

Plus, Samuel is our spy with the highest rank within the O'Leary clan. He's become Caleb's right hand when it comes to finding Lauren.

Another half hour passes, and my phone finally buzzes. I glance at it, but it's a video instead of an address or coordinates.

Since I need petrol, I exit the motorway and pull into a station. I get out of the car, stick the pump into the tank, and press play on the video.

"Oh fuck," I mutter in horror, staring at Samuel's bleeding face.

Caleb's voice comes in the background, and a knife appears by Samuel's eyes. He seethes, "Was I not clear what we do to traitors?"

Samuel cries out, "I'm not a traitor! I'm an O'Leary!"

Caleb snarls, "Really? Seems like you're awfully close to Devin O'Connor." He presses the tip of the blade into Samuel's eyeball.

Samuel's agonizing scream fills the air. "Stop! Ya don't know what you're doing! Ya got it wrong!"

Caleb flicks the knife, and the eyeball flies out of its socket. Blood fills the screen.

Samuel's painful shout makes me wince.

I continue staring at the screen as Caleb takes a knife and flips it from Samuel's forehead, down the middle of his nose, then over his lips.

The sound of Samuel's screams intensifies.

I don't watch any more. I turn off the video and throw the phone inside my car, screaming, "Goddammit!"

A lady at the pump across from me jumps.

"Sorry," I offer.

Pull it together.

The pump clicks, and I take it out of my tank. My anxiety grows.

He's going to get to Lauren first.

He's not.

I don't know what bed-and-breakfast she's at, and he does.

For the first time since she disappeared, I hope Samuel was wrong. I want nothing more than this Maeve lass to be a liar.

I pull out of the petrol station and speed toward the town. I'm not a God-fearing man, but I pray a miracle happens and I find her before Caleb does.

Disturbing thoughts about what he'll do to her and my child, plague me.

He thinks it's his baby.

He won't do anything to harm his own blood.

I don't put anything past him. He's a monster.

Visions of Caleb touching Lauren, or my child, only make me more determined to kill him. I drive faster, and a garda siren fills the air.

I look in my rearview mirror, muttering, "Fuck." I keep driving and read the exit sign, which says *Recess*.

This can't get any worse.

Recess is an O'Leary territory, which means the garda aren't on any O'Connor's side.

I don't have to think about it. I speed up, and a chase begins. It takes four exits and several cars banging into each other before I veer off the motorway.

I don't know where I'm going, and the garda stays close on my tail.

I speed through a town, beeping my horn so that a handful of pedestrians move out of the way. The garda slows to maneuver around them, and I turn in front of a rubbish truck at the right time.

There's a loud crash. I glance into my mirror in time to see steam coming out of the hood of the garda's car.

"Finally," I shout but continue to drive fast, trying to figure out where I'm at and making my way back toward the motorway.

It takes longer than I want to find the entrance, and I curse myself for so many things.

We should've gotten more men to infiltrate the O'Learys.

I should have protected Samuel better, not that I know how.

Then more questions appear.

How did Caleb even find out he was an O'Connor?

His death is on my hands, but I push the guilt away. I can't worry about him right now. The only people who matter are Lauren and my baby.

I continue driving toward the seaside. Rain starts to pour so thick I can barely see. My tires skid across the pavement, and I almost lose control of the vehicle. It forces me to slow down, and I grow antsier.

The remainder of the drive turns torturous. Every second that passes makes my skin crawl, and I wonder if Caleb's already there. Does he have her in his possession?

When I finally exit in Clifden, it's dark from the storm, and I have to slow down even more. I realize I have no plan. I don't know anything about this town. I've never been here. I don't know how many bed-and-breakfasts there are here, nor can I pinpoint the one Lauren's hiding out in.

I grab my phone and pull up a list of options, and my gut drops.

I stare at a dozen options. I switch to view them on the map, figure out where I'm at, then drive to the closest one.

I pull up, but it's shut down as if no one's been here for ages, so I don't waste any time going inside. I drive to the next one, park close to the steps, climb them, and ring the bell.

A dark-haired young woman opens the door, asking, "Hi, can I help ya?"

"Aye. I'm looking for Lauren. She might call herself something else. Strawberry-blonde hair. Blue eyes. Tall. She's pregnant."

The woman looks like she has no idea what I'm talking about and shakes her head. "I'm sorry, but I don't know."

I'm not taking any chances. As far as I know, she could be the best liar in the world. So I shove past her, calling out, "Lauren!"

"Sir, I don't know who you're talking about," she claims in a scared voice.

A man appears. "Can I help ya?"

"Aye. I'm trying to find the mother of my child. Where is she?" I demand, feeling crazed.

He shakes his head. "There's no one here but my wife, a few older guests, and myself."

I shove past him, unconvinced, feeling desperate. I open every door I pass while they object, following me.

The man threatens, "I'm calling the garda if ya don't leave."

I spin on him, grab his shirt collar, and push him up against the wall.

The woman yells, "Don't hurt him!"

I offer, "I won't hurt him, but I want to know where she's at."

"There's no one here by that name or fitting that description. I swear," she claims.

"There's not," he agrees.

I peer closer and finally release him. I finish making my way through the entire house. When it's clear she's not there, my gut falls further, and I leave.

I go to the next bed-and-breakfast on the list, but it's the same situation. Lauren is nowhere in sight, and nothing changes as I make my way through the list.

No one seems to know who she is or has any information about her. It doesn't matter how much I scare or threaten them. I'm at the eighth one when a woman glares at me, threatening, "Call the garda, George."

Anger fills me, swirling with my frustration. I grab my knife and push her up against the wall. I press the blade to her throat, warning, "I don't have time for your antics."

Her eyes widen and her lip quivers.

A man begs, "Don't hurt her, please. That's my wife."

I keep a hold of her and turn my face toward him. I assert, "Then I want to know where Lauren is."

He holds his hands in the air, claiming, "We don't know any Lauren. I swear!"

I slowly release her.

Her husband pushes her behind him.

I order, "You two. Show me every room."

The man says, "Follow me."

I point to his wife. "She comes too."

They obey, but Lauren is nowhere.

I leave the house, get in my car, and speed to the next place on the list. But I can't help wondering if I'm on another wild goose chase or if Lauren's really anywhere near here.

23

Lauren

"This looks amazing," I declare, glancing around the room. The walls have been painted blue. A border runs in the middle with multi-colored baby socks. A brown crib and a rocking chair are in the corner, and my bed is next to it. The closet is a mix of my clothes and the baby's. Diapers fill the shelves.

Annie beams. "We're so glad ya love it. I wasn't sure about the border, but I'm glad we went with it!"

Dominick slings his arm around her and grins, declaring, "Annie has a knack for these things."

"She does," I agree and get teary-eyed. It happens all the time now. I add, "I can't thank ya enough. You've been amazing through all this, and I'm so grateful for ya."

"Stop saying 'thank ya' all the time," Annie states.

Dominick nods. "Aye. We told ya. We're completely selfish. This is fun and exciting for us."

I smile, glancing at the room again. So much has changed. As soon as Annie and Dominick found out, they became like parents to me.

From time to time, I think about my mum, and while I still love her, I know this is a better situation than what she would want for me.

And I still can't believe she told Caleb it's his baby when I told her not to. I have so many mixed feelings about my mum. I know she means well, but she's crossed the line. She knows Caleb's evil and is capable of anything. I don't trust him near me or my baby. So the knowledge of what she's done sent a new level of determination through me to make sure that I always stay here with Annie and Dominick.

Annie asserts, "Well, I think it's time we start dinner. The guests will be hungry."

"Oh, I got a head start and already fixed the casserole. I put it in the oven when ya shooed me from the room," I chirp.

"Very well. I'll go mix the muffins," she says.

I lift my chin. "I did that too! They're in the tin."

She pats me on the shoulder. "Thank ya. Let's go finish it up."

The three of us walk down the stairs and into the kitchen.

"Smells delicious," Dominick proclaims.

"Aye, it does. Too bad ya won't be eating it," a voice I know too well and makes the hairs on my neck rise booms into the room.

My pulse skyrockets and my skin crawls. Nausea hits me. I put my hand on my belly, spin, and my nightmare's in front of me. I stutter, "C-Caleb, what are ya doing here?"

Dominick stands in front of me. "You're not welcome here."

Caleb's eyes turn wilder. They're red like he's not slept in days, and he lunges toward us. He grabs Dominick by the shirt, lifting him so he's on his toes.

Annie screams and smacks Caleb's back.

It doesn't stop him. He takes his fist and slams it into Dominick's head.

Dominick goes flying across the room.

I cry out, "Don't hurt him!" I attempt to help Dominick, but Caleb grabs me, pinning me to his chest.

Annie runs to Dominick, seething, "Ya bastard! What have ya done?"

Dominick's eyes are closed. His head rolls, and blood covers the floor.

I shout, "Why do ya have to hurt everybody? This isn't necessary!"

Caleb tightens his grip on me and spins me into him. His breath stinks of stale Guinness and whiskey. The scent of smoke covers his clothes, and my nausea heightens. He snarls, "You'll pay for leaving, especially with my child."

"It's not your child," I blurt out.

A sinister grin fills his face, which scares me more. "Isn't it? Your mum says it is."

Something about his words makes my stomach pitch. I open my mouth, but I can't speak. He leans into my ear and threatens, "I know ya got an O'Connor inside of ya, but ya know what? The world is going to think it's my blood. You'll be mine. And every second that passes, that bastard will know that his child is growing up with me as his da. It'll kill him to know his blood is loyal to the O'Learys and not the O'Connors."

New horror fills me. I swallow down bile. How does Caleb know Devin is the father? I barely get out, "Ya don't know what you're talking about."

"Don't I?" Caleb challenges.

Annie sobs, "Wake up, Dominick. Please wake up."

I dart my eyes over at them, feeling helpless and hating how Dominick looks dead. I ask, "Is he breathing?"

"Hopefully not. He's a fucking pussy," Caleb says, uncaring.

I try to push away from him, but I can't. He's holding me too tight.

Caleb snorts. "You're coming with me."

"Leave her alone," Annie says, and I can see her torn expression between trying to help Dominick and me.

There's only one choice. What Caleb wants, he gets. Dominick's life is the most important thing right now. So I assure her, "I'll be fine. Get him to a hospital."

He pushes me toward the door.

Annie screams, "Let her go!"

He drags me out the front door.

Annie shouts, "Lauren!"

Caleb shoves me into his car and then gets into the driver's side. He turns on the engine and peels out of the driveway.

I beg, "Caleb, please. Ya don't know what you're doing. There's no reason to take me away from here. It's not your baby."

"We've already established that fact. But you'll tell the world it's my baby. Do ya understand, Lauren?"

"No! I won't!"

His eyes darken. He threatens, "Then I'll cut that baby out of your stomach, and ya will never see it."

Horror fills me. It's worse than I thought. And I curse my mum once again for telling Caleb her lie. Then I wonder again how he knows it's Devin's. Did my mum tell him?

No, that wouldn't make sense.

Then who did?

I try to think about how to escape, but what can I do? The car's moving. I don't want to hurt the baby. And Caleb will follow through on his threat if I try anything.

He lights up a cigarette and barely inches the window open. More nausea fills me. I close my eyes and lean against the window, my heart pounding, wondering how to escape. It's my job to protect my baby, but how can I?

Caleb turns up the music. The darkness deepens the farther away we get from my safe haven. All I can think about is if Dominick's alive. And I curse myself for staying in one place for so long and thinking I could be safe.

Maeve. She must have told him. She's the only one who knew where I was.

Still, I ask, "How did ya find me?"

310

He glances at me. "Did ya think ya could run and hide and I wouldn't? God, you're stupid. I will always outsmart ya."

I glare at him, firmly repeating, "But how did ya find me?"

He reaches over and smacks my face. The sting erupts over my cheek. I cry out, "Ow. Why are ya hurting me?"

"Ya will be respectful to me at all times. Do ya understand, ya fucking whore?"

I try not to cry, but I can't help it.

"Oh, now you're going to sob. Oh, poor baby Lauren," he mocks.

I try to stop my tears and stare out the window. This can't be happening, but it is.

"Your mum's going to be happy to see you," he states.

I swallow hard, fighting the feelings of hating her and wanting to see her just because she's my mum.

Disgust fills his voice. "Your mum knew the right thing to do. She knows where her loyalty lies. She would never spread her legs for an O'Connor."

I focus on the window, staring into the darkness, trying not to gag from the smoke. If I throw up, Caleb's only going to be angrier. I'll be in another position I don't want to be in.

My insides continue to quiver, and the baby kicks. I put my hand over my stomach, trying to soothe him, wondering if he can sense he's in danger.

Caleb turns up the music and drives faster. More fear fills me. He knows I hate it when he drives crazy. But I refrain from asking him to slow down.

It's a long way. We're hours into the drive when I finally ask, "Where are we going?"

He arrogantly states, "To my house. Where do ya think we're going?"

I don't know why I would think he would take me anywhere else. It's not like he's going to keep me hidden. He'll let all of Dublin and Belfast now he has me as his.

I beg, "Caleb, please listen to me. I didn't mean to hurt ya. And I don't know what ya think ya know—"

"I know everything, Lauren. I know it's an O'Connor inside you and not an O'Leary. Do I need to know anymore?" he interjects, scowling with hatred.

"It's not," I say in my most convincing voice.

"Don't lie to me," he screams, and the crazed look on his face intensifies.

I take a deep breath, pleading, "Please don't hurt my baby."

He snorts. "Here's what's going to happen." He lights up another cigarette and takes a drag. He blows the smoke toward me and asserts, "You're going to marry me. The baby will be named Caleb. He'll be known as my son, and ya will not tell anybody anything different. Do ya understand me?"

My entire body quivers. My chest tightens to the point I can barely breathe. "Please, Caleb. Just let me go. Ya don't want me. There are so many women better for ya than me."

He grunts. "Oh, I know there's better lasses out there, but you're still going to be mine. Whatever I say for the rest of your life, you'll do. And if ya dare disobey me, that abomination inside your belly will pay for it."

Tears continue to fall down my face, and I turn back to the window, not wanting to be in this position but unable to figure out how to get out of it.

Now, my fate is different than what I wanted. Everything I was scared of is coming to fruition, except it's a thousand times worse.

Mum. Maeve. They both betrayed me. It hurts what they've done. And I vow to make them pay, even though I've never considered myself vengeful. Yet the lines have been crossed. They took things too far, and now my child is in danger. So if it kills me, I will eventually figure out how to make them regret ever telling Caleb anything.

My only thought of how to keep my son safe is to find Devin, but that still scares me. I wish I knew the O'Connors wouldn't take my baby, but I don't know what to believe.

I need to take my chances with Devin.

How?

I curse myself for getting rid of my phone. I don't know his number. Plus, I doubt Caleb's going to give me a phone. I'm going to become his prisoner.

At some point, I doze off. It's hours later when we finally pull up to Caleb's mansion.

"Get out," he orders, jerking the door open so my body almost falls out of the car.

I groggily sit up, realizing I'm still in this nightmare.

"Now," he demands.

I obey him, knowing there's no point in doing anything but what he wants. His house is full of guards. Everyone works for him, and their loyalty is only to him. No one would dare disobey him. And even though I didn't disobey him by leaving, he surely sees it that way.

He leads me up the stairs and puts me in a guest room instead of going to his bedroom. It surprises me. He must be able to tell from my expression.

He chuckles, then seethes, "Ya thought I'd let ya in my bed and give ya the privilege of sleeping with me while that bastard's in your stomach?"

I protectively put my hand over my belly, unsure what to say or what he has planned for me.

He shakes his head and mocks me, "Tsk, tsk, tsk. Lauren, what would your uncle Tommy have said?"

I stay quiet, knowing my uncle Tommy would be just as ruthless as Caleb. Neither man has any heart or soul. I've known that for a long time. And both of them hate the O'Connors more than anything.

"Strip," Caleb demands.

I stand frozen in shock.

"I said to strip. Don't make me say it another time," he warns.

I don't know what else to do. I slowly remove my clothes until I'm in my bra and underwear.

"All of it," he demands, scowling at my belly.

My hands shake so hard I can barely unclasp my bra.

He points to the floor. "Pick up your clothes."

I do as instructed, feeling vulnerable and wishing I could crawl into a hole.

He grabs them from me. "You'll get fresh clothes when you've earned them."

Fresh panic fills me. "What are ya talking about?"

He glances over my body, lingering for too long on my belly, and then locks his eyes with mine. Disgust fills his face. "Like I said, when ya earn clothes, ya can wear them. Till then, ya can be the filthy whore that ya are, and whores don't deserve anything." He leaves the room, taking my clothes with him.

I turn and stare at the bed. It's just a mattress. There are no pillows or blankets. It's the only thing in the room.

I completely break down, sitting on the mattress and sobbing. I don't know how long it lasts, and I try to sleep, but I can't.

When the sun barely peeks over the horizon, I realize no blinds or drapes exist. I go to the window, look down, then step back. Caleb's men stare up at me, and I realize how exposed I am.

I go to the other side of the bed and sit on the floor, not wanting to be anywhere someone might be able to see me. I'm unsure how long I'm in there before the door opens and one of his maids walks in with a tray.

I pull my knees to my chest tighter, trying to cover myself.

She looks at me with disgust. "Caleb says you're a traitor. Why would ya do that? Tommy was your uncle."

"Shut your fucking mouth and mind your own business," I seethe.

She gives me a haughty look. "Don't worry. I serviced him last night for ya."

Does she think I'm going to be jealous? She can service him all she wants. I just glare at her and shake my head. "Ya disgust me."

She scoffs. "No, Lauren. I'd give ya respect and call ya an Ahern, but you're no longer worthy of being Tommy's niece. Here's your food. Caleb said to make sure ya eat it." She leaves it and walks out of the room.

I don't move for a while, then I hear Caleb's voice seemingly come from nowhere. "You've been ordered to eat. I suggest that ya do. And every last bite."

I look around the room and then glance up. In the corner, there's a small speaker and camera. I swallow hard, lift the tray, and gape at the tiny wiener-shaped pieces of meat. The small card states, Squirrel Dick.

I squeeze my eyes shut in disgust. I try to swallow the bile down but can't. I run to the en suite bathroom and throw up in the toilet.

I stay in the bathroom a long time until Caleb's voice orders, "I said to eat it. If ya don't eat it in the next ten minutes, I'm cutting the baby out of ya."

I force myself to get off the cold tile. I go back into the room and stare at the overcooked organ.

There's no way I can eat it.

I have to.

No, I can't.

Caleb's voice booms, "It goes down ya, or I'm cutting the baby out. Last warning. Take your pick, whore."

There's no choice. Caleb doesn't make threats he doesn't follow through on.

Somehow, I force myself to eat the food, swallowing down the bile every time it tries to come back up, until everything is eaten.

"Now go take a shower," Caleb's voice orders the moment I set the fork down.

I obey, happy to escape the empty plate reminding me what I just ate.

I go into the bathroom and scrub my body five times, trying to wash away all the filth Caleb's subjected me to. I've never felt so violated, but nothing helps.

When I finish brushing my teeth, he appears. He holds a towel out for my hair and one for my body. He announces, "There's a dress on the bed. Put it on. Your mum's here."

A burst of hope fills me.

Maybe she can talk sense into Caleb and get me out of here.

What am I thinking?

She will. She's my mum.

I dry off, go into the bedroom, and put on the dress while Caleb's beady eyes watch me. When I'm clothed, he escorts me through the house, down the stairs, and into a sitting room.

My mum's standing at the window. She spins. "Lauren, oh, thank Jesus Caleb found ya."

She runs over and pulls me into her arms, but I shove her back, resisting the urge to hug her. Letting my anger flow, I seethe, "How could ya have told him?"

She stares at me and puts her hand on my cheek. "Why are ya so ungrateful, Lauren? This is who we are. You're meant to be Caleb's wife."

"Mum, ya don't know what you've done."

"I've given ya your birthright. The position will give ya everything ya could ever want in this world."

I scoff. "Are ya kidding me?"

Her eyes darken. "Ya should be grateful. You'll have more than I ever had. More than I could give ya."

Any part of me that thought maybe my mum could help me or that she wouldn't be the one who really did this to me disappears.

How can she care about me when this is now my destiny?

She went against all my wishes, didn't listen, and insisted that Caleb was the one for me, even though I told her all the horrible things he did to me. And now she stands here continuing to believe this is best for me?

I shake my head. "Don't come back here."

Horror fills her face. "What are ya talking about?"

"I want nothing to do with ya."

She stands in shock. "Ya don't know what you're saying, Lauren."

"I do. Now, get out!" I scream, pointing at the door.

She doesn't move.

Caleb claps, laughing. "Bravo. Bravo."

Mum and I turn to him in question.

He states, "Kathleen, ya heard your daughter's wishes. You're no longer welcome in this house."

My mum gapes at him. "Caleb, ya don't mean—"

"Sure, I do. After all, ya told me ya wanted me to be good to your daughter, right? If that's what she wants, that's what she gets."

"I want you to let me go," I declare.

He takes his hand and slaps me.

The sting crawls up my face like it did in the car. I squeeze my eyes shut. My chest tightens and my heart pounds faster.

He grabs my chin and forces me to look at him, warning, "Ya better learn how to respect me. Ya will be my wife, and my wife will never speak to me in that tone. Now get your ass back upstairs and get your clothes off."

Tears fall fast down my cheeks.

He turns toward Mum, stating, "And you..." His smile turns more sinister. He orders, "Don't ever step foot in my house again."

24

Devin

*P*atrol cars are everywhere. Someone called the garda. Every bed-and-breakfast I go to, they're crawling around, so I have to wait for them to leave.

I'm almost to the last place when an ambulance flies past me. Goose bumps break out on my skin, and I follow it.

I park down the street and see caution tape is blocking off the front yard of the bed-and-breakfast. I watch, hoping to spot Lauren, but she never appears.

Instead, an old man on a stretcher and a sobbing woman, who I guess is his wife, get into the ambulance. When it takes off, my gut tells me to follow it, so I do.

I don't know what happened, but surely Caleb's been there. Why else would there be a crime scene?

The ambulance drives fast to a hospital and pulls up to the emergency doors. A staff of medical people rush out and help get the man inside. The woman follows, still distraught.

I park my car and go inside, keeping a low profile, hoping to catch the woman when she leaves the room.

The night turns into morning. I grow antsier, but she finally steps out and walks down the hall to the beverage machine. She slides some coins into the slot for a cup of coffee.

I cautiously approach her, saying, "Ma'am, I don't want to scare ya."

She freezes, and tension mounts in the air between us.

"Ma'am," I restate.

Her shaking hand reaches for the cup of coffee. She takes a sip, then spins toward me. The lines on her face are deep and she looks tired, but something about her also screams that she's kind.

She must know Lauren.

I wait for her to speak, but I'm also suddenly tongue-tied and afraid I'll spook her.

She stares at me and finally asks, "You're him, aren't ya?"

I nod, not knowing what she knows, but state, "If ya mean Devin O'Connor, then yes, I am."

She doesn't look scared but doesn't look comfortable either. Her eyes well with tears, and she blinks so they don't fall. Then her expression turns angry. She seethes, "Did ya come to hurt her too?"

My heart pounds harder. "What did he do to her?"

She swallows harder, informing me, "He took her."

"I need to know what happened."

She studies me further, as if unsure whether she should trust me or not.

I glance behind us, then lower my voice even more. "I know I'm a bad man, but he's worse. And I can assure ya I will not hurt Lauren or her baby."

She stays quiet.

I add in a firm voice, "*My* baby."

Her eyes narrow.

More determined than ever to find her, I add, "If Caleb has her, it's not good. Ya need to tell me everything so I can help her."

The woman's expression shows her helplessness. "We tried to protect her. We did. But he knocked my husband out, and, well..." She turns away, wiping tears off her face.

I wait.

She sniffs hard and lifts her chin, announcing, "He's still not awake." She turns, squeezing her eyes shut as if trying to control her emotions, then her shoulders tremble.

I put my hand on her arm.

She takes a minute, then gives me a hardened look. "What do ya want with her, Devin O'Connor?"

"I want to protect her and my baby."

"How do I know ya don't want to hurt her?"

"I've never tried or wanted to hurt Lauren," I insist.

She doesn't move. I wait for her to speak, trying to gain her trust, not breaking my gaze from hers.

She finally says, "We've always stayed out of trouble. We never wanted anything from the O'Learys or the O'Connors. We just wanted to live our lives in peace. I think that's what Lauren wants too."

My stomach curls. "Ma'am, I assure you I will not hurt Lauren. But if Caleb has her—"

"He does," she interjects, solidifying what I already know. And then she adds, "If ya know he has her, why are ya here?"

It's a good question. I should've gone straight to Dublin. But I admit, "I need to know details in order to rescue her. Is the baby okay? Has Lauren been okay?"

Something passes in the woman's eyes. I don't know what it is. Is it compassion? Pity, maybe? Whatever it is, it quickly disappears. She lifts her chin, straightens her shoulders, and says, "She was fine. But now, that thug has her. And..." She stares at me.

"And what?"

She cautiously declares, "He knows it's not his baby. He knows it's yours."

I jerk my head back, and everything inside me drops. My chest tightens so fast I can barely breathe. "What do ya mean?"

"He knows. He told her he knows," the woman repeats.

I let it sink in, but it's worse than I thought. If Caleb knows it's my child, he'll use the baby to get to me. I question, "You're sure he knows?"

She nods. "Yes. Please don't hurt her."

"I promise ya I will not hurt her," I state again.

She swallows hard. "Then why are ya here? Go find her. She doesn't deserve to be treated the way he'll treat her. He already slapped her once."

Rage fills me. I curl my fists at my side, asking, "When?"

"At our place."

I tighten my fist, wishing Caleb's face was in front of me. I vow, "I will find her. And thank ya, ma'am. Ya will be rewarded for your loyalty to her and my child."

"I don't need to be rewarded. I just want Lauren and your son to be okay," she claims.

I freeze, gaping at her.

She studies me and confirms, "It's a boy."

A chill runs through me. "She's having a boy?"

The woman smiles and tears up again. "Yea."

I take a deep breath and assert, "I'll make sure they're taken care of, I promise."

"Ya better," she warns.

I nod and turn to leave but stop. I spin, adding, "I hope your husband's okay."

Her eyes glisten again. She doesn't say anything and walks away from me back toward the room.

I leave the hospital and pick up the phone, calling Brody.

He answers, "Devin, where are ya? I've been calling ya all night."

I blurt out, "Caleb has Lauren, and he knows it's my baby."

Silence fills the line.

Brody clears his throat. "Where are ya?"

"On my way back. I need as many men as we can get."

"For what?" Brody asks.

"To go to Dublin."

"Ya can't just storm down there," he declares.

"I can and I will," I claim.

"No, we need a plan. The last thing ya want to do is something that gets her or the baby injured."

I snarl, "He's already hurt her. He slapped her. Who knows what else he's done with her?"

Brody sighs. "Devin, get back here. Alaina and I will figure out a plan."

"We don't have time for your plans. I need to get her out of Caleb's control," I insist.

"We have men inside who—"

"Samuel's dead."

"What are ya talking about?" Brody demands.

I pull my phone in front of my face, find the video Caleb sent me, and forward it to my brother. "Watch." A few minutes pass, and I can hear the video playing on the phone.

He stops it and orders, "Ya need to come home. We'll figure out how to retrieve her, but ya can't go down there alone. And we can't send men to meet ya. We need a strong plan so no one gets hurt."

"He has her and my baby," I say again, as if Brody doesn't know.

"Get home. That's an order. Don't ya dare do anything stupid. If ya do, you'll get Lauren and the baby killed. Think before ya do something ya can't undo." He hangs up.

I toss the phone on the seat next to me, frustrated, angry, and annoyed at the world. I debate about what to do.

I drive as far as I can until it's time for me to choose my path. I can continue on to Belfast or go to Dublin. My phone rings. I pick it up.

Alaina commands, "Devin, come back home. Do not go to Dublin. You'll get her killed. I know how my brother works."

"Your brother is a dead man walking," I declare.

"No one wants him dead more than me."

I huff. "That's a big statement to make, Alaina."

She asserts, "We both have our reasons. Now, get home so we can come up with a plan. Otherwise, you're going to get her killed and your baby. Ya don't want that, do ya?"

"Of course I don't."

"Then get home. Don't be stupid, Devin." She hangs up.

I debate some more and almost turn toward Dublin but decide she's right. I can't go in there by myself. I need more than my own manpower, and I don't want to get Lauren or our son killed.

My son. I'm going to have a son.

Caleb's going to be the father over my dead body.

I grip the wheel tighter.

"Why didn't Lauren come to me?" I mutter, asking myself for the millionth time. I would've protected her, would've made sure she and our child were safe.

I slam my hand on the steering wheel, tired and beyond frustrated, wanting nothing more than this situation to end. I want Lauren in my arms and my son to be safe.

I drive as fast as I can, getting back to Belfast, ready to do whatever we need to do to ensure that Caleb never sets eyes on anyone again, much less Lauren and our son.

I go directly to Alaina and Brody's. I pull up, and there's a car I don't recognize. It's nothing fancy, and I wonder who it belongs to.

I step into the house and go directly to Brody's office. I don't knock, just throw open the door. My brother, Alaina, and Kathleen are there.

"What have ya done, ya stupid woman?" I accuse.

Kathleen turns her grim expression on me. "I did what every O'Leary would do."

"And what's that gotten ya? What's that gotten any of us? Your daughter is now in Caleb's hands. Do ya know what you've done?" I shout.

Her face hardens. She turns back to Alaina. "What can I do to make your brother change his mind? Tell me."

Alaina shakes her head, her eyes in slits. "Kathleen, ya know Caleb as well as ya knew Tommy. Ya know how they act. Did ya really think he wouldn't discard ya the moment he could?"

"Discard? What are ya talking about?" I question.

The room goes silent.

Alaina gives me an uncomfortable look.

"What are ya talking about?" I demand again.

She glares at Lauren's mum. "Kathleen went to Caleb's today. Lauren said she didn't want to see her again, and Caleb banned Kathleen."

"Serves ya right," I snarl, ready to show her my wrath. This is all her fault. Caleb would never have known Lauren was pregnant if it weren't for her.

Kathleen huffs. "I don't expect ya to understand."

I seethe, "Ya also told him that it's not his baby, didn't ya?"

Kathleen's head jerks back. "What are ya talking about? Caleb doesn't know it's yours."

"He does," I inform her.

She shakes her head in confusion. "No, that's not right. He thinks it's his baby."

"No, he knows it's mine."

The blood drains from her face. She weakly accuses, "No, he wouldn't have gone to get her if he knew. He wouldn't want her if he knew it was an O'Connor she was carrying."

Spit flies out of my mouth as I snarl, "Are ya ridiculously stupid? Of course he would go get her. Do you not think he would use my child to hold over her head? To hurt her? To hurt me?"

Kathleen swallows hard. "No, he..."

"He knows. It's been confirmed. And it's your fault."

She shakes her head. "I didn't tell him!"

"If you didn't tell, then who did?" Alaina asks.

Confusion fills Kathleen's face.

I press, "Aye. Who would've told Caleb if it wasn't you?"

She shakes her head. "I-I don't know. No one. No one would've told him. No one knew she was pregnant but me."

Alaina asks, "What about the other barmaids? The ones who were there the night that Devin showed up?"

"If ya hadn't stepped foot in my pub, none of this would've happened," Kathleen seethes at me.

"It's no longer your pub," I remind her.

Alaina raises her voice, ordering, "Let's stay on track."

Kathleen agrees, "Yea. This isn't about me. It's about you and what you've done. Remember?"

I bark, "No, it's about what *you've* done."

"Enough! This isn't helping anything," Alaina reprimands. "What about the barmaids? Did they know she was pregnant?"

Kathleen shakes her head. "No, of course not. Nobody knew."

"No one?" I question.

Kathleen insists, "No."

"Then who would've told her?" I ask.

"I don't know. But if Caleb knows..." Kathleen shoots Alaina a helpless and fearful expression.

My gut dives further. "Is there anything else that ya need to tell us before ya let the door hit your ass on the way out?"

Kathleen looks between the three of us, then shakes her head in defeat. "No, but, Alaina, please do what ya can to convince Caleb to let me see my daughter."

I roar, "Why would Alaina convince Caleb of anything? They're not even on the same side anymore. Are ya that daft?"

Alaina interjects, "Devin's right. What were ya thinking, Kathleen?"

Her mum's hardened expression breaks. She starts to sob. "He told me he would care for both of us."

"And ya believed him?" Alaina questions. "Ya know how he is. Why would ya ever believe anything that he says? He's full of lies."

Her mum just cries quietly.

"If there's nothing else ya have to add to this, get out of here," I order.

Her eyes dart between Alaina and me.

I assert firmer, "I said get out. You're not welcome here."

Kathleen finally caves and quietly walks past me, not saying a word.

"One more thing," I call out.

She spins and arches her eyebrows.

"If anything happens to my son or Lauren, you're the one who's going to pay for it."

25

Lauren
Three Weeks Later

"*P*ush. Come on, Lauren, you can do it," the doctor encourages.

More pain fills me. I've been in labor for the last twenty-four hours and never felt so tired or hurt so badly.

"One more," the doctor claims.

Another cramp hits me, and I push with everything I have, screaming in pain.

"Again!" he orders.

Tears drip off my chin, and I cry out, "I can't!"

"Ya can! Now do it," the doctor commands.

A nurse holds my hand. She's the only other person in the room and adds, "Last one. Almost there, Mum."

"It hurts. I can't breathe. I... Oh Jesus." I moan as more pain fills me.

"Push, push, push," the doctor yells.

Somehow, I manage to do it. I swear a watermelon passes through my lower bits, almost making me pass out. Then a wail rings through the air.

"It's a boy," the doctor proclaims, holding up the baby.

His cries intensify.

I stare at him, muttering in awe, "He's so tiny."

"He's at least seven pounds," the doctor claims.

I hold my arms out. "Give him to me."

The nurse strokes my head. "Shush, now. We have to clean him up."

"Just give him to me," I repeat, afraid they'll take him from me. All I've heard in the last few weeks since Caleb kidnapped me is his threats. Over and over, he used the baby to scare me.

After a week, he finally gave me clothes and let me move around the house. But it was false freedom. He never lets me forget he can hurt me or my child.

"Shush now." The nurse grabs the baby from the doctor.

He pats my ankle, asserting, "Ya did good. Now, hold still. I have to sew ya up."

"Please give me my baby," I beg, fearful I'll never see him again.

The nurse moves over to the side of the room, stating, "He's right here. Don't worry, dear." She moves in front of my son so I can't see him.

He continues to cry, and it feels like forever that I'm in stirrups with the doctor sewing me up.

The nurse finally brings the baby over, all cleaned up.

When she hands him to me, he curls into my chest, still crying.

"Shh," I tell him, trying to calm him. I stroke his head and stare at the red hair, amazed he's finally here. I count his little fingers and toes. He tries to find my breast and immediately does.

"Oh, he's hungry." The nurse laughs as the doctor leaves the room.

The baby takes to my breast and starts feeding.

The nurse places a blanket over him, asking, "Ya know what you're going to name him?"

"Caleb Junior," Caleb booms, appearing in the doorway.

A shiver runs through me. I can't imagine calling my baby Caleb. Yet I don't really have a choice.

"He's beautiful. Ya did well, sir. Looks just like his dad." The nurse beams.

I almost tell her he looks nothing like Caleb. He looks like his real father, Devin. I see it in my baby's nose, cheekbones, and jawline. He hasn't opened his eyes yet, so I don't know what color they are, but I know he resembles his father.

I hug my son tighter, afraid Caleb will grab him from me and disappear, just like he's threatened so many times.

Instead, Caleb comes closer and orders the nurse, "Ya can leave the room now."

"Oh, sure," she says and quickly scurries away.

I don't loosen my grip on my son and meet Caleb's eyes.

He leans down and murmurs in my ear, "Little Caleb sure seems hungry. But so is Daddy."

A new chill flies down my spine.

He adds, "As soon as the doctor gives the okay, you're moving into my bedroom."

Horror fills me. I knew the day was coming. I stay quiet, knowing it's pointless to fight.

Caleb rises and stares at me. "Ya really do look a mess. Ya should clean yourself up." He turns and walks away.

I try not to cry. I'm tired of being emotional, but I can't help it. I hug my son tighter, watching him feed.

He eventually moves to the other breast, and the same thoughts I always have go through my mind.

Why didn't I go to Devin?

The O'Connors would have taken the baby.

They wouldn't have. Would they?

Regardless, I can't dwell on it. I made my choices, and now I'm here. The only thing I can do now is everything in my power to protect my son. Caleb's going to use him as a weapon. I know he will. He's pretty much told me so, and I hate it. I hate myself for being so cowardly that I stayed in Ireland. I should have left the country.

I scold myself for what I should have or could have done. Then I think about Annie and Dominick, and another wave of sadness passes me.

I never stop wondering if Caleb killed Dominick. I hope he's okay, but I also know he might have permanent damage from Caleb's blow.

Then I think about how excited they were about the baby. I glance at my son, and it all makes me more emotional, remembering how they were willing to welcome him as a grandchild with open arms. All the kindness they showed me was in vain. It only wreaked havoc over their household.

My son looks up and coos.

It pulls me out of my thoughts. I look down, whispering, "Hey, sweetie."

He opens his eyes, and they're as green as Devin's, making me emotional again.

I try to pull it together and kiss my son's head. I vow, "Hi, sweetie. I promise I'll take care of you."

It seems to appease my baby. He puts his head back between my breasts, as if tired, and closes his eyes.

I don't know how long I'm there, stroking his head, trying to fight sleep, afraid that somebody will come in and take my son from me the moment I do.

It's well past midnight, and besides the nurse who comes in to check on us every so often, no one else has been around. Every few hours, I doze off slightly, but my son is always there, hungry, wanting to feed, and I can't help but smile.

Seeing so much of Devin in him makes me sad and happy, but I also know Caleb will probably see it. At some point, he'll hate it.

I have to figure out how to escape him.

My worries never fade. My fears of waking up without my son never do either, and it's well into the next morning when there's a knock on my door.

I'm exhausted. I look over, and Maeve is standing in the doorway with a bunch of flowers.

I seethe, "What are ya doing here?"

Her eyes widen. She asks, "Can I come in?"

I don't say anything.

She steps inside, shuts the door, walks over, and puts the flowers on the table.

"I asked ya what you're doing here," I snap.

She furrows her eyebrows. "I came to see the baby. Caleb said it would be okay."

"Ya sure are buddy-buddy with Caleb, aren't ya?" I accuse.

Her face falls. "No, I'm not. Nor do I want to be buddy-buddy with him."

"Sure could have fooled me."

She glances between my son and my face in confusion.

I grip my son tighter, warning, "Don't touch him."

She holds her hands in the air. "Okay. I really did come to see how ya were doing."

"Why do ya care? Ya didn't seem to care when ya told Caleb where I was, now did ya?"

Guilt fills her face.

I lash out some more. "Ya even told him that my child wasn't his. Now he's using that information as a weapon against me. Are ya happy?"

She glances behind her, but the door is still shut. She looks back and shakes her head. "No, Lauren, I'm not happy. Do ya think I had a choice?"

"Ya always have a choice," I declare.

She takes a deep breath and shuts her eyes, shaking her head. "No, I didn't. He was going to kill my father."

"So ya threw me and my unborn baby under the bus?"

She squeezes her eyes shut, begging, "Please, ya have to understand. My da owed a debt that he couldn't pay. He really was going to kill him."

I huff. "Your father made a debt he couldn't pay. He should have dealt with the consequences. Instead, you made me and my baby deal with them. I hope you're proud of yourself."

She steps closer. "Lauren, please. I didn't mean to harm ya. I really didn't. I just... I didn't know what to do. It was my father. It was the only way I could save him."

I stare at her, with more hatred filling me. I'll never forgive her. How can I? She might have killed Dominick. She could have killed Annie. She could have killed me and my baby. It could still happen because of whose control we're under now.

She swallows hard. "I want to help ya, Lauren."

I scoff. "Help me? How exactly are ya going to help me? Are you going to get me out of the prison I'm now in for the rest of my life? Or are ya going to try to take my son from me the way everyone else wants to?"

She wrinkles her forehead. "No, of course I don't want to do that. I would never try to harm you or your baby."

"Really? That's not very convincing after what ya did."

"Please. Ya have to understand," she pleads.

My son starts to whine, and I move him over to my breast. He immediately begins to feed, and I hold him tighter, threatening, "Don't ya dare come near my son ever again. If ya do, I'll kill ya!"

"Lauren, I promise you, I will try to make this better."

"Ya can't make this better. Do ya not get that? I know you're young, but you're not stupid, Maeve. Ya understand the ways of Caleb and how this works. Ya know how evil he is and that he would show me and my son no mercy."

Tears well in her eyes. "I'm sorry! I never meant to harm ya!"

I lash out, "Ya didn't just tell him where I was. Ya told him my baby wasn't his."

"I told him it wasn't his because I thought he wouldn't come after ya," she blurts out.

I sarcastically laugh, then hurl out, "Ya seriously thought he would just forget about me? That he wouldn't come after me, especially knowing that I slept with his enemy and was impregnated with his baby? Ya didn't think he'd use that against me just for his own sick pleasure?"

She bites her lip, looking defeated.

I almost feel sorry for her. Almost. Then I remember what she's done.

She lifts her chin and squares her shoulders. "I promise ya I will help ya take care of this."

"How? How are ya going to help me, Maeve?"

"I'll talk to Devin. I'll find him."

"For what purpose? So the O'Connors can take my baby?"

She gives me a confused look. "Do ya really believe they'll take your baby?"

"Yes. No. I don't know. But ya can't just walk up to the O'Connors and talk to Devin. Is that what ya think you're going to do?"

Wrinkles form on her forehead. "I... Well... I know Alaina. I could go talk to her. She'll help us."

I laugh again. "She's an O'Connor now. We're O'Learys. Have ya forgotten that?"

"No, but she's not heartless."

"Sure she is. She's Alaina O'Connor. Jesus, ya really are naïve, Maeve."

Her face flushes. She lowers her voice, and hurt fills it. "I only wanted to save my father. I really do want to help ya. I didn't mean to put ya in any bad position."

I stare at her, feeling so many emotions that should only be directed at Caleb, but I can't forgive her for what she's done. I understand her father was in a bad position, but he made his own bed. She should have let him sleep in it and left me and my son out of it.

She adds, "I'll go tell Devin. I promise ya, he'll help ya. He has to. It's his son."

My eyes fill with tears. "Don't ya get it, Maeve?"

She stays quiet.

I continue, "Nobody can help me. Devin can't help me. I'm Caleb's prisoner. For the rest of my life, I will be his prisoner. And every waking moment, all I will do is try to protect my baby. The one he knows isn't his child but his enemy's. And he'll do everything in his power to use my son as a weapon for some sick, twisted game of revenge he has against Devin and the O'Connors. And ya helped do this."

A tear falls down her cheek. She swipes at it. "I'm sorry. I really am."

I seethe, "Tell it to my son."

She glances at the baby, opens her mouth, then snaps it shut.

"What, there's nothing else ya want to say?" I goad in anger.

She waits a moment. Intense silence fills the air. She finally just states, "I really am sorry, Lauren. Your baby is beautiful." She turns, walks out, and shuts the door.

My insides quiver harder.

My son looks up and whimpers.

"Hey, there. What's wrong, sweetie?" I ask, stroking his head and giving him another kiss. It takes a moment for me to get him settled in my arms, but he finally does.

As much as I wish I could forgive Maeve or forget what she did, I can't. And part of me thinks maybe I should have let her go to the O'Connors, but it's just asking for more trouble.

They can't do anything.

I'm Caleb's now.

Anything Devin tries will only make things worse. This is my fate.

Now, my only goal in life is to protect my son.

26

Devin
One Month Later

*B*rody scrubs his face, asking, "What do ya mean, we lost the last one?"

Alaina relays, "They killed him. We have no more men inside right now."

I bark, "How could ya have let this happen?"

She shakes her head. "Come on, Devin. I know you're upset, but—"

The anger I've been holding inside me for too long explodes. "He has my son! He's telling the world my blood is his! And the mother of my child is his hostage. What part about this do ya two not get?"

Brody crosses his arms. "Let's not get into this again. Ya know we understand what's happening."

I point to Alaina's now empty gut. "If it were your child—"

"Leave Caireann out of this," Brody snarls, curling his fists at his sides.

Alaina shoots daggers at me with her eyes.

Tense silence fills the room.

I love my niece, but whenever I look at my brother or Alaina holding her, it's another reminder my son isn't with me.

Alaina's expression softens. She asserts, "Let's all stay focused."

I grumble, "We shouldn't have no men inside their clan. We've had no issues infiltrating them in the past. Caleb isn't smart, so how is he finding out who our men are? Somebody's a snitch."

"I agree. Ya two have dropped the ball," Tynan declares, walking into the room.

"Nobody asked your opinion," Brody barks.

Aidan steps into the room behind my brother, his voice booming, "There's something you need to know, Devin."

The hairs on my neck rise. "What?"

He fidgets with his lighter, letting the flame ignite, informing me, "Scarlet just told me she saw one of the O'Leary lasses."

"So?" I question.

He glances at the flame, letting it burn longer than anyone else would, declaring, "Scarlet claims the lass knows information about Lauren and your son."

I step closer. "Who is she?"

"Someone named Maeve."

"Maeve? Why did she come into Belfast?" Alaina asks in surprise.

"What do ya know about her?" I ask, wanting more details about this woman.

"Her father works for the O'Learys. He's a big-time gambler, always running from his debts and then figuring out how to make more," Alaina says.

"What did she tell Scarlet?" I ask.

Aidan flicks his lighter again, and a new flame erupts. "She didn't say much. She insisted she needs to meet with ya and has information about what Caleb's planning."

My stomach churns. I try to push all the bad thoughts about what he might do to Lauren and my son out of my mind. I demand, "Where is she?"

Aidan hands me a piece of paper. "She gave that to Scarlet. She told her ya need to meet her there alone at eight tonight."

I open the paper and look at it. It's a pub in a bad area of town. It's an O'Connor pub, but no one I know ever drinks there. I ask, "Why'd she pick this place?"

Aidan shrugs.

"It's probably a trap," Tynan states.

"Good. You're coming with me, then."

He groans. "Seriously? I have a date tonight."

"I don't give a shit about your date. My son and my woman are in Caleb's hands. What part of this don't ya understand?"

He shakes his head. "Of course ya don't care. Another night lost for me."

"You're such a selfish bastard. It's your nephew," I remind him.

"*I'm* selfish? You're the one who's stopping me from getting pussy."

"Jesus. Really, Tynan!" Alaina reprimands.

"You're such a dick," I mumble, brushing past him.

"Spoken from the king himself," he mutters.

I glance at my watch. There's only a half hour until it's time to meet this girl. I ask, "Scarlet thinks this is legit?"

"Aye, she does," Aidan confirms.

"Let's go, Tynan."

Aidan calls out, "I'll follow you, just to make sure."

For the millionth time, my hope ignites. I try to shut it down, but all I can see in my mind is Lauren and our child.

I've seen pictures of him. Caleb's been releasing photos online, touting him as his. It only makes the situation worse.

I never thought I wanted kids, but all I want to do is hold him and Lauren and know that they're safe and away from Caleb forever. Whenever I think I'm going to get that and then fall short, it deepens my craving to the point it's painful.

Tynan's car is in front of mine. He slides in his driver's seat, and I get into the passenger side. We make our way through town, barely speaking. When we pull up to the pub, I direct him to pull into the alley.

We wait until it's almost eight o'clock and then I tell him, "Make sure ya shut your mouth. I'll do the talking."

345

"Whatever. Just hurry it up. I still want to go out tonight."

I refrain from smacking him. I need to focus, so I enter the pub from the back door. It's dark and reeks of stale alcohol, cigarettes, and cigar smoke.

I glance around, my eyes adjusting to the dim light. All I see are men, except for the shadow of a person in a hoodie in a back corner booth. I mumble to Tynan, "I think that's her."

He doesn't say anything and follows me to the booth. I slide across from the woman, and Tynan sits next to her.

Her eyes widen as they dart between my brother and me.

Out of the corner of my eye, I see Aidan step inside and sit at the bar where he can view the entire room. I lean closer to the young woman. "Assuming you're Maeve?"

Her lip trembles, as does her voice. She nods, confirming, "Yea."

"Well, we don't have all day. Spit it out, lass," Tynan demands.

I kick him under the table.

He grunts.

The fear in Maeve's expression grows.

Tynan eyes her over, adding, "Ya are a pretty thing, for an O'Leary."

"Shut up, Tynan," I warn.

He keeps his focus on Maeve.

Even though my insides are boiling over, I calm my voice, asserting, "It's okay, lass. Just tell us what ya know."

She takes a deep breath and relays, "I have information about Lauren." She glances at Tynan and then focuses on me. "You're Devin, right?"

"Aye."

"So ya know it's your son, right?"

More rage flares in me. "Of course I do, lass. Now spit out whatever it is ya know."

She blurts out, "Lauren doesn't want me to tell ya anything."

Hurt and confusion fill me. Surely she doesn't want to stay with Caleb? Or does she?

I question, "Why? She doesn't want to be saved?"

Maeve shakes her head. "She thinks it'll make it worse. That there's no saving her and her son. Is that true, or do ya think you can?"

My mouth turns dry. I tap my finger on the table and lower my voice. "Come hell or high water, I will get possession of my son and Lauren. So whatever it is ya know, ya need to tell me."

"Will ya take the baby from her?"

I stiffen. "Is that what she thinks?"

"Her mum told her that."

"So? Her mum's the same evil bitch who told Caleb she was pregnant."

Maeve asks, "So ya won't take her son from her?"

"Ya mean *my* son?"

Maeve's face darkens.

Tynan puts his hand over Maeve's.

She inhales sharply and refocuses on him.

He claims, "Lass, no one in our clan is taking her baby from her. Now tell us what ya know. Time's ticking."

Maeve pulls her hand out from under his and glances behind her. Then she looks back at me, admitting, "I overheard my father talking to Caleb's men."

"And?" Tynan prods.

"He's going to force Lauren to marry him."

Horror fills me. It's not the first time an O'Leary has forced someone down the aisle. Scarlet's only with Aidan because she was forced to marry Tommy and he rescued her.

My gut churns faster. Who knows what Caleb's threatening to do to the baby. And I know what happens to those women. They have no choice in the ceremony and how other men will speak for them during their vows.

I swallow the bile moving up my throat, demanding, "Where?"

Maeve slides a piece of paper across the table. "The details are all here. You'll help her, right?"

"It's probably a trap," Tynan states.

Maeve glares at him and seethes, "It's not a trap."

"Sure it's not," Tynan adds.

She questions, "Why would I want to trap ya?"

"You're an O'Leary," Tynan says in disgust.

She blinks hard and looks down. "I promised Lauren I would help her, even though she doesn't want my help."

My brother is right in some ways. She is an O'Leary. So why is she here? So I question, "Now, why would ya do that, lass, when you're an O'Leary?"

It takes a moment for Maeve to look up, and regret and guilt swirl on her face. "I did something bad."

I curl my fist under the table. "What was that?"

Her lip quivers harder. She opens and shuts her mouth, squeezing her eyes so tight wrinkles form at the corners.

"Tell me," I demand.

She finally opens her eyes, locking them on mine. "Caleb was going to kill my father. He gambled more money than he had. And I knew where Lauren was."

"How did you know?" I question.

"I was at the bed-and-breakfast. It was just a coincidence. She made me promise her I wouldn't tell anyone. But I didn't know how else to save my father."

Tynan whistles. "So you ratted her out? Nice friend ya are."

"I didn't have a choice," Maeve declares.

"Ya always have a choice. Ya should learn that," Tynan claims.

"Shut up," I order, giving him a warning look.

He shakes his head in annoyance.

I refocus on Maeve. "So you're how Caleb found her?"

She looks ashamed but nods. "Yea. And I'm sorry. I just want to make it right. I didn't want my dad to die, and I didn't want to hurt Lauren or the baby, but I didn't know what to do."

I ask what I hope is a no. "Has he hurt the baby?"

Maeve shakes her head. "Not that I'm aware of."

"And Lauren? What has he done to her?" I ask, fearful of so many things.

And it hits me how much I want Lauren as mine. How much it's been bugging me that she's not with me and I haven't protected her.

Maeve swallows hard. "She's okay right now, but he's going to force her to marry him. I-I thought maybe ya could stop it."

I take the piece of paper and glance at it. Then I slide it into my pocket. "How do I know you're telling the truth?"

"I am telling the truth. Why else would I come here and risk my life?"

"Because ya want to trap us," Tynan repeats.

I slap the back of my hand on his thigh. He shuts his mouth.

Maeve glares at him again and insists, "I'm not trying to trap ya. I'm just trying to help ya so that Lauren and the baby can escape Caleb's claws."

My stomach flips. "I'll tell ya what. I'll do what I can. However, if this is a trap, I guarantee ya that ya will pay for it with your and your father's lives. Do ya understand me?"

"I'm not lying. I just want Lauren and the baby to be safe. It's the least I can do after what I did."

"Now you have a conscience," Tynan taunts.

Maeve's face turns red.

"Get up," I order my brother.

He slides out of the booth.

I follow, rising, then I put my hands on the table and lean down. I threaten, "Don't go too far, Maeve. Remember, if anything is false about this information ya gave me, or if this is a trap, my people will find ya. Any wish to be happy you're on this earth will vanish. Do ya understand me?"

She nods.

I take my phone out and demand, "Now, tell me your phone number."

She scrunches her face. "Why?"

"Your job isn't to ask why," I warn.

She hesitates and then rattles it off.

I program it into my mobile, pat her shoulder, then leave. I get into the car.

Tynan follows, whistling. "She's a looker."

"You're such an asshole. What the fuck is your problem?" I bark out as he starts the engine.

He grunts. "I didn't say anything that's not true. This could totally be a trap."

He's right. I know he's right, but I won't give it to him. I just declare, "It's not a trap."

"How do ya know?"

"I just know. I can feel it."

He snorts and pulls out of the alley. "Sure. Just like all the previous false information ya got that sent ya on those dozens of trips ya made to find Lauren."

"This is different," I declare.

"Is it?"

"Aye. And why wouldn't Caleb make her marry him? It makes total sense."

Tynan shrugs. "I don't know. Where do ya want me to drop ya off? Your place or back at Brody's?"

"Brody's," I answer.

"Sucker for punishment, huh?" he asks.

I groan. "God, ya need to grow up."

"Whatever."

I add, "The only thing we're focusing on between now and Saturday is ensuring I have anything I need to rescue Lauren and my son. Don't go too far, Tynan. You're going to be part of this."

"Of course I am," he grumbles and speeds up.

I sit back, drumming my fingers on my thigh, feeling more antsy than I've felt in a long time.

Is this really it? Am I finally going to get my woman and baby back where they belong?

I have to kill Caleb.

It's got to be part of the plan, but I've got to make sure she and the baby are safe first.

A million thoughts go through my mind in a debate about the logistics to make this happen. When Tynan finally pulls into Brody's driveway, I get out of the car.

One thing is clear as I climb up the steps to the house. Come Saturday, I will have Lauren back in my arms as well as my son.

27

Lauren

"There we go. Ya look like a bride now." Stella, the maid who hates me and sleeps with Caleb all the time, smirks, pushing the final pin into my hair to attach my veil.

I stare at my reflection in the mirror, feeling sick. There's no choice. I have to marry Caleb. He already warned me that if I don't say my vows and someone else has to for me, that I'll never see my son again.

Stella adds, "Don't worry, ya won't be the only one servicing him."

I shoot her a look. The thought of touching Caleb makes me ill. So far, he's not touched me in that way. But he already told me he's saving it for after our ceremony. I seethe, "You're disgusting."

"At least I know where my loyalty lies."

"Get out of here," I say to her.

She gives me another nasty yet haughty look and leaves.

I go over to the bassinet and pick up my son. "Hey, sweetie."

He looks at me, and my heart swoons. He's the only thing that holds me together. But I still can't look at him and not think of Devin.

I add, "Hey, baby, we have to be strong today, okay?"

He tilts his head, peering at me.

I coo, "Look at ya all dressed up, handsome man." I lean closer and whisper, "Your real da would love to see ya, I bet."

He tugs on his onesie tux.

I kiss his cheek and add, "I need ya to be a good little lad at the ceremony today. Okay?"

He snuggles into my neck.

I hug him tighter, wishing today wasn't happening but knowing I need to get through it.

The door opens, and Caleb's voice booms, "There's my bride!"

My skin crawls, and I spin to face him. I point at Maeve and question, "What's she doing here?"

Caleb taunts, "Now, is that any way to treat your new nanny?"

I gape and hold my son tighter. "Nanny? I don't need a nanny. And she's not touching my child."

"*Your* child? Don't ya mean *our* child?" he asks, arching his eyebrows, challenging me.

I step back, repeating, "She's not touching him."

"She's the new nanny, and ya will hand over Caleb Jr. to her."

I cringe inside whenever he says Caleb Jr., but I'm also dying. No one has touched my baby except me unless I was in the room and Caleb forced me to allow it.

I state, "She doesn't even have any qualifications."

"And how would ya know that?" Caleb questions.

Maeve gives me a pleading look, but I won't back down. I won't forgive her for what she did, and I won't have her in charge of my child if I can help it.

Caleb's sinister grin grows. He declares, "I'll leave you two, so Maeve can get acquainted with the baby."

"She's not touching him," I insist again.

Caleb crosses his arms. "Is this going to be the day?"

I bite my lip and look away, squeezing my son tighter. He says it all the time, meaning is this going to be the day my son is taken from me and I never see him again.

"I asked ya a question. I expect an answer," he declares.

I sigh and force myself to look at him, which he requires. To appease him, I state, "No, it's fine. Everything's fine."

"Good. I'll see you at the church."

He shuts the door, and I glare at Maeve, snarling, "How dare ya?"

She holds her hands in the air. "Lauren, I'm not here to hurt ya or your son."

She looks behind her to double-check that the door is shut and then steps closer.

I retreat until there's nowhere to go and I'm against the window.

She quietly says, "There are cameras. Give me the baby, and we can talk."

I glance up at the ceiling and realize there's no other choice. I warn, "If ya hurt him—"

"I would never hurt Caleb Jr."

I want to tell her not to call him that, but I know all my words are being monitored.

I kiss my son and begrudgingly hand him to her, feeling like my entire world's about to implode. My voice shakes, and I plead, "Please make sure he's taken care of. Do not let them take him from me." I start to cry.

She grabs the baby, puts him on her hip, then grabs a tissue. She hands it to me and states, "Lauren, don't cry. Your makeup will run."

She's right. Nothing but perfection's acceptable for Caleb. I take the tissue and dab at my tears.

She vows, "I promise ya I'll take great care of him. Everything will be fine. You'll see."

"Everything will be fine?" I sarcastically laugh. "Yea, thanks to ya, everything will be fine."

Hurt and guilt fill her face.

I don't care. Until the day I die, I'll never forgive her for what she did. I'm in this situation because of her. I could be with Annie and Dominick right now, having my baby and me loved and cared for. Instead, I'm here, scared every moment of every day that I'll have my son taken from me, never to see him again. On top of that, I'm dealing with Caleb's abuse.

Maeve says in what should be a reassuring voice but doesn't make me feel it, "Lauren, ya look beautiful. Trust me, everything will be fine."

"Don't tell me to trust ya," I seethe and then turn in the mirror. I wipe a bit of mascara from under my eye to ensure I look presentable, according to Caleb.

There's a knock on the door, and it opens. One of Caleb's men announces, "It's time to go."

I take a deep breath and hold my hands out to Maeve.

"Let me see my son again."

She hands him to me.

I hug and kiss him, willing myself not to break down and praying that he'll be in my arms once today is over. I whisper in his ear, "Be a good boy today, okay?"

"We need to go now," Caleb's man repeats.

Maeve holds her hands out.

I hesitate but hand my son to her.

We walk through the mansion, down the staircase, and every step feels like I'm approaching my death. We step outside, get into the limo, and I take my son from Maeve.

The driver heads toward the church. It's the one all the heads of the O'Learys are married in. It's the place where women have been forced to say vows. It's a building I never wanted to step foot in, in the position I find myself. Today I will have to willingly say vows and do what I can to keep my son.

The ride goes too quickly. At every traffic light, I will it to turn red, but it doesn't. I'm soon standing outside the church.

I hand Maeve my son, warning, "Ya better take care of him."

"I will," she confidently declares, then adds, "Stop worrying, please."

Stop worrying? I'll never stop worrying, I say to myself, glaring at her.

We walk side by side into the church, and I swallow bile, feeling sick, trying to focus on my son. The moment we get inside, music starts to play.

Maeve's ordered to go to the front of the church and sit in a pew. The doors shut, and she disappears with my baby.

Anxiety spins to the depths of my soul. I blink hard to not cry.

When the doors open again, I step past them and cringe.

There are only six people in attendance. Caleb, his two brothers, Maeve, my baby, and the priest.

I swallow hard, and my knees wobble as "The Wedding March" plays. Somehow, I force myself down the aisle, trying to stay confident and keep my eyes locked on Caleb's so I don't upset him. He's warned me too many times that if I do anything to embarrass him, my son will pay the price.

When I reach the front, he takes my hands, and the sick feeling in my stomach grows. I know what's to come later tonight, which adds to my panic and fear.

My son starts to whine, and Caleb turns, shooting him a dirty look. He orders Maeve, "Shut him up!"

I turn as well, and a tear escapes. I wipe it before Caleb sees it.

Maeve holds my son close to her, cooing, trying to shush him.

I offer, "He's probably hungry."

Caleb snarls, "Didn't ya feed him before ya came?"

"Yes, but he's growing."

Caleb glowers at me.

The priest clears his throat. "Are we ready to begin?"

Caleb turns to him. "Aye. Ya may."

The tremor in my hands grows worse, even though Caleb squeezes them tighter. I barely hear the priest or Caleb as he says his vows. I watch his mouth forming the words, but everything feels like I'm in a tunnel, and I don't know how I'll repeat the same things to him.

It comes time for my vows, and the priest touches my shoulder. "Lauren?"

I snap out of it. "Yes, I'm ready," I assert, not wanting to harm my baby, knowing there's no getting out of this. So I stand taller, straightening my shoulders, lifting my chin, and focusing on the priest.

He booms, "Repeat after me. I, Lauren Byrne, take you, Caleb O'Leary..."

My voice comes out barely audible as I repeat the words.

Caleb scowls in disapproval.

I clear my throat, claiming, "Sorry, I have a lump in my throat," and then repeat the phrase.

The priest continues, "Take you, Caleb O'Leary, to be my forever husband."

My chest tightens, and the air in my lungs feels stale. I repeat the words, "Take you—"

The lights go out.

Caleb releases me, shouting, "What the fuck is happening?"

I step back and immediately look toward where Maeve and the baby are, but everything is pitch black. I back away from Caleb.

He and his brothers shout, and somebody grabs me. I scream, but they put their hand over my mouth. I'm dragged through the church while listening to my son's wails.

The boom of a gun being fired echoes through the church, and I scream, but the hand is still over my mouth, muffling the sound. Something's familiar about the arms around me and the person's scent.

It's Devin.

It can't be. My mind's playing tricks on me.

Confused, I'm led through the church halls, out the door, and shoved into a car so fast I can't register what's happening until it pulls away. It takes me a moment to realize I'm staring at Devin.

It's like he's a ghost. I never thought I would see him again. Never thought I would feel him or be this close, but all my internal alarm bells are going off.

I cry out, "My baby! Maeve has my baby. Please, ya have to find her. Go back. I have to get our baby. It's yours."

"Shh," Devin says and tugs me into his chest. "I know, angel."

Angel. How long has it been since I've heard that?

I push away from him. "Devin, Maeve has the baby. We have to get our son. Ya have a son."

He puts both hands on my cheeks. "I know, Lauren. Don't worry. It's fine."

"It's not fine. She has the baby. We're in the car, and she has the baby. Go back," I hysterically beg.

"She's bringing the baby to us. Don't worry."

"What? She can't. She's an O'Leary under Caleb's command. What are ya doing? Our son will get killed!"

"She came to me so we could rescue both of ya. Just trust me. Our son will be back in your arms. I promise ya."

I insist, "He'll die. She's how Caleb ended up finding me. Ya have to trust me on this, Devin. Please go back. I need to get our son."

"Lauren, she's bringing our son to us. I promise ya."

"Devin, please. Ya don't understand the stuff Caleb has threatened to do to him. Please. We'll never see him if we don't go back."

He declares, "We can't go back, angel. But I promise ya, she's bringing him."

"I don't trust her. What about this do ya not understand? Go back," I cry out.

"Trust *me*," he says.

But I can't. My baby isn't in front of me. So I push at him. "Please. It's your son. Do ya not understand?"

"Lauren, you're hysterical right now. You've got to calm down."

"Don't tell me to calm down."

"Listen, angel, ya have to take a breather. She's bringing the baby."

"Then call her right now," I order.

He shakes his head. "There's no contact. Ya have to trust me. She's bringing us the baby."

I continue to fret the entire way to Belfast. The driver speeds down the road. Cars are cut off. Horns blare. A few accidents happen, but we make it in record time and then pull up to a huge mansion.

"Where are we?" I question.

"We're at Alaina and Brody's."

New panic erupts. "Alaina?"

Devin nods. "Aye. She's waiting for us and the baby. Don't worry. Everything will be fine. Ya will have our son in your arms again soon."

I stare at him in horror.

Whoever was driving gets out and slams the door. Neither of us move for a moment.

Devin puts his hands on my cheeks again. "I've missed ya, angel. So much."

Tears just fall down my face. I've missed him more than anything. Yet all I can think about is our baby. "Devin, please. We have to get our son back."

He tries to reassure me again. "Everything's going to be fine. You're never going to have to hide anything again. Okay? I'm going to protect ya and our son. I promise ya."

They're the words I dreamed of hearing, but they don't calm me. I blurt out, "But Alaina will take the baby too."

"No, she will not take the baby. It is *our* baby. My baby as much as yours. She would never do that."

"But my mum—"

"Your mum's an evil woman. She never deserved ya or loved ya the way she should have."

I confess, "She told me ya would take the baby. That the O'Connors would, and that's why I didn't tell ya."

"Shh." He pulls me into him. "Everything's going to be fine. I promise ya, no one's taking the baby."

Fresh tears fill my eyes. "But where is he?"

Devin keeps his voice low, claiming, "Maeve has him. She's bringing him. Just calm down, angel. Calm down."

I can't stop sobbing into his chest.

At some point, he gets out of the car, pulls me with him, and leads me into the house and to a sitting room.

Alaina comes in, and there's a mix of happiness to see her—from old memories—and fear. It's like she can sense it. She stands a good distance away and holds her hands up. "I'm not here to hurt ya, Lauren. We're here to protect ya. I promise."

"Where's my baby?" is all I can ask.

"He's on his way. Don't worry."

"Ya can't trust Maeve."

"We can, and we have. She's bringing your son," Alaina calmly states.

Devin tugs me closer and kisses my head. He repeats, "Everything's fine, angel. Just take a breather."

I push away from him. "Do not tell me to take a breather. Until my son is in my sight and in my arms, I will not take a breather. Do not tell me that."

He sighs. "Okay."

I order, "Get Maeve on the phone. I want to talk to her. Get her on the phone *now*."

He shakes his head. "Angel, we can't. I told ya there are no phones on this one."

"Why are there no phones?"

He answers, "Because she didn't want Caleb to take it and see our messages. Ya have to trust that she's coming."

I question, "Is one of your people following her or with her?"

His face hardens. "No. She slipped out a different door. But trust me, she's coming."

"She's not, and you're never going to meet your son," I warn and sob again, feeling like my entire world's crumbling and my worst nightmare has just come true.

28

Devin
The Next Day

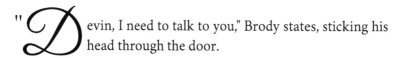

"*D*evin, I need to talk to you," Brody states, sticking his head through the door.

My gut falls. Something is wrong. I can tell by his expression. I stay calm and kiss Lauren on the forehead. "Angel, everything will be okay. Trust me. I'll be right back."

"No, don't go," she begs, gripping my hand.

Alaina sits down next to her and puts her hand on her thigh. "Lauren, let him go. Something's come up that he needs to deal with, but I'm right here."

Lauren turns to her. "But ya want to take my baby."

Alaina shakes her head, reiterating the same thing we've told her since she arrived. "No, Lauren. I would never take your baby, and it's Devin's baby too. I would never do that to either of ya. It's *your* baby. Ya will be the only one raising your baby."

Lauren's eyes tear up and she looks at her lap, twisting her fingers together.

Alaina grabs her hand, ordering, "Devin, go. I'll stay with Lauren."

"Maeve can't be trusted. You're all disillusioned," Lauren mutters.

I can't blame her after what Maeve did to her. I understand why she's paranoid. God only knows what Caleb has put her through.

"She's bringing the baby," Alaina calmly states again.

I rise, declaring, "I'll be right back." I step into the hallway and shut the door.

Brody's expression hardens. "We've got a problem."

"What is it?" I ask.

"Lauren's mum. She's made a deal with Caleb and is on her way here."

I snarl, "What are ya talking about?"

Brody clenches his jaw and shakes his head. "We'll find out when she gets here."

"If she made a deal with Caleb, it's regarding Lauren or the baby. She's got some balls coming here," I snarl.

"Agreed."

I glance back at the closed door. "She's not coming near Lauren. How far away is she?"

Brody glances at his watch. "Few minutes."

I don't say anything, processing the information, trying to figure out what to do.

"You've got a decision to make," Brody states, giving me a knowing look.

I sigh, scrubbing my hands over my face. I don't like that my son's not here yet either, but I have to trust Maeve. It's not her fault that she got separated. The smoke was too much, and our guys didn't get to her fast enough.

Still, the more time that passes, the harder it gets to reassure Lauren that everything is okay.

Brody asks, "Well? Are ya killing her? It's your call."

I don't want any more grief in Lauren's life. I'd happily take out Kathleen for all she's put Lauren and my son through. But I know it has to be Lauren's decision. So, I begrudgingly go back into the room.

"Is it Maeve?" she questions with a mix of hope and fear in her voice.

"No. But I need to talk to you regarding another issue," I inform her.

"About our son?" Her voice cracks.

I hold my hands up. "No, our baby's fine."

"How do ya know?"

I sit next to her and tug her closer to me. "Lauren, please. A decision has to be made, and ya need to be part of it."

Her eyes turn to slits. "What's so important if it doesn't concern our son?"

"I need ya to stay calm."

She takes a deep breath and nods. "Okay."

I debate for a moment and decide the cold hard facts are the best direction to go. "Your mum's met with Caleb."

A mix of disgust, hatred, sadness, and betrayal overtakes her features. "About what?"

I don't take my gaze off her, stating, "She made a deal with him to come here."

Lauren glares at me. "Why?"

Brody interjects, "She told him she has access to Alaina and can get in here to take the baby."

Lauren's eyes widen. "She wouldn't."

"She has," Brody insists.

"But..." Lauren turns away, her lip trembling.

My brother adds, "Caleb made a new pledge to her."

Lauren stares at me in horror. "What did he promise?"

Brody answers, "If you return, she'll have full access to you and the baby again. She'll be back in his good graces, and he'll take care of her."

"No, she wouldn't do that," Lauren denies.

I tug her closer.

Brody adds, "It's been confirmed. She's on her way here."

The color drains from Lauren's face.

I quietly tell her, "I need to know what ya want me to do."

She swallows hard.

I continue, "There are two options. Listen carefully and then decide. This is your mum."

Her lips tremble harder. She whispers, "What are the options?"

"We can keep her alive in a cell until she dies, or I can take her out today. What do ya prefer?"

She gapes at me, then her expression hardens.

I give her a few moments to process, then say, "I don't want to make this decision, Lauren. She's your mum, so it's your call. But I won't let that woman return to Dublin since she's willingly trying to put ya and our son back in enemy hands."

Lauren remains speechless.

"Give us the room," I direct Alaina and Brody.

They leave.

Once the doors shut, I pull Lauren onto my lap. I stroke her cheek and gently say, "There's no right or wrong answer. You can tell me to put her in a cell and kill her later if ya want. But those are the only two options."

Her eyes darken. She shakes her head and, in a firm voice, confirms, "My mum wants to take our child and me and put us in danger because she cares more about the O'Learys than her own blood."

I'm unsure why I play devil's advocate, but I do. Maybe it's the sadness I see in her eyes. But whatever the reason, I declare, "In fairness, she's doing it because she wants to see ya and be in your life."

"But only if I'm an O'Leary." Fresh tears fall down her cheeks. She swipes at them.

I kiss her on the lips and tug her into me. In her ear, I murmur, "Angel, what do ya want me to do?"

She barely gets out, "How could she do this?"

I don't answer her.

There's a knock on the door. Brody and Alaina reenter the room. He announces, "She's here."

Lauren's body stiffens.

"I'll put her in a cell for now," I say.

"No. Wait," Lauren orders.

I freeze and study her for a moment. Then I ask, "What do ya want to happen?"

She stays quiet.

I reiterate, "We can keep her in a cell until you make up your mind."

Lauren puts her hand over her face. "Why is she so evil? Why can't she just love me more than O'Learys? She's as bad as Tommy, isn't she?"

Alaina interjects, "It's hard, Lauren. Your mum was born during a different time. Ya know how it is for the women and how it was for her."

"But she's willing to take my baby and give him to Caleb," Lauren seethes.

Alaina nods and affirms, "Yes."

Lauren lifts her chin. "What would ya do, Alaina?"

She stares at Lauren for a moment, then answers, "It's not about what I would do. It's about what ya would do."

Lauren sniffs hard, then squares her shoulders. "You wouldn't think twice. You would kill her."

"Yes, I would. But that's me, not you. You have to decide and live with that decision," Alaina says.

Lauren turns to me and orders. "Kill her, Devin. Take her out. Send a message that anybody who comes after our son does not deserve to live."

Shock fills me. Perhaps I shouldn't be surprised, but I didn't think Lauren had it in her. Yet I also know she'd kill for our son. And it's the answer I wanted to hear, but I question, "Are ya sure? Once I do it, it can't be undone."

"There will be one less person trying to harm our child. So, yes. Do it and let me know when it's done."

"Ya sure?" I ask again.

"Yes. Stop asking me," she asserts.

"Okay." I kiss her head, rise, and leave the room with Brody. As soon as the door shuts. I order, "Have them take her to the warehouse."

"Done." He picks up his phone and puts it to his ear, and as I exit the house, I hear him say, "Warehouse."

When I get to the warehouse, I don't have to wait very long. In the few spare minutes, I debate whether I should torture her mum or just kill her quickly. Part of me wants to torture her for hours, but I also want it to end. My focus has to be on Lauren and our son. Plus, I still need to hunt down Caleb.

The moment she enters the room, I stop debating. I order, "Put her in cell B."

She has tape over her mouth, and her eyes widen. She tries to resist but can't. They put her in the tiny room and strap her to a chair.

She tries to fight again, but she's no match compared to my men.

As soon as they step back, I point a gun at her head and state, "Ya had the best daughter in the world, but ya couldn't see that. Ya couldn't choose her over the O'Learys. Now ya want to come after my son? Ya don't deserve to live. But just so ya know, Lauren made this choice."

Shock and fear fill her expression.

I shoot her between the eyes. Blood pools everywhere, and I direct my men, "Clean it up." I leave and get in my car.

I'm almost to Brody's when he calls.

I answer, "I'm almost back."

He snarls, "Caleb's on his way."

My pulse skyrockets. "Where is he?"

"Few kilometers from the border. I'll send you the vehicle he's in, but several of them exist. We're sending all the guys we have that way. There's going to be a full-out war."

I drive like a madman through the city. Within ten minutes, I get another call from my brother.

"Our men just took a dozen of them out. He's in the third to the last car."

"I'm on it," I say, accelerating until I spot our men in their vehicles and positioned on top of buildings, ready to shoot. Then I hear gunshots, and Brody was right. I'm driving straight into a war zone.

I stay back, letting my men take the O'Learys' cars out one by one as they use guns and bombs to explode the vehicles. But the O'Learys just keep coming. Thick smoke fills the air, to the point I can barely see. And then I get another call from Brody.

He directs, "Surveillance has three cars left. The next one is his."

"Order the men to stop shooting," I state.

"Are ya crazy?" Brody asks.

"Order them. He's mine," I remind my brother.

"Don't do something stupid," he warns.

"I'm not. Order that they can take out the last two cars, but Caleb is mine."

"Fine," he grumbles and hangs up.

The shooting slows and then goes quiet. I drive faster and spot Caleb's vehicle coming toward me on the bridge.

I accelerate and brace myself. I slam into his car head-on and then jerk my wheel to the right.

His vehicle skids against the metal railing, and I reverse into it hard, pushing it off the road.

The car flies through the air and then somersaults down the cliff.

I pull over and watch it until it hits the rocks at the bottom. Then I drive quickly through town until I reach the crash site.

Smoke fills the air. I take my gun and shoot the driver in the head, then pull out my knife and tug at Caleb's door.

He's barely conscious. Blood oozes everywhere, and his body is trapped between the metal.

He barely gets out, "Please."

I crouch down and push the blade's tip into the side of his cheek.

An ear-splitting sound flies out of him.

I lose all control and stab him in the face, over and over, until Aidan tugs me back.

His voice registers, and I don't know how long he's been saying my name.

I glance at him.

Aidan orders, "Tynan."

My other brother steps into view and tosses the contents of a can of petrol over the car.

Aidan holds out a box of matches.

I stare at them and then Caleb's bloody face. I turn toward my brother. "You do it. I'm done with this piece of shit."

Aidan's lips curve.

I take several steps when the heat of the fire hits the back of my neck. I glance at the flames and then continue to my car, wanting to do nothing but get back to Lauren and, hopefully, my son.

29

Lauren
Two Days Later

*I*t's been three days, and I still don't have my son with me.

"He's coming," Devin keeps trying to reassure me.

"It's been over seventy-two hours. How can ya keep saying that? I don't understand why you're not doing anything," I accuse.

"Angel—"

"Don't, angel me!" I shout and walk out of the room. I go into the den, then freeze.

"It's time ya got married. You're getting too old," Tully, Devin's father, says to Tynan. He arrived yesterday, claiming he wanted to see his grandbaby. He seems just as unhappy as I am that my son's not here.

The strange thing about Tully is that I like him. I already trust him. He's kind, and it's confusing to me because I don't expect anyone in the clan that's male to be nice, but he is. He's made an effort to try to get to know me. And according to Alaina and Scarlet, he did the same thing when he met them.

"Oh! Sorry to interrupt," I blurt out.

Tully and Tynan jerk their heads toward me.

"It's okay. Come in," Tully says, motioning to me.

"No, it's okay," I say.

He insists, "No, please sit down. I'm almost done with this conversation anyway." He scowls at Tynan.

Tynan mutters, "That makes two of us."

I take a few steps toward the sofa.

He looks at Tynan again. "I mean it. Ya can't stay a playboy forever."

"Whatever. I'm done with this conversation," Tynan grumbles and shoves past us.

Tully points, ordering, "Have a seat, Lauren."

My heart beats faster. I ask, "Am I in trouble?"

"No, of course not." He picks up his cigar and doesn't light it but moves his thumb over it, stroking it. It's something I've noticed he does quite a bit.

"Don't smoke in here," Devin warns, entering the room.

"I know the rules," he barks.

I bite my lip. It's an ongoing fight between all the brothers, Alaina, and Tully. They always remind him not to light up his cigar in the house and go out onto the porch they deemed his smoking area.

Tully locks eyes with me. "I just got a phone call that you'll be happy about."

Hope rises within me. "Have they found my son?"

He nods, smiling.

"Maeve's on her way?" I question, not believing it.

"Aye."

I glance at Devin, then back at Tully. Then I ask, "You're going to punish her, right? There needs to be consequences for what she's done to me and my son, just like with my mum.

His face falls. He declares, "No. She did exactly what she was supposed to do. Why would I punish her?"

"What do ya mean she's done what she's supposed to? She was supposed to be here days ago. My son—your grandchild— has been missing for over seventy-two hours."

Tully shakes his head. "No, he wasn't missing. He was with Maeve the entire time. She had to hide. She did everything correctly. You'll see."

"Then why isn't she here?"

His voice sharpens. "Because they were chasing her. But now, she's with our men. They're escorting her here, and she's happy to have their protection. She risked her life for your son—my grandson. So we will not punish her. Do ya understand?"

I keep my comments to myself, trying to process this information but not wanting to challenge Tully based on his tone.

Is it possible that Maeve did keep my son safe?

Devin sits down. "Lauren, I told you Maeve is on your side. I know she told Caleb where ya were, but she really was in a bad spot."

"So that's an excuse for her endangering our child?"

"No, I'm not saying that," Devin firmly states.

I cross my arms, glaring at him. "But you're telling me I should just forget about it and let it go?"

He sighs and scrubs his face.

Tully sits down next to me on the other side. He says, "Lauren."

I turn toward him, my heart beating faster. I wait for him to speak.

He asserts, "Sometimes, we must put ourselves in the other person's shoes."

I start to laugh.

"What's so funny?" he asks.

I argue, "Since when do clansmen put themselves in other people's shoes?"

He arches his eyebrows.

"Well?"

He offers, "I do."

"So do I," Devin echoes.

"Do ya?" I challenge.

He shrugs. "Sometimes."

I stare at my lap and fidget with my fingers.

Tully reiterates, "Maeve risked her life to try to make a right for the wrong that she did. So, try to go easy on her. Okay?"

I grip my fingers tighter.

Devin puts his hand over mine. "Lauren, let's look at the positive. Within a few minutes, our son will be with us."

I look at him, blinking hard. Then, with an emotion-filled voice, I ask, "Is he really coming? Please don't tell me he is and not have him show up." Tears drip down my cheek.

Devin swipes at them, affirming, "Angel, I promise ya, in a few minutes, he will be in your arms."

Those few minutes take forever. I rise and pace the room as time seems to stand still. When a car pulls up, I leave the den and go to the foyer. I bolt out the front door, run down the steps, and the moment the car parks, I fling open the back door.

Maeve and the baby are in the back seat. My son is in her arms.

I cry out in relief and joy. I reach in, and she hands the baby to me. I grab my son, pull him into my chest, and sob.

"I'm sorry, Lauren. I really am. I tried to get here as fast as possible, but they were chasing me. It was hard. The baby was crying, and I didn't know who to trust. I had to hide," Maeve rambles out.

"Ya did well, Maeve," Tully says.

She freezes, her eyes widening in fear.

Tully reaches into the car, ordering, "Come on inside."

She swallows hard and asks, "Who are ya?"

"I'm Tully O'Connor."

She shrinks back a bit, as if she's unsure if she should be scared.

I don't blame her. I understand it. Tully's the opposite of what we've known.

He adds, "I won't hurt ya. We're very grateful that ya brought my grandson back. Now, please come inside."

Maeve reluctantly gets out of the car, and they disappear into the house.

I spin, and Devin's staring at us, eyes full of emotion and wearing an expression I've never seen before. I choke up even more.

His eyes lock on our son's head.

I turn our baby around and state, "This is your son."

Devin keeps his gaze on him as if he's unsure what to do. Then he holds his hands out and cautiously asks, "Can I hold him a moment?"

I don't want to let my son go, but I do. "Of course ya can." I hand him to Devin.

He pulls him close to his chest, murmuring, "Hey, buddy, I'm your real da."

I can't see. My eyes are too blurry from my tears.

Devin takes his other arm and pulls me into him. He continues, "You're safe now. I'm going to make sure I protect ya and your mum." He kisses both of us on the head and then leads us inside.

I take a deep breath, trying to calm my residual fear.

Devin quietly asserts, "It's over. We can now begin."

"Begin what?" I question.

He kisses me on the lips and answers, "The rest of our life."

30

Devin

"*I* wake up and roll over, but Lauren's not beside me. I groan, grip my raging hard-on, then mutter, "Fucking wedding rules."

Fuck this.

I leave the guest bedroom and wander naked down the hall, wondering what time it is, knowing it's still early.

I sneak into our bedroom. Lauren's quietly sleeping. She's probably exhausted. I know she's been feeding the baby several times in the middle of the night. But I'm a selfish bastard, and I want my soon-to-be wife.

I stare at her for a moment, thinking about how lucky I am. I finally have everything I want—her and our son, whom she named Dominick Devin O'Connor. There's nothing else in the world I'll ever need. And I'm never letting either of them out of my sight again.

She moves her hand, and the diamond ring peeks out from under the pillow.

Warmth fills my heart. I assumed marriage was for the weak. That it was a noose around a man's neck, and I swore I'd never tie the knot.

Yet here I am, counting down the hours that stand between Lauren and me saying our vows.

I sneak over to my dresser, quietly open the drawer, and pull out a pair of handcuffs, knowing exactly what I want to do to her. She's lying on her stomach, so I carefully maneuver the handcuffs. I attach one to her wrist, slide it around the headboard bar, and then attach the other. She barely stirs.

Yep, she's exhausted, I think, licking my lips. I go to the end of the bed and lift the covers, sliding my hands over the backs of her calves and licking her inner thigh.

She moans and twitches.

I continue upward until I reach right between her thighs, inhaling deeply.

"Devin," she softly mumbles, still half asleep.

"Shh, angel. Daddy needs to take care of you this morning."

"What time is it?" she asks, shimmying her lower body toward my face.

Happiness fills me. I chuckle, answering, "I don't know, but it's our wedding day."

Her body stiffens. "Devin, ya can't see me. It's bad luck."

"Fuck that. We don't have bad luck, angel. Now, be a good little vixen and come for Daddy."

I flip her body, and she gasps. I move my face toward her clit, licking it, sucking it, taking it as mine.

In under a minute, she cries out, "Sweet Jesus, Devin."

I move her thigh up, slap her ass, and suck her so hard she convulses harder.

"That's my vixen," I praise, then slide my tongue up her stomach and between her cleavage before I enter her in one thrust.

She whimpers.

I push my tongue into her mouth, taking all of her, and wrap my hand around her throat.

Her eyes widen, and the flare of excitement and lust I crave lights up in their depths.

I thrust over and over into her, tightening my grip and watching her eyes. Right before she can barely kiss me back and loses all control, I cut off her air supply.

Her entire body quivers and then collapses under mine, convulsing violently. Her walls squeeze me into perfect oblivion.

I come inside her, thrusting deep, grunting, "Fuck, ya little vixen."

Her eyes roll, and I bury my face in her neck as our bodies shudder against each other, then I release my grip around her neck.

In the aftermath, I roll off her, keeping her restrained.

She wiggles her wrists, and the metal clinks. She asks, "Ya gonna unlock me?"

I grin. "No."

She arches her eyebrows, her flush growing deeper again. "No?"

I glance at the clock. "It's only five a.m. We have two more hours until you have to get up and get that pretty white dress on."

Her lips twitch. "What if it's not white?"

"What other color would it be?"

"Maybe red."

I chuckle. "I don't care what you show up in as long as you say 'I do.'" I take my index finger and trace her jawline.

She smiles. "Of course I'm going to say yes."

I dip down to her breast and start sucking it.

She arches her back and moans.

I go to the other one, do the same, and she presses her body into mine. I murmur in her ear, "Daddy needs to taste your pussy again."

She giggles, and I slide down her body, eating her out until she comes like a freight train.

And I love every minute of it. I relish knowing how to work her body to make her feel this way.

We spend the next couple of hours together. We're both a hot, sweaty mess and get into the shower together. Then we dry off.

I come out of the bathroom with a towel wrapped around my waist, and there's a knock on the door. I state, "I guess that's my cue to go."

She reaches her arms around my neck and pulls me down for a kiss.

I retreat and warn, "Get your pussy prepared. I'm going to devour it all night."

She softly laughs. "You're so dirty."

I squeeze her ass cheeks. "That's right. I'm your dirty soon-to-be husband. You're going to be Mrs. Devin O'Connor. So don't ya forget it."

She beams. "I won't."

I give her a peck on the lips and release her. I open the door.

My sister Bridget's eyes narrow. She's flown over from New York, and my niece Fiona stands beside her with my son. Bridget shakes her head at me and scolds, "What the hell are you doing here, Devin?"

"I think all of you guys have issues," Fiona adds.

"And why is that?" I question.

Bridget interjects, "Because you and your brothers can't seem to understand wedding day rules."

I turn back toward Lauren. "Have fun. I'll see ya soon."

"Bye," she chirps, waving.

I step out into the hallway, and Alaina and Scarlet approach me. They both have grins on their faces.

Alaina's lips twitch. "I see Bridget's not happy."

"Ya know it." I step out and grab Dominick from Fiona, saying to him, "Hey, buddy. I think ya need to come with me."

"No, I want to see him first," Lauren calls out.

I grin. I should have known that would happen. I go back in and hand him to her.

Her face lights up. She kisses him on the forehead and coos, "Hey there, Dominick. How ya doing, sweetie? Today's the big day. I want ya to be really good for Daddy. Okay?"

He looks at her and tilts his head.

She kisses him again and beams.

I pull both of them into me, kiss Lauren's head, then say, "Okay. Time for me to have a day with my son. You'll see him later."

"Okay," she says reluctantly, which makes me want to chuckle again. She's a really great mum. Even though she knows he's safe, I still sense her anxiety sometimes.

I grab her ass and lean into her ear, murmuring, "Everything will be fine. I won't let him out of my sight, I promise."

She looks up and smiles. "I know."

"All right, angel. Have fun." I kiss her cheek and grab Dominick. "Come on, son. We've got manly things to do today."

Bridget looks at me and orders, "Out. Now."

"I'm leaving." I step into the hallway, and the door shuts. I toss Dominick in the air and tickle him until he laughs. I'm happier than I've ever been, knowing my life is finally complete.

And come hell or high water, no one, and I mean *no one*, will ever touch my son or wife again. I'll protect them no matter what I have to do, and if anyone even tries to come for them, they won't be breathing for long.

Dominick's laughs subside, and I hold him close to me. "Let's go, buddy. Today's going to be the greatest day ever."

EPILOGUE

Lauren

*D*evin leans down and kisses our son on the head, then gives me a peck on the lips. "I'll be back soon." He leaves the den.

Annie picks up the baby and coos, "He's adorable. I just can't get over him."

"I can't believe ya named him after me," Dominick states for the hundredth time, grinning from ear to ear.

"Well, Devin didn't want him to be called Devin Jr., and there wasn't any other name I would even consider," I admit, so happy I finally get to call my son what I wanted instead of Caleb Jr.

Annie kisses my son and hands him to her husband, saying, "He's such a good boy. Look at that smile."

I add, "I'm so happy ya could come stay for a while."

Annie nods. "We are too. We're just glad you're okay. Both of ya."

"I really am sorry for everything I put ya through," I repeat for the tenth time today.

"Hush, dear. We've already gone through this," Annie insists.

Guilt eats at me. I confess, "I know, but I keep thinking about when Dominick got hurt."

He waves his hand in front of me. "Oh, shush. I'm a tough man."

I laugh. "Yea, ya sure are."

The phone rings, pulling me out of my trance. I jump up. "Oh, Devin forgot his phone. Let me go give it to him." I grab his phone off the desk and run after him, shouting, "Devin!"

He turns back toward me. "What's up, angel?"

"Ya forgot your phone. Oh, it's... What?" I stare at the screen.

"What is it?" he asks, his eyes turning to slits.

I show him the screen. "Why is Tynan sending a picture of Maeve?"

Devin swipes on the glass and opens the message. The blood drains from his face. He mutters, "Ya have to be kidding me."

"What's wrong? Is she okay?" I fret.

It took me a while to get over everything Maeve did, but I finally gave her a pass. Tully was right. She was in a crappy position. While it's still hard sometimes to think about the fact that Caleb was there because of her, she did risk her life to save my son. I've never been happier than now, having Devin and Dominick with me. I can't deny she had something to do with my happiness. So, I'm letting the past be the past, and I'm just concentrating on the future.

"That son of a bitch," Devin seethes.

"What?"

He shows me the screen.

> Tynan: Tell Dad I got myself a bride.

The hairs on my arms rise. "What does that mean?"

Devin closes his eyes and shakes his head.

"Tell me," I demand.

He opens his eyes and swallows hard. He admits, "Maeve's da has been placing bets with Tynan."

"Why would he do that? He's an O'Leary."

"It doesn't matter. Gamblers are gamblers. They go where the games are. And he must not have had anything else to pay with," Devin states.

I argue, "Ya can't let him do this. He can't take Maeve as payment! Stop him!"

Devin's face hardens, and he says, "Ya didn't see the rest of the message?"

Fear fills me, and goose bumps break out on my skin. I shudder, replying, "No, I didn't. What does it say?"

He clenches his jaw and then hands the phone back to me.

My gut dives as I stare at the message.

> Tynan: Tell Dad we just finished taking our vows.

. . .

Thank you for reading Illicit Heir!

Are you ready for the final book in the Mafia Wars Ireland series?

Download Illicit Monster here.

ILLICIT MONSTER

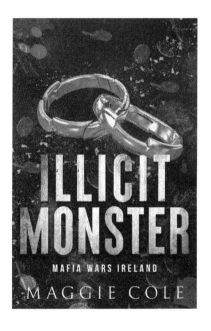

My father sold me to his enemy.

He stole my innocence—right after he dressed me in white and made me vow to be his for all of eternity.

Now I'm cut off from my family.

Subjected to my husband's warped rules and laws.

At the mercy of a tyrant who leers at me with green heated eyes until I beg him for things I shouldn't.

Every day, I promise myself I'll grow stronger and resist the urge to appease him.

It's a losing battle I can't win.

All I want is to love him, but I tell myself not to be foolish.

After all, a monster will never love.

He'll only go deeper into his sinister ways.

READ ILLICIT MONSTER-BOOK FOUR OF MAFIA WARS IRELAND

CAN I ASK YOU A HUGE FAVOR?

ould you be willing to leave me a review?
       I would be forever grateful as one positive review on Amazon is like buying the book a hundred times! Reader support is the lifeblood for Indie authors and provides us the feedback we need to give readers what they want in future stories!

Your positive review means the world to me! So thank you from the bottom of my heart!

CLICK TO REVIEW

READY TO BINGE THE ORIGINAL MAFIA WARS SERIES? GET TO KNOW THE IVANOVS AND O'MALLEYS!

He's a Ruthless Stranger. One I can't see, only feel, thanks to my friends who make a deal with him on my behalf.

No names. No personal details. No face to etch into my mind.

Just him, me, and an expensive silk tie.

What happens in Vegas is supposed to stay in Vegas.

He warns me he's full of danger.

I never see that side of him. All I experience is his Russian accent, delicious scent, and touch that lights me on fire.

One incredible night turns into two. Then we go our separate ways.

But fate doesn't keep us apart. When I run into my stranger back in Chicago, I know it's him, even if I've never seen his icy blue eyes before.

Our craving is hotter than Vegas. But he never lied.

He's a ruthless man...

"Ruthless Stranger" is the jaw-dropping first installment of the "Mafia Wars" series. It's an interconnecting, stand-alone Dark Mafia Romance, guaranteed to have an HEA.

Ready for Maksim's story? Click here for Ruthless Stranger, book one of the jaw dropping spinoff series, Mafia Wars!

MORE BY MAGGIE COLE

Mafia Wars Ireland

Illicit King (Brody)

Illicit Captor (Aidan)

Illicit Heir (Devin)

Illicit Monster (Tynan) - October 15, 2023

Club Indulgence Duet (A Dark Billionaire Romance)

The Auction (Book One)

The Vow (Book Two)

Standalone Holiday Novel

Holiday Hoax - A Fake Marriage Billionaire Romance (Standalone)

Mafia Wars New York - A Dark Mafia Series (Series Six)

Toxic (Dante's Story) - Book One

Immoral (Gianni's Story) - Book Two

Crazed (Massimo's Story) - Book Three

Carnal (Tristano's Story) - Book Four

Flawed (Luca's Story) - Book Five

Mafia Wars - A Dark Mafia Series (Series Five)

Ruthless Stranger (Maksim's Story) - Book One

Broken Fighter (Boris's Story) - Book Two

Cruel Enforcer (Sergey's Story) - Book Three

Vicious Protector (Adrian's Story) - Book Four

Savage Tracker (Obrecht's Story) - Book Five

Unchosen Ruler (Liam's Story) - Book Six

Perfect Sinner (Nolan's Story) - Book Seven

Brutal Defender (Killian's Story) - Book Eight

Deviant Hacker (Declan's Story) - Book Nine

Relentless Hunter (Finn's Story) - Book Ten

Behind Closed Doors (Series Four - Former Military Now International Rescue Alpha Studs)

Depths of Destruction - Book One

Marks of Rebellion - Book Two

Haze of Obedience - Book Three

Cavern of Silence - Book Four

Stains of Desire - Book Five

Risks of Temptation - Book Six

Together We Stand Series (Series Three - Family Saga)

Kiss of Redemption- Book One

Sins of Justice - Book Two

Acts of Manipulation - Book Three

Web of Betrayal - Book Four

Masks of Devotion - Book Five

Roots of Vengeance - Book Six

It's Complicated Series (Series Two - Chicago Billionaires)

My Boss the Billionaire- Book One

Forgotten by the Billionaire - Book Two

My Friend the Billionaire - Book Three

Forbidden Billionaire - Book Four

The Groomsman Billionaire - Book Five

Secret Mafia Billionaire - Book Six

All In Series (Series One - New York Billionaires)

The Rule - Book One

The Secret - Book Two

The Crime - Book Three

The Lie - Book Four

The Trap - Book Five

The Gamble - Book Six

STAND ALONE NOVELLA

JUDGE ME NOT - A Billionaire Single Mom Christmas Novella

ABOUT THE AUTHOR

Amazon Bestselling Author

Maggie Cole is committed to bringing her readers alphalicious book boyfriends. She's an international bestselling author and has been called the "literary master of steamy romance." Her books are full of raw emotion, suspense, and will always keep you wanting more. She is a masterful storyteller of contemporary romance and loves writing about broken people who rise above the ashes.

Maggie lives in Florida with her son. She loves sunshine, anything to do with water, and everything naughty.

Her current series were written in the order below:

- All In (Stand alones with entwined characters)

- It's Complicated (Stand alones with entwined characters)
- Together We Stand (Brooks Family Saga - read in order)
- Behind Closed Doors (Read in order)
- Mafia Wars (Stand alones with entwined characters)
- Mafia Wars New York (Stand alones with entwined characters)
- Club Indulgence Duet
- Mafia Wars Ireland

Maggie Cole's Newsletter
Sign up here!

Hang Out with Maggie in Her Reader Group
Maggie Cole's Romance Addicts

Follow for Giveaways
Facebook Maggie Cole

Instagram
@maggiecoleauthor

TikTok
https://www.tiktok.com/@maggiecole.author

Complete Works on Amazon
Follow Maggie's Amazon Author Page

Book Trailers
Follow Maggie on YouTube

Feedback or suggestions?
Email: authormaggiecole@gmail.com

twitter.com/MaggieColeAuth

instagram.com/maggiecoleauthor

bookbub.com/profile/maggie-cole

amazon.com/Maggie-Cole/e/B07Z2CB4HG

tiktok.com/@maggiecole.author

Printed in Great Britain
by Amazon

30173324R00231